Florida
Shakedown

Oh what tangled webs we weave....

Kerry Costello

This book is a work of fiction. Names, characters, places and incidents, are either the product of the writer's imagination or are being used fictitiously. Any resemblance to any actual persons, living or dead, and events or locations, is entirely coincidental

For my wife Lyn and our sons Andrew, Timothy and Alexander

ACKNOWLEDGEMENTS

Lyn Costello

Jasia Painter

By the same author

No Way Back

The Long Game (Gibson series, book 1)

Florida Clowns (Gibson series, book 3)

You Owe Me

CHAPTER 1

Gibson woke up, and held his hand up to shield his eyes from the searing late afternoon sun. The sky was solid blue. A gentle cooling breeze blowing off the bay made the heat just about bearable. Across the other side of the pool he could see and hear a large elderly man, snoring loudly, slumped in a chair under a canvas sun canopy. There was no one else around.

He got up a little unsteadily, walked down the steps of the kidney shaped swimming pool and made his way into the deep end, gradually submerging himself in the lukewarm water. He wondered how easy it was to drown yourself, and sank to the bottom resting on his knees, staying perfectly still until he started to run out of air.

He opened his mouth to breathe in the water and gagged. A reflex action caused him to straighten his legs and propel himself upwards, coughing and spluttering loudly as he broke the surface. The man who'd been asleep under the sun canopy got to his feet looking concerned, and walked over to Gibson, who was still in the water, arms resting on the edge of the pool, gasping, and trying to recover his breath.

'You okay buddy?' said the man in a distinctive southern drawl.

'Yes, breathed in some water by accident,' he said in between gasps. The man looked at him intently then said 'Okay, well you be careful now young man,' he lingered as if he was going to say more, then walked away towards the door of the apartment block. Gibson waited until he'd gone, then hauled himself out of the pool and lay down on his sunbed. He closed his eyes and laughed involuntarily *'Young man' only in Florida could someone of sixty be referred to as 'young man'.*

The sun did its work and after a few minutes he was dry. He got up, grabbed his towel, picked up the now empty plastic tumbler he'd brought the vodka down in, and made his way back to his rental unit. Tiny lizards skittered out of his way as he walked along the concrete pathway to the building entrance. Bay View on Park Shore Drive was appropriately named, as all the apartments had views over Venetian Bay, a man-made development based on Venice, with homes on stilts painted in pastel shades of yellows, pinks, browns and creams.

The apartment was spacious and far too big for his needs, but he'd booked it at the last minute and got a bargain. It had three bedrooms, two bathrooms, shower room, a large fully equipped kitchen, a huge lanai and all mod cons, including wireless broadband. He'd brought his laptop, intending to revive the book he'd been writing prior to Jill's death. It was based on his experiences as a policeman, but he couldn't work up any enthusiasm for it anymore and just used the laptop these days for emails, and to surf the internet for news.

He checked his emails now, nothing, closed the laptop and went over to stand at the floor to ceiling window that overlooked the bay. The sun was getting lower, soon to disappear behind the high rise blocks of luxury apartments on Gulf Shore Boulevard opposite. He watched a small motorboat leaving one of the condo's boat docks, for a sunset cruise. The five occupants armed with bottles, snacks and plastic containers. It was likely to be another spectacular sunset over Naples Bay. *How Jill would have loved it here* he thought.

He went back to his laptop, fired up ITunes and found Jill's favourite song, Jerry Butler singing For Your Precious Love. The speakers were tinny but he didn't care. He sat their listening and thinking back over their life together.

*

The next morning dawned bright and sunny. Gibson felt a little more positive, relaxed, better than he'd felt for a while. He went to the bathroom, looked in the mirror and didn't like what he saw. A red booze bloated face stared back at him, complete with crooked nose and small scar under his right eye.

He brushed his teeth, pulled on some shorts and a tee shirt, put his trainers on and made his way downstairs. There was a full length mirror at the bottom of the stairs.

He stood and turned sideways, *hmm, put a bit of weight on, but still got my hair, bit greyer maybe?*. The beach was just a ten minute walk away and despite the early hour, he guessed the temperature to be already in the low eighties. Walking along Park Shore, he soon came to a beach access point, strolled through the car park area and on to the beach. The turquoise sea was flat calm, small waves lapping gently on to the pale sandy shore. Gibson took some deep breaths then turned south and walked briskly along the shoreline. After a hundred yards or so he felt energised and broke into a gentle jog, gradually increasing his speed until he was running, pounding the sand.

His lungs complained and legs ached as he sweated and strained, but he kept going at a reasonable pace, his mind made up. It had been a year of misery and too much booze and introspection, *but no more he thought, no more, enough, fuck it, no more self-pity.* He got back to the condo showered and went to see what was in the fridge, some eggs, bread and orange juice. The coffee machine took some figuring out but he finally produced an acceptable drink, then he made a breakfast of boiled eggs on toast. Afterwards he tidied the apartment, made some more coffee, sat down in a comfortable armchair and read for a while.

He woke with a start, the book on the floor. Standing up he stretched and looked through the window. *How long have I been out?* He looked at his watch and saw that he'd been asleep for nearly an hour. *This is no good, I can do that in rainy Manchester.* He went to the bedroom, changed into his swimming trunks, slipped a linen shirt on, grabbed a beach towel and went down to the pool for a swim.

'Good morning,' he said to two matronly ladies sunning themselves by the pool. They stopped their conversation briefly and greeted him warmly as though he were an old friend, despite him never having met them before.

'Hello and how are you?' the first one said, the second one smiling at him fondly.

'Very well thanks. Beautiful day,' he replied. Then walked over to one of the sunbeds, draped his towel over the back of it before walking down the steps of the pool and into the tepid water. *Wow, this is warm as a bath.* He swam for a good fifteen minutes, crawl then backstroke, then back to a fast crawl for the final length. Getting out, he showered and towelled himself dry before laying his towel on the sunbed, then lying down on it and closing his eyes. His leg muscles still ached in response to his early morning run, the first for over a year, but he felt good. He was drifting off to sleep again when he sensed a presence nearby and opened his eyes, squinting in the strong sunlight.

'How ya doin', didn't wake ya did I?' said a large portly man standing by his sunbed, a tin of beer in each hand. One tin was open and the other one was being offered to Gibson. The man was tall, tanned, wore red flower patterned shorts, no shirt and sported a huge belly. He had an engaging smile, grey thinning hair and a round open face.

'It's a bit early for me, thanks all the same' Gibson said in as pleasant a manner as he could.

'Well, the beer's nice an' cold and it's four in the afternoon somewhere, but don't let me force ya.' Beads of condensation were running down the beer cans, sunlight glinting off the tin tubes. Gibson suddenly felt thirsty, *what the hell, I'm on holiday* he thought, and propped himself up on one elbow to take the offered can of beer. 'Thanks, you're very kind,' he said

'No problem, my name's Jack by the way, Jack Otterbein.'

'Nice to meet you Jack, my name's Gibson,' he replied and sat up as he peeled the tab off the top of the tin and took a swig of cold beer.

'Yeah I know, John Gibson, mind if I sit down?' He pulled a chair over without waiting for a reply.

'How do you know my…'

'Name?' Jack finished the question for him. 'Simple, I'm the chairman of the apartment association so I get to see the details of anyone coming to stay here, you know, the form you filled in on line when you rented the place?'

'Oh yes right, I see, well just call me Gibson, people never use my first name so if you don't mind?'

'No Gibson, I don't mind, anything to oblige, cheers,' said Jack and knocked his can against Gibson's, then took a long draft of his beer' 'Ahh that's better,' he said smacking his lips. Gibson took another swig of beer.

'So you're here for nearly two months, that's quite a vacation.'

'Yes well I'm retired now,' said Gibson, 'so I have plenty of time on my hands, and you?'

'The same, retired well sort of, we've spent the winters down here for as long as I can remember, can't beat it. You were a policeman weren't you?' Gibson was taken aback.

'That wasn't on the form, so how ….?'

'The internet, nothing's private any more, I was just curious and put your name in, plus Manchester, and up you popped. Well to be fair, there were quite a few John Gibsons, but there was a newspaper report and a photograph of a Chief Inspector Gibson and it was quite a good likeness.'

'Oh right, I see.'

'Yeah, well look, I know we've only just met, but I'm sorry for your loss, must have been tough, losing your wife like that.'

Gibson looked around to make sure no one was within hearing distance 'Yes it was,' he said, but I'd appreciate it if you didn't mention it to anyone else. One of the reasons I came here was to get away from, well to get away, you understand?'

'I do, and don't worry I won't say a word, but don't think the other residents won't figure out who you are eventually, like I say, nothing's private anymore.'

'I suppose you're right.'

'I am. Most of the people here have nothing much to do, so anyone new is of great interest, but they're a nice crowd, so be patient, just play it cool and they'll eventually leave you alone.'

'Okay thanks for the advice…., em, Jack.'

'No sweat. You had, what did they call it, a distinguished career? I mean especially catching that son of a bitch serial killer in ninety, that was something else, some detective work huh?'

'Yes, well maybe I just got lucky.' Gibson frowned. He was starting to feel awkward and beginning to wonder if it had been a mistake to stay there.

'Lucky? Well I'm with Gary Player on that one, what'd he say? The more I practice, the luckier I get.' Gibson smiled weakly at the re-telling of the well-worn anecdote.

'Look, I can see I'm crowding you a bit here, so I'll leave you alone to get some rest and some sun but there is something you might do for me when you have a few minutes to spare. I'd like you to look at something and just give me your opinion, won't take more than ten minutes I promise, okay?' Before Gibson could reply, the man called Jack strolled off waving his hand, saying 'See ya later.'

Gibson lay back on his lounger closed his eyes and tried to relax again, but he was agitated by the conversation he'd just had. Jack was right though, no one had any secrets any more, not even a private life, especially if you'd held any kind of public office. Pretty soon, everyone in the apartment block would know about the tragedy of Jill's death. He could still see the headlines in the newspaper – Police Chief's wife dies in plane crash.

He pushed the image away, opened his eyes and looked around. Jack had stopped to talk to the two ladies by the pool. Gibson had reluctantly agreed to see a grief counsellor after Jill's death, and at the time he dismissed her advice, but now he was beginning to think he should take notice, otherwise he was going to become more and more miserable, unsociable and isolated. He sat up and shouted.

'Hey Jack.' Jack looked up and Gibson waved for him to come back. Jack finished his conversation and strolled back to where Gibson was.

'Sorry Jack I didn't mean to be rude or anything, what was it you wanted my opinion on?'

'Well if you're sure I'm not imposing, I mean later would be fine if it's inconvenient now.'

'No now's fine, I can honestly say that apart from a vague idea about going fishing, I have absolutely nothing planned, so what can I help you with?'

'That's real nice of you Gibson, come up to my apartment and I'll show you, like I say, it won't take long.'

Jack shouted as soon as they got through the door. 'Mary Lou, you there? Come and meet Gibson, the English guy you were so curious about.' Their apartment was much the same layout as the one Gibson was renting, but much more opulent, with heavy brocaded furniture, dark wood and rich burgundy coloured curtains. Mary Lou appeared and told Jack off.

'You're not supposed to say things like that. You embarrass me Jack.' Mary Lou Otterbein could only be described as tr5uly beautiful, thought Gibson. She was petite had dark red hair cut in a bob a copper tan and a figure that spoke of lucky genes, or hard work in the gym. Turning to Gibson she introduced herself.

'Hello I'm Mary Lou and it's very nice to meet you, er, Gibson did you say?'

'Yes, my last name, but it's what everyone calls me.'

'Okay Gibson, like the cocktail, I can remember that. Would you like a coffee, I know Jack will want one?'

Jack had disappeared into one of the rooms. A voice shouted 'Come in here Gibson, in the den, Mary Lou can we have some coffee please?'

Mary Lou smiled. Gibson said he would love a coffee, and made for the door Jack had just disappeared through. The den was a sort of cross between an office and a hobby room. There was stuff all over the place, books, trays with papers, some golf trophies on a shelf, a desk with a PC and printer on, a two seater sofa that had seen better days and a battered leather chair with an extension for resting your legs on. There were lots of framed photographs adorning every available space on the creamy green painted walls, in addition there was a huge wide screen TV mounted on the wall opposite the sofa. The room had a restful if slightly scruffy feel to it. Jack was attaching a long cable running from the computer, to the television.

'Take a seat Gibson I'll have this sorted out in a minute. I could show you on the PC, but you'll see it better on the bigger screen.'

Gibson sat on the sofa and waited.

'Okay ready to roll, hang on let's get the coffee first I don't want your concentration interrupted.'

Gibson was intrigued and tried to guess what he was going to see then gave up. Jack leaned out of the door and shouted to Mary Lou to ask if the coffee was on its way. There was a muffled reply which Gibson couldn't quite hear but he got the intonation – as in don't be so impatient. Gibson laughed to himself, they were a comical pair. Jack checked his remote, looked at Gibson and raised his eyes to the ceiling. Mary Lou came in and set a small tray down on the table, with two mugs of black coffee a jug of cream and a bowl of sugar lumps.

'I'm off down to the pool now Jack, see you later Gibson.'

They both said their goodbyes and helped themselves to coffee. Jack went over to the vertical blinds and half closed them to cut out the bright sunlight. He moved the foot rest and sat in the leather chair with the remote, leaning forward, changing the settings on the TV to connect with the cable from the computer, then he got up went back to the PC and clicked the mouse. A picture appeared on the television as a video started.

'What you're going to see now is not very pleasant. I won't say any more until you've seen it all,' said Jack.

*

The video showed a well-lit beige coloured wall with some clear plastic sheeting attached to it. The sheeting continued to the bottom of the wall and then out on to the floor, covering a fairly large area directly in front. There was no movement and Gibson began to wonder if the video had frozen, but then a figure came into view and stood in front of the camera.

The man was wearing a black sweat shirt, black jog bottoms and a black ski mask He was in focus and it was a good quality picture. Gibson could now make a guess at the size of the area covered by the plastic sheeting. He looked quickly at Jack to make sure this wasn't some sort of elaborate joke, but the expression on Jack's face convinced him this was deadly serious. The preparations with the plastic sheeting told Gibson he was about to witness something brutal and bloody.

The man spoke, and despite him using some sort of voice altering device, he was easy to understand. *All very professional so far*, thought Gibson. Despite the altered voice, it was obvious the man had an American accent.

'You were told not to go to the cops. Did you think we were joking?' And with that, the man stepped sideways and a few seconds later a hooded man came into view being pushed and dragged towards the wall by two large masked men. Gibson could hear the muffled voice of the man, sounds of angry cursing as he was manoeuvred into place. The victim was wearing a grubby looking white sweatshirt and faded blue jeans, no shoes.

He was running to fat, but quite tall. His hands were tied behind his back but he still struggled in vain to break free of the men. He kept trying until the man on the right put the muzzle of a revolver to his temple and spoke into his ear. It wasn't possible to hear what was said, but the hooded man stopped struggling and allowed the men to position him where they wanted him to stand.

He wasn't up against the wall but about a yard in front of it, standing on a plastic sheet. The man on the left bent down and secured the hooded man's legs together at the ankles with a plastic tie. Gibson was beginning to feel queasy. The hood was pulled off the man's head to reveal his pasty white face. He had a distinctive anchor shaped beard and moustache, longish dishevelled grey hair and deep set eyes. His age was hard to judge, over sixty maybe thought Gibson.

The man's expression was one of defiance as he looked straight at the camera. Someone shouted and the men holding him moved quickly to the side, then came a loud explosion and simultaneously the man was propelled backwards with the force of the blast, from what Gibson judged to be a shotgun.

The victim's upper body area exploded, blood spurting out in a gush as he collapsed and fell sideways to the floor. The body twitched once then went still. Blood continued to spread slowly on the plastic sheet as it drained from what was now certainly a corpse. One of the men came back into view and threw a large grey blanket over the prone form, then the first man re-appeared in front of the camera and spoke again.

'Your fault,' he said, then the screen went blank.

CHAPTER 2

As a police officer, Gibson had experienced many horrific sights, bodies of people who had been the victims of the most hideous attacks, small children and even babies who had died as a result of violence and sometimes what could only be described as torture. Rape victims horribly assaulted, young men stabbed or beaten unmercifully to death, car crash victims with the most dreadful injuries, you name it he'd seen it, but he had never experienced the cold blooded execution of another human being. He remained silent for a while wondering about his fellow man's apparent unlimited capacity to visit violence, death and suffering on others. He shook his head and looked at Jack.

'So why was he killed, when did all this happen?'

'Last September, but before I go on, can I ask you a question first?' Gibson nodded, 'Go ahead.'

'Was that all genuine, I mean could that have been a set up, you know, staged?' The question threw Gibson. It had never entered his mind to question the authenticity of the video. He re-ran it through in his mind and couldn't see how.

'Well it seemed genuine enough to me Jack but your question means that you think it might be otherwise, could you explain?'

'Look, do me a favor and look at the video again, then we can talk, I'll go and get some fresh coffee while you watch it.' Jack went back to the computer, set the video back to the beginning, started it running and left Gibson alone while he went for some fresh coffee. Gibson watched the video again, but with less emotion and a more cynical attitude this time. The video came to an end and a few seconds later Jack came back into the room with two cups of freshly brewed coffee and set them down.

'Help yourself to cream Gibson, what do you think now?' Jack sat back down on his leather chair.

'As far as I can tell it's genuine. There's no doubt about the force of the shotgun blast propelling the victim back to the wall. You just couldn't fake that. The blood, obviously, everything about it seems genuine to me. Why? Do you know different?'

'You're sure about that Gibson, absolutely sure?'

'As sure as I can be, yes, so c'mon Jack you obviously think there's room for doubt, so let's have it.' Jack looked down at the floor, then directly at Gibson.

'Unfortunately I agree with you. I think it's genuine, can't see it any other way.' His eyes were wet when he spoke. 'The guy they killed was Rick, Richard Boswell, my friend for over forty five years and my business partner for not much less. They kidnapped him and sent me a ransom demand. I went to the police but they didn't really seem to know what to do. They suggested a few things, but I was scared they'd kill Rick so I paid up. Other than telling the police, I followed the kidnapper's instructions to the letter and handed over the diamonds.'

'Diamonds?' said Gibson.

'Yeah diamonds, they insisted on diamonds, clever see, can't mark 'em or trace numbers like you can with cash. Anyway, instead of releasing him like they promised, they sent me that video. I don't see why me going to the cops made any difference to them, I mean they got the diamonds and the cops weren't in a position to interfere, so why kill him?'

'I'm afraid they probably used you going to the police as an excuse, they probably planned to kill him all along, that way there's no witness is there? No one who can give the police any information about the kidnappers?'

'Yeah, you're probably right, the cops here said more or less the same thing.'

'Unfortunately that's always a big risk in these situations' said Gibson. 'So there was no follow up at all from the kidnappers, I mean after they sent you the video?'

'Not to me there wasn't, but a day later, the sick bastards sent a copy to CNN and Fox News. Both of them played edited versions of it over and over again. Everyone pretending they were horrified, but they loved it, just the sort of stuff these media people thrive on, it was horrible.'

'I wonder why the kidnappers would do that?' said Gibson, more to himself than to Jack, 'I mean I can see why they might if they intended to kidnap again, to warn whoever, that they were serious about killing their victims if they weren't paid, but what purpose would it serve in this case? I mean I presume the news channels said you'd paid the ransom?'

'Yeah they did, they always started the report with something like "despite a ransom of millions being paid, the kidnappers still went ahead with their threat to kill Richard Boswell etc., etc...."'

'So', said Gibson, 'what was their motive for sending the video to the news channels? All it would demonstrate is that you pay the ransom, but we still kill the hostage, doesn't make any sense?'

'I don't know what their motive was; your guess is as good as mine Gibson. I have no idea why, but there it was, all over the news for days. 'Because I'd insisted on paying, the cops were really pissed with me. They didn't say we told you so, exactly, but I got the message, you know, but then again, I understood their attitude, and to be fair, after that they did really try to find the guys who did it, but they had nothing to go on and it soon became just one of their unsolved cases.'

'I'm really sorry about that Jack, and listen, I hope this doesn't sound heartless, but why did you ask me to look at this video, not just to confirm what you already know surely, I mean I can understand you being upset, anyone would be but…?'

'No Gibson, please just bear with me. I just want to show you something else, then you'll understand.' Jack pressed a button on the remote and changed the settings on the television to DVD player then pressed the remote again and looked over at Gibson. 'Don't worry this isn't bad, just a news report, bear with me here.' The TV showed the start of a program on extreme weather. Jack fast forwarded to a CNN news report on Hurricane Sandy, then fast forwarded it again, then reversed it until he was at the place he wanted. He pressed the start button. The presenter was in mid commentary about the devastation that Sandy had wreaked on the north east coast of America, and this section was primarily about New Jersey.

It showed street scenes of cars blown over, flood damage and the destruction of buildings. Then it panned into a close up of some officials being helped, by what looked like passers-by, dragging a woman out of a collapsed building. The commentator was talking about unsung heroes who were helping each other and how such disasters brought out the best in people etc., then the commentary stopped abruptly as Jack stopped the picture in freeze frame.

'See here,' he got up, went to the big TV screen and pointed at the face of one of the men in the picture, 'see this man here, that's Rick, right there, look.' Gibson stood to see if he could get a clearer view of the man Jack was pointing to. He could see the likeness to the man in the previous video, but this man had no beard, unshaven yes, but no anchor shaped beard, his hair was darker as well he thought. Despite the likeness, he couldn't swear it was the same person.

'I see what you mean Jack but lots of people have doubles, you hear about it all the time, people being mistaken for other people.'

'Yeah I know, and this guy hasn't got a beard, but that's easy enough to get rid of, but see here, look, how many doubles have the same scar on their face as the original guy? If you look at the video showing the shooting, you'll see a white scar over Richard's left eye which cuts across his eyebrow here,' said Jack pointing at his own left eyebrow 'and if you look closely at this guy on the news report, he has the same scar, see? And I should know about that scar, I gave it to him when we were kids. And look at those eyes, those deep set eyes' Jack pointed again at the man's face on the screen.

Gibson moved closer to get a better look but had to back away until he got a clearer view. He could what Jack meant, and he could see that there might be the white line of a scar over the man's left eye, it was difficult to be absolutely sure, but he had to admit, the man did have the same unusually deep set eyes as the man on the previous video.

'Show me the video of the shooting again and let me see his face on that one please.'

'Sure thing,' Jack said. We can see it on the PC monitor this time so you can compare the two images of Rick's face.' Jack went over to the PC, started the video again, fast forwarding until he found the place he was looking for and freeze framed it. 'See here, the same scar, now tell me it isn't Rick on both pictures.'

Gibson looked at the picture of Rick's face on the PC, then went over and scrutinised the image of the face on the television again. Jack waited then went over to the blinds and opened them to let the light in. Gibson sat down again, sipped his lukewarm coffee and pondered. He wondered just what he'd got himself into, but he couldn't deny being intrigued. He needed to know where this was all going though. Jack came back and sat down on the leather chair looking at Gibson waiting for him to speak.

'Well Jack I admit the likeness is there.'

'Likeness?' Jack exclaimed. It's too much of a likeness Gibson, I think it could be Rick, maybe he's still alive.'

'I assume you've shown all this to the appropriate authorities?'

'Yep and they don't wanna know.'

'Well I don't know what to say Jack, I mean you asked me to look at the original video and I gave you my honest opinion. But I agree, the man on the news report does look like the same man, but obviously, if your friend was abducted and killed in September, he couldn't possibly have been alive during Hurricane Sandy, which was when, November?'

'Well, end of October when it hit.'

'So if you're absolutely convinced that your friend might still be alive, it seems to me you need to pursue this with the authorities, and make them listen. But to state the obvious, if he is still alive, then the execution was staged, So the question is, why would that be? Perhaps it's more likely that there are in fact two people who look alike and who both have a similar facial scars Jack. I mean scars like that are not uncommon, I've got a scar under my eye as you can see and I guess there are lots of other people with similar facial scars.'

'Yeah, but do they look exactly like you as well? C'mon Gibson, there's something hinky about all this.'

Gibson realised he was being drawn in, and began to think how he could extricate himself, before this went any further. He stood up ready to leave and said.

'I can see where you're going with this Jack and I really wish you the best of luck. I just hope I've been of help, though I'm not sure how. But I'd better be off now, lunch to make and maybe some fishing to arrange.' Jack stood.

'Help me Gibson, help me find Richard, I'll pay you.'

'Look Jack, I can't even if I wanted to I wouldn't know where to start. I'd love to help, but it's impossible, look I'll have to go.'

'You were a cop Gibson, sorry a detective, you know the ropes, it's not like we speak another language over here, lots of things are pretty much the same. And, I'll make it worth your while, seriously, I'll pay you well either way, but if we could prove Richard's still alive then you'd get a small fortune. The insurance company alone would pay big-time. At the moment they're looking to pay my company well over half a million bucks for a key man insurance claim, you could expect to get maybe a third of that if you find him alive.'

'I really can't. I admit the money's tempting and I'm flattered you think I could do the job, but I just couldn't. Anyway why ask me, I'm sure there are lots of American private detectives available, people who know the ropes over here, I wouldn't even know where to begin, so even if I did agree you'd be wasting your money.'

'Yeah but you do have contacts over here don't you, I mean in the police. I read your bio on the net and it said you did three months secondment or whatever the right word is, with the NYPD. I read all about how they asked you to help in a serial killer case they had, after you'd cracked the case in the UK. And as I understand it they did eventually catch the guy and gave you a lot of credit for your help, so c'mon Gibson what do you say?'

'That was different. I was just in a consulting role, never operational, so it doesn't change anything, I just couldn't accept your offer, sorry Jack.'

'Okay Gibson, but just promise me you'll think about my proposition. I won't say another word about it. I'll leave you alone to get on with your vacation. You can relax by the pool whatever. And if you don't bring the subject up with me I'll never mention it again to you. But thanks for your time today I really appreciate it.'

'That's fair enough Jack I'm happy to have helped, if that's what I did, and please understand, I'd love to help you further, but I can't see how I could. I'm sure an American private detective would be much better placed to do the job.'

'Yeah maybe you're right, it's just that when I checked on the internet and read all about your career, I thought this is fate, this guy has arrived just as I found out Rick might not be dead.'

'But surely, that CNN report was a few months ago, so why have you only just found out?'

'By accident, I was watching this TV program on hurricanes last week and they played an extract from CNN news, and that's when I saw Rick or at least someone who looks incredibly like him. Fortunately it was a program they were repeating, so I had the opportunity to record it the next day and study it more closely. Then I went to the cops, and like I said, they didn't want to know, then the same day I received your booking details, looked you up on the internet and found out you were a cop, fate Gibson, I'm a great believer in it.'

CHAPTER 3

Bay View was a low rise three story block of apartments, containing just thirty units in total. There were two buildings built at right angles to each other. The large gardens were laid to lawn, lush with hibiscus and bougainvillea. The gardens stretched all the way down to the edge of Venetian Bay. Royal palm trees were scattered here and there, giving it a Caribbean feel. There were individual boat docks built into the retaining wall of the bay. At the front of the complex were visitor's parking spaces and under cover parking for the resident's cars.

The apartment he'd rented had use of one of the boat docks, but there was no boat included in the deal, so he'd called the local bait shop who also rented out boats, to see what prices were like. At three hundred dollars a day, Gibson concluded funds wouldn't stretch to hiring a boat, so he decided to buy some fishing tackle instead and make do with fishing off the boat dock for the time being.

He made himself a ham and onion sandwich for lunch, washed it down with a diet coke, then drove the short distance to the bait shop on Park Shore where he kitted himself out with a rod, reel, line, bait and all the other essential bits of tackle he needed, then drove back to Bay View and made his way down to the boat dock where he spent the next two hours happily relaxing in the sun, catching fish and throwing them back.

Afterwards, back in the apartment he felt relaxed, the fishing had occupied his mind completely for a while and now he was rested and refreshed. He found it hard to believe that only twenty four hours before, he'd felt so low that that he thought life wasn't worth living. He sat on a stool in the kitchen glugging some bottled water and reflected on the strange meeting with Jack earlier in the day. The pull of curiosity tempted him to consider the proposition, but another internal voice cautioned him, telling him to put it out of his mind completely, that he'd be barking mad to even consider taking on such a thing, relax and enjoy yourself in the sun, there's lots of fish to catch, places to see all this lovely weather to enjoy…

He went to the bedroom and through into the huge walk in wardrobe where he'd stored his luggage, found his cabin bag, brought it out and placed on the bed, then searched through it until he found his address book. Sitting on the edge of the bed, he ran his finger down the tabs stopping at the letter R. He opened the book, looked down the page, then picked up the phone.

'NYPD how may I direct your call?'

'Bureau Chief Tom Romano please.'

'Please hold and I'll put you through to his secretary.'

'Bureau Chief Romano's office, can I help you?'

'Yes, could I speak to Chief Romano please?'

'I'll see if he's free. Who may I say is calling?' Gibson gave his name and was put on hold again. A man's voice came on the phone.

'Is that really you Gibson, you limey cocksucker?'

'And a very good afternoon to you too Chief Romano.'

'Yup it's you alright, you calling from that little island of yours, now what's it called again Great Brittany, something like that, right?' Romano was the original wind up merchant and knew only too well where Brittany was, but he still made Gibson laugh with his pretend insults.

'As a matter of fact I'm back in the USA, Naples Florida to be precise.'

'Wow Gibson, you've become a snowbird. So did you just call to tell me how wonderful the weather is down there or to ask after my health?'

'Neither, I wanted your advice, well opinion really; do you have time to talk?

'For you Gibson old buddy, I have all the time in the world. It's partly due to you that I've got this fancy bird and stars on my uniform. Oh and by the way, I assume you got my letter about Jill?'

'Yes I did Tony, thanks for all the kind words.'

'So my friend, I'm sitting down, go ahead, what's the haps?' The chief's voice was a bit husky to begin with but soon cleared.

Gibson explained his strange morning meeting with Jack, leaving nothing out. The chief remained quiet and let Gibson tell the story without interruption, then said.

'Yeah I remember that, they showed the execution video on the news, well edited bits of it, like one of those terrorist beheading type vids, pretty vile. So why are you calling me - as if I couldn't guess?'

'Well what do you think Tony?'

'You mean do I think it's possible the guy's still alive, or do I think you're crazy to think of taking this on?'

'Both.' There was a brief silence at the other end of the phone, then, 'Well partner, the answer to both is yes. I think it's possible he could still be alive, unlikely, but possible. And yes you'd be crazy as a coot to take it on,'

'So will you help me, if I decide to go ahead?'

'I was afraid you were going to ask me that. Jesus Gibson, it'll be like looking for a needle in ten haystacks, for Chrissakes, why do you want to do this?'

'To get my life back. Since Jill died, I've been in a funk, more like a depression you know…, and well, I need to do something, something that will take all my attention and energy, something challenging and this will be challenging.'

'You can say that again partner. Look you know the answer, I couldn't refuse you, so what do you want me to do?'

'Well I'll need some sort of authority to ask questions. Can I get some sort of official designation, you know like when I was seconded to your department the last time?'

'This is a bit different old friend, but…, yeah okay I'll work something out, and…?'

'And, I'll need access to records and any stuff pertinent to my investigation, could you assign someone in your department as a contact, someone I can call when I need information, that sort of thing, I obviously can't keep calling the big smell at the top, whenever I want something.'

The chief laughed heartily down the line, 'well Gibson, I've been called some things in my life, but never the big smell at the top, you really are a one off partner.'

'So that's a yes then?'

'Yeah that's a yes, as you put it. I'll get Margie my secretary to get things organised. I'll brief her on the background and she can appraise whoever I designate for the job, in fact I know just the right person, Bonnie Ledinski, a very bright junior detective, she's cute and smart.

'Thanks Tony, you're a pal.'

'Yeah sure I'm a pal, big smell at the top, wait till I tell my wife, she'll just love that, bye you crazy limey bastard, and good hunting.'

CHAPTER 4

He put the phone back in its cradle and went to stand at the large window overlooking the gardens, the swimming pool and Venetian Bay. The sky was deep blue, devoid of any cloud, the late afternoon sun sparkled on the breeze rippled water in the bay. A squadron of pelicans flew in a low formation, skimming the surface looking for shoals of fish to plunder.

'Crazy limey bastard', he repeated out loud to no one in particular. Then went over to the kitchen table, sat down and started up his laptop. He checked the mass times at the local catholic churches. It was Sunday tomorrow and St Anne's on 9th Street Naples had a mass at eleven, perfect.

Gibson was converted to Catholicism late in life. Jill was a catholic and Gibson found himself occasionally attending mass with her on Sundays. Eventually the priest persuaded Gibson to go the whole hog and become a catholic himself, which he did, as much to please Jill as anything else. But then found mass a place where he could meditate and reflect, and he began to appreciate the new perspective it gave him on life, and maybe more.

That was until Jill's untimely death, when he fell out with God big time, but now for reasons he couldn't fathom he felt the need to re-connect. He went back over to the window and gazed out, looked up at the sky and sighed.

'Well', he said, 'I suppose you think I'm crazy too'. Jack answered the door and looked at Gibson nonplussed.

Hi Gibson, come on in, I'm working in here.' Gibson followed Jack into the den. Jack had his glasses pushed back on top of his head and there was a pile of paper on his desk and other piles of papers on the floor. 'Please sit down and excuse the mess, just doing the domestic bills and some paperwork from the company. I'm not really involved day to day but I sometimes wonder if they realise that – so is this visit what I think is?'

'Well I'm not sure if either of us has thought this through properly and common sense tells me that this is a crazy thing to do, but on the other hand, you're right I was a good cop and a good detective and truth to tell, I miss it, I miss the action, so if you still want me to do the job, then I'm in.'

Jack's face split wide with a huge grin. 'I knew you would' and he thrust his hand out for Gibson to shake. Jack was strong and his enthusiastic handshake nearly pulled Gibson's shoulder out of joint. 'C'mon let's have a drink' said Jack and headed out of the door, Gibson followed. They went into the lounge which had a large open kitchen to the rear.

'Mary Lou, Mary Lou,' Jack yelled. 'No Mary Lou, must be still down by the pool, loves the sun that girl. What'll you have, sit down anywhere, I'm having bourbon with ice?'

'The same' said Gibson and sat down on the sumptuous gold and red braided settee. Jack got two cut glass tumblers out of a dark oak display cabinet, took some ice out of the huge silver steel fridge freezer in the kitchen and poured two generous slugs of Four Roses bourbon into the tumblers. He passed one to Gibson and said 'here's to success Gibson.' They clinked glasses and Gibson said 'to success' then they both took a swig of bourbon. The deal was sealed.

'Okay, so you'd better tell me the whole story Jack, have you got a pad and pen so I can make notes?'

'Sure thing Gibson, in fact let's go back into the den where I have all my papers, dates and things.' Once they were seated in the den and Gibson had a pad and pen, Jack began.

'Rick and I grew up together in a little place called Janesville Wisconsin. Rick's mom and mine were best friends and we lived just a few doors from each other, went to the same school and all that. He was a couple of years older than me but after his dad was killed in the Korean war he ended up spending a lot of time at my house, we were close, more like brothers than friends. Then we both got caught in the draft lottery in sixty nine and served a year's tour of duty in Nam. We were both in the infantry, thrown in at the deep end and we'd only been there a couple of weeks when the shit went through the fan and we found ourselves on the front line in the battle of hill nine three seven otherwise known as Hamburger Hill, you heard about that right?'

'I'm afraid not, I was only what, fifteen years old then and I was more concerned with taking my exams than noticing what was happening on the other side of the world.'

'Right, yeah of course, well it was one of those crazy pointless military objectives that achieved sweet nothing other than the unnecessary slaughter of American troops. Know why it was nicknamed Hamburger Hill?' Gibson shook his head 'Because when we attacked, we were chewed up like hamburgers.' Jack stopped talking, looked down and drew a long breath through his nose, then he looked up and his smile returned, 'anyway I won't go into detail, but it was rough, but we both survived and that's the main thing. So when we came out of the army we decided to start up in business together. I'd worked in a travel agency as a kid and Richard had worked in a bank.

We decided to open up a travel agency, mainly 'cos it needed very little capital and there was no stock to buy. We just called it JARIC, combination of our initials and eventually added a bureau de change to the business and the way things went meant that we ended up specialising in big groups rather than individuals. Oh I forgot to say that soon after starting the business, we moved to New York, big city, big bucks we thought, and we were right. One thing led to another and we grew the business into a big multimillion dollar organisation, and I mean big. After about five years hard slog we were able to ease up a bit and then we both met our respective future wives.

I met Mary Lou, she was only seventeen at the time and Richard met a girl called Sally. All this happened within a couple of months. So it ended up where we both got married the following year, on the same day, same church the lot, a double wedding. As you know I'm still married to Mary Lou, but Richard split up with Sally about five years ago, shame really as they were great together. I don't think he ever actually got divorced, but still.

So, back to the business. We had fantastic hotel deals all over the world that our competitors just couldn't match. Richard used his expertise to work the foreign exchange bureau and unknown to me started, dealing in currency speculation, you know, essentially betting on exchange rates. If I'd known, particularly if I'd known the size of the sums involved I have crapped myself, but as it turned out, Richard had the touch and we made even more money.'

'And do you still both own the business?' Gibson asked, as Jack stopped talking briefly to take a drink of his bourbon.

'Yeah pretty much, I mean Rick and I are still the major shareholders, well we were, Rick's shares are going to be the subject of probate I guess. We gave some equity away to key staff a few years ago as we were getting on and we wanted to do less, at least I did. Richard was hooked on making more and more money so he stayed more involved with the foreign exchange side. That side of business was more like a bank and Richard was handling all sorts of big international financial transactions through it.'

'Okay' said Gibson scribbling the last of his notes. 'I get the general picture, so what happened, I mean when was Richard kidnapped, how did that all come about?'

CHAPTER 5

FIVE MONTHS EARLIER

Jack and Mary Lou were strolling arm in arm along the promenade deck of the Celebrity Constellation, on its way back to Miami after cruising round the Caribbean. The sea was calm and flat, the air warm and balmy. Stars twinkled against a backdrop of a solid black sky; it was a perfect September night. They were due back in Miami the following day and had just had dinner with the people they'd shared a table with for the past two weeks. Everyone said how much they'd enjoyed each other's company and they all promised to keep in contact, swapping phone numbers and email addresses, the more experienced among them knowing it was unlikely any of them would hear from the others again.

They'd been married for thirty six years and Mary Lou booked the cruise as a surprise, to celebrate their wedding anniversary and also Jack's sixty fourth birthday, both of which had occurred earlier that month. Mary Lou was ten years younger than Jack and still looked good for her age. She stood five foot five without heels, had well coiffured auburn hair and took care of herself. Jack was nearer six foot, overweight, with greying hair, but he still cut a handsome figure.

'Well Jack, I'll be glad to get back home, it's been a perfect cruise, absolutely perfect,' she turned and gave him a peck on the cheek.

'Yeah,' he said, 'makes you feel lucky to be alive, like you say, just perfect.' Then Jack's cell phone warbled.

'Jack, how many times have I told you to switch that damn thing off when we're out?'

'Yeah I really should do that, sorry, better answer it all the same.' The voice was indistinct, muffled and gravelly.

'Jack Otterbein?' the voice asked.

'Uh huh' said Jack.

'Listen and listen carefully, we've taken Richard Boswell and unless you do exactly as we say, he'll be executed.'

'Yeah yeah yeah okay, I'll play.' Jack said smiling and looking at Mary Lou, pointing at his head with his free hand, making a circular motion with his finger. 'So kill him, I mean, as if I care.' Then he laughed. Mary Lou looked at him enquiringly.

'Okay if that's the way you want to play it,' said the voice, 'we'll send you a finger, or maybe an ear when you get back from your cruise, then we'll call back, see if you're still laughing.'

'Hold on, whoa, just hold on,' said Jack, the smile turning quickly to a worried frown. 'Hello, hello, are you still there? Hello, hello….Jesus.. answer me….are you still there?'

Eventually the gravelly voice replied. 'I'm still here,'

'What do you want?' asked Jack.

'What do you think we want, we want money.'

'I don't understand.'

'What's to understand? We have your partner and we'll kill him if you don't pay up. Is that simple enough for you? Now shut up and listen. We'll contact you again to give you your instructions. I warn you now, if you go to the police, or try anything clever, then all bets are off, understand?'

'Yeah, I understand, but....'

'But what?' said the voice in an exasperated manner. Jack had recovered some of his composure now.

'How do I know you've got Richard, put him on the phone.'

There was a muffled conversation, a scream in the background, then a strangled voice, a couple of octaves higher than normal, 'Jack you've got to help me....' The first man came on again.

'That's it, so do as you're fuckin' told and he goes free, try to fuck us over, and he's gator food.' And with that the line went dead.

Jack turned to Mary Lou, lost for words. 'What was that all about Jack?'

'They've got Rick.'

'Who's got Rick, what are you talking about Jack, you're not making any sense.'

'He's been kidnapped; they said they'll kill him, execute him if I don't do as they say.'

'Who is it, who's going to kill him?'

'How the fuck do I know? He didn't give me his name and address!' Mary Lou looked shocked and about to cry.

'Sorry, sorry honey, I didn't mean to…, oh sweet Jesus, c'mon Mary Lou,' Jack put his arm around Mary Lou's shoulders, 'we'd better go back to the cabin, I need a stiff drink.'

They arrived back into Miami the following day and were disembarked by cabin number order. Jack and Mary Lou fidgeted while they waited for their number to be called. Neither of them could face breakfast. Eventually they were allowed to get off and made their way down the walkway and on to the dockside, then along to the luggage hall to collect their bags. Jack signaled a porter and Mary Lou went to look for their luggage.

They found their bags and were leaving the luggage hall, porter in tow to collect their car from the car park when Jack saw a little black boy holding a placard with Jack Otterbein written on it.

'You looking for me kid?'

'If you Jack Ottobeen man, then yeah I lookin' for you, here,' he said and thrust an envelope out towards Jack. Jack took it and was about to ask some questions, but the boy ran off weaving in between the other passenger and porters and was soon lost to sight. He sighed and opened the envelope. There was a single sheet of paper with neat writing on it.

Follow these instructions to the letter or you get to arrange a funeral, not that you'll have a body to bury. At nine a.m. on the 8th September leave your apartment in Naples (yes we know where you live) drive alone, along the Tamiami Trail to County road, the junction of 41 and 29. Park in the Gas station and wait. Bring $2m dollar's worth of diamonds, each diamond to be worth approx $5,000. Put them inside a small secure hold-all. They won't weigh much. They will be professionally valued before we release him so don't do anything stupid, but an allowance will be made if you're a little under or over in the total value. Take an additional $1,000 in $20s and $50s unmarked bills and keep separately in your pocket. If we suspect you've told the cops, or we find any electronic tracking devices in the bags, any tricky stuff at all and Richard Boswell will be executed.

Mary Lou saw Jack reading the note. '

What is it Jack?'

'Later, let's get the car first.'

They left Miami and made their way to the Interstate for the hour and a half drive across Florida from the east to the west coast along Alligator Alley and on to Naples on the Gulf of Mexico where they lived in the winter. They hadn't spoken to each other since leaving the docks, other than to check road directions but once they were settled on the Interstate Jack said.

'The letter's in my inside jacket pocket on the back seat, grab it will you and read it to me.' Mary Lou read it out loud, stopping abruptly at the part where it specified the sum of money being demanded by the kidnappers. 'two million dollars' worth of diamonds! Holy shit Jack, where're you going to get that many diamonds from, and where are you going to get the money to pay for them?'

'Good questions.'

'Do you think they're serious?'

'I don't know, but I think they are.'

'Are you going to tell the police?'

'Well, they say they'll kill Rick if I do, but I've been thinking. If I don't go to the cops, I won't be able to make any kind of insurance claim for the ransom and I'm sure we have some kind of cover for stuff like this. I know we have key man insurance for each of us, but I think that only kicks in if either one of us dies. I need to check, but I think I have to go to the cops, it doesn't mean we won't still have to pay though. Let's see what they say, Jesus Christ I can't believe this is happening.' Mary Lou looked disapprovingly at Jack.

'And what about the money, do you have that much money in the company?'

'Well yeah we do, at any one time we have somewhere around a hundred million dollars in cash at the bank, maybe more. It's not ours, its forward cash flow, basically pipeline cash, you know, money clients have paid for stuff we've booked, plus any money we're holding on the forex side. We don't give credit but we get credit, so we probably owe ninety five per cent of the cash we have in the bank.'

'Well I knew you made lots of money Jack, but I never knew just how much.' Mary Lou was quiet for a brief moment while she did the math, 'you mean you make five million profit a year?'

'Yeah, well that's gross, net, its' a lot less, lots of costs to come out of that and it depends on the year, this year's been particularly good. Rick has done some amazing deals on the banking and forex side of the business, so I guess we can kind of borrow the money out of the cash flow, it's how to get it out without it amounting to fraud or whatever, I'll talk to the accountants, I'm sure they can figure something out. As for buying diamonds, I wouldn't know where to start, but I guess we can employ some kind of expert for that. What day is it today and when's the eighth, I've lost all track of time while we've been away?'

'It's Monday today, the third, so it's this Saturday, six days from now, including today.'

'Jesus Christ Almighty'

'Don't blaspheme Jack.'

CHAPTER 6

PRESENT DAY

'So?' Gibson asked, 'were you able to get the money and the diamonds in time?'

'Yeah that wasn't too problematic as it turned out. Our accountants arranged for me to have access to the necessary funds within forty eight hours and buying diamonds is easier than you think. There's lots of people buy diamonds instead of gold as an investment these days, so we soon found a respectable source and that was pretty well it. There was a bit of a problem getting the right number of diamonds at the right value range demanded by the kidnappers but we got there in the end.'

'Why do you think they specified the value of the diamonds?'

'The cops said it would be easier for them to dispose of them in small quantities, rather than trying to offload large value ones, and I could see that made sense. I tell you, it was quite scary for a couple of days though, having two million bucks worth of diamonds hidden in our apartment.'

'And what happened with the police?'

'Well that was a bit more difficult. When I told the cops in Naples, they got a hostage specialist guy over from Miami. He interrogated me and I was sure he thought I was involved. I suppose they have to think like that, but it pissed me off. Anyway they wanted to do all sorts of things, electronic tags on everything, including me, bug my phones, all that kind of shit, but to be honest I thought it was all a waste of time and too risky. My feeling was we were dealing with some really smart guys and it wouldn't take them long to figure out if I'd followed their instructions or not, so I told the cops I was going to pay up.'

'And?'

'They were furious, but I know that even governments pay ransoms on the quiet, even though they all say they don't, they do. I mean, if you're dealing with smart ruthless guys, then what choice do you have?'

'How did you hand the diamonds over?'

'Well I drove to the gas station like they told me to. The cops had insisted that they at least monitor my cell phone and use it to track my movements, but the kidnappers weren't that stupid. There was a taxi waiting at the gas station and after I'd been parked for a couple of minutes, the driver, Hispanic looking guy, he gets out and walks over to me and asks if I'm Jack Otterbein. I says yes and he hands me another cell phone and he tells me he has instructions to tell me to leave my own cell phone in my car.

He watches me leave my cell then I get in his taxi then he drives me down the 29, and the cell phone he's given me rings. It's the same guy that called before, same muffled sounding voice. He tells me I'm going to the Everglades

Airport where I'll find a helicopter waiting for me. You know Gibson, I don't think I ever realised there was an Everglades airport, but it was huge, stuck out in the middle of nowhere and apart from a couple of light planes there was just the one helicopter So the taxi man has a word with the guy in the Airport office and they open the gate and let us drive right up to the copter. The pilot, an old guy, he tells me to get in and the taxi driver says he'll wait for me.

The pilot tells me he has the coordinates for where we're going and he'd been paid a deposit but he'd been told I'd pay him the balance in cash. He wanted five hundred bucks so I handed it over. He didn't ask me what this was all about and I didn't tell him. We took off and the pilot tells me about the airport, something to talk about I suppose, but he tells me it's big enough to land a jumbo or even the space shuttle, but it's mostly used by blue herons and gators who sometimes sunbathe on the runway.

Anyway, we fly out into the everglades and over the ten thousand islands, man what a view. It was a beautiful Florida day, blue sky hardly any clouds. I'd always wondered if there really were ten thousand islands, and I think there probably are at least that many. He looks at some notes on his lap and checks it with his instruments then says, here we are, and we begin to descend on to one of the larger islands. We land next to a wide sand beach and there's a small yellow and white fishing boat moored just offshore.

A guy on the boat waves three times, then the pilot tells me to take whatever it is I'm supposed to leave and place it on the beach along with the cell phone. I do as he says then get back in and off we go. I asked the pilot if he knew the guy on the boat and he says, 'no and I don't want to, okay? I'm just doing the job I'm paid for.'

Fair enough, I think. and in no time we're landing back at the Everglades airport, I get back in the taxi and he drops me off at my car. That's it, or so I thought.

'So did you hear from them again?'

'No, well no phone call or anything, just a letter in the mail three days later with a flash card in it. You can guess what was on it,' said Jack looking at his PC.

'What did the police say when you showed them?'

'They weren't that sympathetic. They analyzed it and came to the same conclusion as you, that it was all genuine. They had zip to go on in terms of tracing the kidnappers and no chance of tracing the diamonds. They flew me in a helicopter over the ten thousand islands again to see if I could locate where we'd made the drop, but it was impossible to tell, they all look the same from up there.

They also interviewed our staff, particularly those who worked in Rick's division, but nothing came of that. They found out that the last person to see Rick before he disappeared was his secretary. When she left for the day, he was in his office, working late as usual. He'd told her earlier that he was flying down to Naples the following day for some R&R. He has a house down on Gordon Drive in Port Royal. That's where the cops say the snatch took place.

Rick lives, or lived alone and just had a part time housekeeper who did some cleaning for him and looked after the place when he wasn't there. The police found the lanai at the back had a big hole ripped in it and they said the kidnappers got in through that. The house has a swimming pool that's a sort of extension of the living room. It extends into the garden and has this big lanai over it. There's a slider between the pool and the lounge, but people don't tend to keep them locked, I mean this is Naples, one of the most secure places in America, you just don't expect house invasions or burglars round here.'

'What about security cameras, surely he had those?'

'Yeah, but they were covered in white paint and the police say that the kidnapers probably used paintball guns, or some sort of paintbrush or pad on a pole to disable them, something like that anyway.'

'Did they say if there was there any sign of a struggle, in the house itself?'

'No, the cops said they probably woke Rick up with a gun to the head and took him out of the front door. The house has a big hedge around it so you can't see into the front, nice and private. The bed was rumpled they said so that was it and it all came to a dead end, and that's where it's stayed.'

'Okay well I'm going to need to talk to the local police to get details, so I'll get some names off you later. I'll also need to talk to his housekeeper, and any friends or acquaintances he has, or had down here, girlfriends, people, where he went for a drink, all that sort of stuff, but first I need to go and see his offices, interview his secretary and see his apartment, in New York you said?'

'Yeah, the office is in Union Square, between fifth and Broadway and Rick's apartment is quite nearby.'

'Great, I can kill two birds with one stone. I have to go and see an old friend of mine, Chief Romano at NYPD. He's agreed to fix me up with some sort of authority to be able to ask questions, interview people, get information from the police and so on.'

'See, I knew you could pull some strings if you wanted to. Now listen, you're going to need some money to cover your initial expenses, so just wait there I'll go get some cash.'

Gibson started to protest but then thought better of it. He hadn't got a lot of spare money so he wasn't in a position to fund any air fares or hotel accommodation, no matter how temporary that might be. Jack came back and handed over two thousand dollars in cash to him.

'Here take that to begin with. I suggest you keep plenty in cash and put the rest into your checking account so you can use your credit card against it.'

Gibson said it seemed far too much money, but Jack would have none of it and told Gibson it was chicken feed in the scheme of things.

'Okay Jack, is Richard's secretary still working at the company?'

'Betty Matlock, yeah she's still there, works for the guy who took over from Rick.'

'Okay, then can you tell her to expect me, and can you arrange for me to have access to Richard's apartment, that's assuming you haven't got rid of it?'

'No, the apartment's still there, the lease doesn't run out for another six months. I'll call Betty and tell her to expect you, when do you plan to go?'

'It's Sunday tomorrow, so I'll start first thing Monday, might as well get stuck in right away, before I have second thoughts.'

'Great news Gibson great news, I knew you were the man. Are you okay making your own flight arrangements, need any help with that?'

'No, I'd prefer to book my own flights, but could you ask someone to arrange a hotel near your offices, I think I'll only need one night, two at the most.'

'No problem Gibson. You might want to check the weather forecast, its mighty cold up there this time of year and I heard snow was on the way, so if I were you I'd take something nice and warm to wear. I'll make the call now and get someone to sort out your hotel reservation.'

'Thanks Jack.'

'No Gibson, thank you, I can't tell you how pleased I am that you've agreed to do this.'

'Yes well,' said Gibson, 'we'll just have to see how well I deserve your gratitude.'

Sunday morning Gibson went for his run along the beach then after breakfast made his way to St Anne's. He found he had to park some distance away even though he was early. He knelt in the pew and prayed. It felt strange being alone in the church. He'd always been with Jill whenever he attended mass before, even at the funeral, he thought. Jill entered his thoughts and she looked happy. He was about to speak out loud to her then remembered where he was. She laughed, then the priest started talking and the spell was broken.

CHAPTER 7

'Jeff, get that blanket and hood off our hostage and cut those ties.'

'Sure thing Dave' said Jeff and took a small folding knife out of his pocket as he went over to the man on the floor, nearly slipping on the bloody plastic sheeting as he knelt down. He removed the blanket then pulled the hood gently off the man's head and cut the plastic ties behind his back. He moved along the sheet to the man's feet, and did the same there.

'You okay Mr Boswell?' shouted the man called Dave, who was now busy taking the camera off the tripod. The man on the floor didn't reply but just rolled over on to his back and lay there for a while, eyes closed.

'You okay Mr Boswell, want some help?'

'Just leave me a minute for chrissakes,' said the man in an exasperated voice. 'Jesus I can't believe I'm paying you fuckers to put me through so much pain.'

'Sorry about that Mr Boswell, we just did as you asked, and if I say so myself, I think we did a great job.' The man turned his attention to the other one who was busy clearing up. 'Frank, make sure you clear up all that blood and put that sheet in the bag over there, we got to leave this place as clean as we found it, okay?'

'Yeah yeah, I hear ya,' the man replied.

'And you Jeff, be careful with that camera, put it back in the case carefully, that's a couple of thousand buck's worth of equipment, and here,' he said holding the folded tripod up, 'don't forget this.' The man called Dave went over to Richard Boswell and extended his hand for him to get hold of. 'C'mon Mr Boswell, we got to be out of here soon.'

Richard grabbed the man's hand and got up to a sitting position, then the man pulled him all the way upright.

'Jesus' said Richard, his face contorting as he got to a standing position. 'Where's the rest room?'

'Over in the corner Mr Boswell.'

'And my bag?' The man went over to the small pile of equipment, got Richard's bag and handed it to him. Richard closed the rest room door, turned, looked in the grimy mirror and couldn't help laughing Jesus what a mess. He opened his bag and pulled out a plastic garbage sack, a flannel, some fresh clothes and a roll of kitchen towel. He dropped the clothes on the floor and hooked the garbage sack on the faucet then he slowly pulled his blood soaked sweatshirt over his head grunting as he did so, and dumped it in the sack. Underneath was the Kevlar vest, held in place with Velcro, it had cost over five hundred dollars, but well worth it he thought as he stuffed that in the sack along with the remains of the bloody plastic bag, his tee shirt, jeans and underpants.

He ran some water, soaked the flannel and wiped himself down. He rummaged in the bag for his shaving stuff and scissors, then chopped at his beard and moustache then used his battery powered razor to get rid the rest of his facial hair. He smoothed his hand over his chin, it felt strange and still a bit stubbly but it would do for now he thought. He put the shaving stuff back in his bag, took most of the hair out of the sink and flushed it down the toilet, then ran the faucet to clear the remaining bits of hair down the plughole. He took some toilet paper wiped around the sink and flushed that down the toilet as well. Satisfied there was no hair left, he tied the plastic sack and went back out, he winced again as he put his sports bag and the garbage sack down on the floor near the door.

'You're going to be sore for a while I reckon Mr Boswell, but think of all that money you're going to get, that should make you feel better.'

'Look, I told you, the money I'll be getting is my own money. I know it's difficult for you to grasp and I'm not going to explain, but that's a fact. Anyway that's not for you to worry about, you and your buddies here are being well paid for your services so just be happy with that.'

'Yes we are Mr Boswell, very happy, but the payment terms, it's been bothering us. We were talking last night and we think you should pay us the whole lot now, we won't say anything I promise, why would we?' Richard Boswell laughed.

'You promise? That's rich, now you listen to me, no, on second thoughts you'd better all hear what I'm going to say, so tell your buddies to stop what they're doing and come over here.' There was an old wooden table and six metal chairs in the corner of the old disused warehouse which the owner rented out now as a film studio, or for any other purpose that he could charge for. Richard Boswell's chest was aching like crazy so he went over to sit down on one of the chairs. Dave followed him telling the other men to stop what they were doing and come over to join them. Richard told them all to sit down. They sat.

'I think I need to impress upon you all just what the situation is so there's no misunderstanding, okay?' He looked quickly at each of them then slammed the flat of his hand down on the table hard, making them all jump. 'I said okay? - that was a question, indicate you understand.' They each mumbled their understanding. 'Now, you second rate no good, out of work, so called actors, this is probably the most you will ever be paid for your work, if you can call acting work that is. So listen, and listen good.'

Dave opened his mouth to speak but Richard Boswell looked at him and he decided to keep quiet.

'I'm not going to change the terms we agreed. I've already given you five thousand dollars between you, which is more than adequate for the expenses to date, the hire of this place, the camera equipment, your time etc. You can keep the change. In addition I'm giving you each fifty thousand dollars which will be placed in three individual offshore accounts in each of your names. You will not be able to draw more than five thousand dollars in any four week period. The reason for this is to make it unlikely that you will go on a spending spree and attract attention' Richard Boswell stopped speaking and rubbed his chest. The man called Dave took the opportunity to speak.

'Look Mr Boswell, you can trust us not to do that, we wouldn't dream of…..'

'Please don't tell me what you wouldn't dream of doing, we're all human and you wouldn't be able to resist, believe me I know about people, so just shut up and listen, this is important. If anyone asks where your new found wealth came from, you tell them you worked as extras in a film and took the option to share in the revenue rather than take wages and it all worked out for you, okay? Should anyone check, the deposits in those accounts will appear to have been paid by a film production company, right?'

'Man you've covered all the bases, I'm impressed Mr Boswell,' said Dave.

'You don't know the half of it. Now what you say about this money to the IRS is your affair, but if you spend it slow and keep it in cash, the likelihood is you'll never be asked to account for it.'

'And when can we draw out the first five grand?' Said Jeff.

'Tomorrow,' said Richard. All three men looked at each other and grinned.

'Awesome,' said Dave and stood up extending his hand to Richard Boswell 'It's been a great pleasure working with you and like I say, you can trust us not to say a word to anyone.'

'Sit down Dave, I haven't finished.' Dave frowned, put his hand down and sat.

'I don't know if it's crossed your mind to wonder why I chose you three in particular.' All three men looked blank. 'No? Well I contacted a theatrical agency and told them I wanted to hire three actors to play tough guys in a new film. They sent me details of a lot of people they considered suitable. I did some initial research on each one who applied and came up with you three, not because of your acting ability, but because you were the first three that fit the criteria I was looking for. Each of you is in a fairly long term relationship, has a relatively stable home life and although only one of you is still married, you all have one important thing in common, each of you has at least one child.' Richard stopped talking and looked at each of them in turn to see if they were beginning to get the message. They had lost the happy faces they had worn when they'd been thinking about the money.

'Now I'm a very rich and powerful man, and well connected. Connected to nice people and some not so nice people, need I say more?' He looked at them all again. They didn't respond but he knew they were all on the same page. He stood up. 'Okay gentlemen time to part company. Enjoy the money keep your mouths shut and you won't have any problems.' And with that he took a Yankee's baseball cap out of his pocket, pulled it low down over his face, walked across the room out of the door and into the warm Florida sunshine.

CHAPTER 8

Jack insisted on driving Gibson to Fort Myers airport, a journey of just over half an hour, during which Gibson was able to ask Jack a few more general questions about Richard Boswell.

'Something I wanted to ask you Jack, not particularly pertinent to the case, but you said that Richard had a house in Port Royal so I looked at some on the internet.'

'Impressive places aren't they?' said Jack.

'That's an understatement.'

'And you're wondering why Mary Lou and I live in a relatively modest apartment, right?'

'You able to read my mind now Jack?'

'Nah, don't worry Gibson, it's been asked before is all. The fact is we like it at Bay View. We bought that apartment when we first started to make money, so it has a lot of sentimental value to us, and its where my friends are. We go back a long way with many of the folks at Bay View. Rick on the other hand, was always more interested in material things than me and he's always been more ambitious. Don't get me wrong, I love money too and we're not exactly poor, we have a beautiful house in Mantauk, Long Island where we spend the summer, so I'm not complaining. Richard has, well had, his house in Port Royal with a garage full of classic cars and his rented apartment in Manhattan, we all have different priorities and that's okay. Anyway, I'm not sure if he owns it or rents it. His divorce cost him plenty, so...'

'Yes, you mentioned he was he was divorced. Did he have a steady girlfriend afterwards?'

'Nah, he played the field I think, but he didn't tell me much about his private life, so you'll need to talk to his drinking buddies, in Olde Naples, to get that sort of information. He was a regular in a couple of the bars on Third when he was down here; Handsome Harry's was his favourite I think, so I'd start there if I were you.' Gibson made a mental note.

'What was Richard like as a person, I mean was he jolly, miserable, sociable, unfriendly, you know...?'

'No, Rick was never miserable, not often anyway, he was always upbeat. An optimist I'd say. He didn't suffer fools though and he could be quite hard when the occasion called for it.'

'Okay, now one thing we haven't discussed, if this other man in the CNN report is Richard Boswell, what would he be doing in New Jersey? Does he have any reason to be in New Jersey that you know of, any friends or anything like that?'

'No, I've racked my brains thinking about that and I can't come up with an answer, maybe he was just passing through, who knows?'

'Are there any other places he might go if he were trying to hide?'

'I know he liked the Bahamas, he went there a few times, and the Keys, he liked going down to fish in Islamorada, but, I don't know Gibson, I just don't know.'

They'd arrived at the Airline Departures dropping off point and Jack pulled over. 'Here we are Gibson and that's departures over there' he said pointing, 'have a good flight and call me when you can with any updates.' Gibson promised he would and bid Jack goodbye

The flight took off ten minutes late for the three hour flight to New York. It was only about two thirds full and Gibson had two empty seats next to him. When the seat belt sign was turned off he took down his bag from the overhead locker. He'd stuffed a jumper and jacket in the bag in response to Jack's warning about the cold weather in New York. He took out his laptop and pulling down the tray from the back of the seat in front, he placed the laptop on it and switched it on. Jack's wife Mary Lou was a bit more computer savvy than Jack and she'd been able to upload files of the execution video and the television program on to Gibson's laptop. She'd also cut the television clip down to a point just before the CNN report showed the man Jack claimed to be Richard Boswell, helping to drag someone out of a building.

He slid the window blind down and clicked on the icon to start the execution video, quickly turning the sound down. After it finished he couldn't help but come to same conclusion as the first time he'd seen it. It seemed one hundred per cent genuine. He then watched the CNN report and let it run without stopping, so he could see the man's face in its natural mobile state rather than trying to freeze frame it. The sequence showing the man Jack claimed was Richard, had the same sort of body shape as the victim in the execution video, a little less heavy maybe, but basically of similar height and build. The deep set eyes too were quite distinctive. Gibson squinted at the picture trying to imagine the man's face with an anchor shaped beard. Just then, the cabin steward stopped by his seat row and asked if he'd like a drink. He ordered coffee, leaned back and closed his eyes.

He was back in St Mary's, kneeling down, eyes tightly closed half listening to the priest droning on about heaven. 'A place where there's no pain, no misery, only peace.' Gibson tuned out, *maybe he's right* thought Gibson, *all the misery's down here, misery by the fucking truckload*. He tried to pray, but could only feel despair and anger. *There' is no God, it's just a grown up's fairy tale, opium for the masses, wasn't that what Marx said? Well maybe he was right.* He looked up at the simple wooden coffin, then felt the pew start to shake, *an earthquake?* Now the whole church was shaking, and they'd all be crushed by the falling masonry, he didn't care.

'Sir, would you please put your laptop away, put your tray table in the upright position and fasten your seat belt?'

Gibson opened his eyes. The plane was vibrating as it dropped through the clouds on its descent into JFK. He looked at his watch and couldn't believe it. He'd slept for nearly two hours. 'Yes sorry' he said suddenly realising how thirsty he was. He hadn't even drunk his coffee. The plane shook and dropped again suddenly as it passed through some more rough air. He remembered his dream.

The taxi dropped him off outside JARIC's offices in Union Square. He stopped to glance briefly at the magnificent statue of George Washington astride a horse, which was mounted on a white plinth in a small garden area, surrounded by trees in the centre of the square. He turned back and pressed the security intercom beside the huge wood and glass door. The security guard on the reception desk telephoned JARIC's office to announce Gibson's arrival and after a brief exchange of words, the guard asked Gibson to sign the guest register then gave him a visitor badge to wear and told him to take the elevator to the fifth floor. A smart middle aged lady dressed in a grey business suite, greeted him as he got out of the elevator. She was medium height, and had dark hair scraped back into a bun.

'Mr Gibson I presume,' she said.

'Mrs Matlock?'

'Oh, just call me Betty we don't stand on ceremony here, please follow me, would you like some coffee or maybe tea?' she asked as they walked along passing through two sets of doors and into a small windowless conference room which contained an large oblong wooden table and ten chairs.

'Coffee please, milk no sugar,' he said 'and please call me Gibson, no Mr necessary.'

She smiled, 'okay, Gibson, please take a seat. Now I imagine you'd like to get down to business, so how can I help? Jack Otterbein told me you're looking into the circumstances surrounding the unfortunate death of my old boss Richard Boswell, and that I was to give you my full cooperation. He told me nothing is confidential as far as you're concerned, so ask away.'

There was a knock on the door and a young man came in with a tray of coffee. Gibson put his laptop on the table and powered it up, then took out his notebook and pen and waited until the young man had left the room before speaking.

'Okay, well I'd just like to ask some general questions about Richard first,' Betty nodded and they began. Gibson soon established that Richard was a workaholic, at least when he was in the New York office. Betty said he did all his socialising down in Naples, New York was strictly all work she said. There were no girlfriends in New York as far as she knew and she went on to say that he worked long hours at the office and went out to restaurants only occasionally, but that restaurant dinners usually doubled as business meetings.

She confirmed that Richard did a lot of dealing in currency speculation and managed a whole host of overseas financial transactions on behalf of the travel arm of JARIC, but also handled transfers on behalf of a range of multinational companies, plus some wealthy individuals. Since Richards's death, Jack had given orders for all currency speculation activity to cease and the man who had taken over Richard's job now dealt with transfers of money on a more conventional basis.

Gibson asked if she'd noticed any changes in Richards's demeanour or habits prior to his capture by the kidnappers, and she said she had noticed that he seemed a bit preoccupied and tense in the weeks prior to his disappearance, but he could be like that when he had a big deal going through. Gibson made notes during the interview and felt he now had as much useful background on Richard as he was going to get from Betty and decided to go to the next stage.

'Right Betty, well I assume you saw the video on the news, the one of Richard being…, there's no real way to say this nicely is there? The video of Richard Boswell being killed?'

'It's okay,' said Betty, 'I've had a few weeks to come to terms with it, so don't worry about my sensibilities, be as brutal as you like if it helps solve the mystery of Richard's death.'

'I want to show you two video clips Betty, and please don't say anything until you've seen both of them.'

He clicked on the video icon on his laptop screen and turned it round so Betty could see. She got up and quickly, dimmed the lights then sat back down and watched the video. She managed to retain her composure, but Gibson could see how upsetting it was for her. The video finished and he clicked on the second icon starting the clip of the CNN report.

'Now just watch this clip and tell me if you see anything interesting.'

Betty watched intently then when it came to the part where people were pulling the woman out of the wreckage of a house, her hand went up to her mouth and she looked at Gibson.

'That's Rick, Richard Boswell….., but that's Sandy isn't it, how could that be…?'

The clip came to an end and Betty sat there, hands in her lap, looking confused, computing the unthinkable in her mind, Gibson waited.

'So Richard's still alive?' she said

'That's what I'm trying to find out. Jack's fairly convinced it's him, but I'm reserving my judgment until there's a bit more proof, certainly more than just a news clip showing someone who looks similar.'

'I must say it looks like Richard and the man seems to have a similar scar over his eyebrow, although I couldn't see clearly enough to be absolutely sure. He hasn't got Richard's beard, and his hair looks a bit darker, but he has exactly the same deep set eyes, and the way he moves, holds himself, I… I don't understand.'

Gibson closed his laptop and put it into his overnight bag.

'I'm afraid I don't have a satisfactory explanation yet Betty, but I need to go and have a look around Richard's apartment, can you take me there, do you have the keys?'

'I can certainly take you to his apartment. I don't have the keys, but I know the building manager and she'll let us in. It's only a few minutes away on Fifth Avenue; Richard wanted somewhere close by to live so he could walk to the office.'

They walked to Fifth Avenue, Betty wore a heavy winter coat and Gibson felt chilly and underdressed in his light summer jacket. Despite the sunshine and bright blue sky, the wind was bitter, but he couldn't be bothered to stop and take out the jumper he'd brought in his holdall. They arrived at the concrete building that spoke of big money. The inside of the entrance hall was pure opulence, onyx and marble, polished brass and huge heavy wooden doors, a crystal chandelier hung from the high ceiling twinkling in the rays of winter sunshine that filtered through the tall side windows.

The building manager was called and immediately recognised Betty. She asked them to wait and went to get the keys. The apartment was located on the twentieth floor which they ascended to in the fastest elevator Gibson had ever travelled in. They entered the apartment and Betty opened the drapes. Light flooded in and Gibson took in the view.

'Wow' he said as he went across to the window and looked down at the traffic on the busy streets. He wandered through the apartment which was furnished in a minimalist Scandinavian style, all light wooden floors, white leather, glass and steel. There were two bedrooms, two bathrooms and a large open plan lounge with an integrated ultra modern kitchen. Gibson looked inside draws and cupboards, took down some books from the bookshelves and tried to get a feel for the man who'd lived there. Then he wandered over to the wall adorned with some expensive looking modern art. After twenty minutes he reckoned he'd seen enough and nothing particularly struck him as out of the ordinary. Betty was sitting on the white leather sofa looking at a wall which had a display of framed photographs on it.

'I've seen enough Betty, shall we go now?' Gibson was stood by the door ready to leave.

Betty got up then turned back to look at the wall of photographs again.

'That's it.'

'What's it?'

'The photograph of Richard with his dad, it isn't there.'

Gibson walked back to where Betty was standing. 'Sorry what do you mean?'

'Richard worked from here occasionally and the first time I had to come to bring him papers to sign he showed me round. On the wall there,' Betty pointed at a space in the display, 'was a framed photograph of a man in army uniform with a little boy stood by his side. The boy was holding a baseball bat and the man was wearing a baseball mitt and had a ball in the other hand. Richard told me it was the only photograph he had of his dad and him together. I asked what had happened to his dad and he told me he'd been killed in Korea when Richard was just seven.'

'And?'

'Well I could tell by the emotion in Richard's voice at the time, just how much he valued that photograph. It wouldn't have any importance or value to anyone else, so I can only think that Richard took it.'

'Maybe he took it to put up in his house in Naples?'

'Yes, I agree that's a possibility, but …..'

'But what?'

'I'm sure I've seen it on that wall since Richard was, you know, executed as you put it. The police came up from Naples a few days after and asked lots of questions. They also asked to look round his apartment, and I brought them here, much the same as I'm doing for you now.'

Gibson remembered something he'd seen in one of the bedside cabinet draws. He went back to the main bedroom and came out holding an empty picture frame. 'Was it in a frame like this?' She nodded.

The taxi dropped Betty off outside JARIC's offices and Gibson told the driver to take him to his hotel. On the short journey from Richard's apartment, Gibson had thanked Betty for her help and said he would probably need to speak to her again. She wished Gibson luck in finding out what had happened to Richard and was obviously confused and upset at the possibility that her old boss might still be alive. It was too late in the day to do anything useful, so he decided to go to his room, take a bath then go down to the hotel bar for a couple of drinks, order room service, watch some old film on the TV, then an early night.

The next morning Gibson got up at seven and went down to breakfast. They had a short order chef on duty making special omelettes. Gibson didn't know when he would next get the chance to eat so he unusually indulged himself in a big breakfast consisting mainly of a four egg omelette with all the trimmings. After breakfast he went to his room and packed then went down to reception and checked out of the hotel, hoping he could get everything done in one day and travel back to Naples later that afternoon.

He ordered a taxi to take him to NYPD's headquarters at One, Police Plaza in downtown Manhattan. On arrival Gibson went through security and made his way to the Bureau Chief's office. He'd called the previous day to say he would be coming. Tony Romano had expressed his regret that he wouldn't be there to see his old buddy from England as he was out of town at a conference, but he said his secretary Margie had everything in hand.

Margie was a slightly overweight matronly looking woman and wore large horn rimmed glasses. Just the sort of secretary any bosses wife would choose, but if I know anything about Tony Romano, thought Gibson, she would be efficiency personified, and he was right.

Margie greeted him warmly and said she'd heard lots of good things about him. He was embarrassed. She sat him down and made a call.

'Officer Ledinski will be along presently, in the meantime let me tell you what Tony has arranged on your behalf. Oh dear, where are my manners, would you like a coffee, a sandwich or anything?'

Gibson gratefully accepted the offer of coffee. She picked up the phone and ordered two coffees, put the phone down opened her left hand desk drawer, took out a thick yellow document file and plonked it on the desk in front of her. She opened the folder and rummaged through bringing out a plastic covered card and handed it to Gibson. It was a private investigator's licence complete with

Gibson's picture on it. It stated that the State of New York, Department of State, division of licensing services, pursuant to provisions etc., etc., that John Michael Gibson had been duly licensed as a Private Investigator. They had obviously used the picture he provided to them when he was previously on secondment with the department. He smiled and looked at Margie.

'How did Tony manage to wangle this?' Gibson asked smiling.

'Oh, you know, leaned on someone as he usually does. The only really tricky part was the fact that you're not a US citizen, so we had to do some fancy footwork to step around that issue, but there you are Private Investigator Gibson, licensed to ask anyone all the questions you like.'

'Well thanks Margie.' Gibson took out his wallet and put the licence in it. Just then there was a knock on the half glass door and a young, slim, attractive, dark haired woman walked into the office holding a small briefcase. She looked to be in her late thirties.

'Ah, Officer Ledinski, let me introduce you to John Michael Gibson, but Tony told me on no account to call him by his first name, so we're just to call him Gibson, that right Gibson?'

'Well it's not anything, you know, not an affectation or anything, just that Gibson is what people have always called me so.....'

Officer Ledinski smiled and thrust out her right hand at Gibson. 'No problem Gibson,' she smiled. 'My name's Bonita Maria Angelina Ledinski, but you can call me Bonnie.'

Gibson took her hand and they shook. 'Very pleased to meet you, er, Bonnie.'

'Likewise, and I'm really looking forward to working with you. Tony told me what a great detective you are.' Gibson felt himself getting embarrassed again, she carried on, 'Tony gave me some brief information about the case, but I think you'd better fill me in on the detail, shall we move to another office and leave Margie to get on?' Gibson thanked Margie again and said goodbye, grabbed his bag and followed Bonnie to the elevator which took them up a floor.

They walked through an open plan office with busy people variously on the phone or typing away on PCs. Gibson couldn't help noticing a number of men's heads turn as officer Ledinski, apparently unaware of the interest she aroused, sashayed past the desks of her co-workers. They carried on walking to the far corner of the room and into an empty glass walled office. They sat on opposite sides of a square metal desk, with two long low stationary cupboards to the side. Bonnie took out a pen and writing pad out of her briefcase. Gibson placed his laptop on the desk. Bonnie looked up and said 'Okay, shoot.'

'I'd like to show you a couple of video clips first,' said Gibson, 'then I can explain, okay?' Bonnie Ledinski nodded and Gibson moved his laptop over to where she could get a good view of the screen. Bonnie flinched a little at the noise of the gun when the victim was shot, then when the first clip had finished Gibson leaned over and clicked on the second one and went back to his seat. Bonnie watched the second clip then said 'Okay, I just need to watch this second vid again' Gibson got up but Bonnie waved him down, 'I can manage,' she said and restarted the video, then paused and freeze framed the picture.

'Okay, like I said, Tony told me some vague details, but I remembered seeing the first clip, or part of it anyway, on the news, a few months ago?'

'Yes, just short of five months ago,' replied Gibson.

'Okay, and the second clip is obviously about the aftermath of superstorm Sandy, and the damage it caused in New Jersey last October, yes?'

'Correct.'

'And the common denominator is one of the guys shown to be pulling that woman out of the building, he looks pretty much like the guy who was murdered, five months previously, right?'

'Correct again.'

'And presumably someone is suggesting that this guy is one and the same person, and if that's the case, then the first vid was a set up?'

'Again correct.'

'And so this someone has hired you to find the guy in the second vid, well actually, the same guy in both vids possibly?'

'Yes.'

'That's a very tall order Gibson, my new found friend. So, how can I help?'

Gibson told Bonnie what he'd found out so far, his visit to the apartment on Fifth Avenue and the missing picture. He gave her all the information he had on the background of Richard Boswell and told her he intended to go back down to Naples and try to pick up the trail from where the kidnap, staged or otherwise, took place. Bonnie made notes as Gibson spoke.

'Okay got the background, now anything practical you need? You'll want stills producing from those vids and I can get our guys to do that,' then she got her own laptop out of her briefcase and handed Gibson a memory stick. 'Put the vid clips on there and I'll get that sorted and send them along to you, tomorrow. Margie gave me your contact details email etc. Have you got a cell number?' Gibson had bought a cheap cell the day before in Wal-Mart and gave her the number. 'Thanks, anything else? She asked'

'Yes, can you get someone to identify the location, the street where the rescue of that woman took place on the CNN report, and could you maybe ask CNN if they got the names of anyone involved in the rescue, the victim maybe, anyone at all? Maybe the CNN reporter spoke to the victim or some of the rescuers afterwards?'

'Yep, I think we can manage that, anything else?'

'Nothing I can think of at the moment Bonnie. Thanks for your time and I look forward to hearing from you. It's been a pleasure meeting you.'

'No problem Gibson the pleasure's been all mine.'

Gibson packed up his laptop and Bonnie walked him back through the office to the elevator. Gibson said he could find his own way out and thanked her again for her time. She said she'd be in touch soon and to let her know if there was anything else she could do to help in the meantime. They shook hands and said goodbye.

Bonnie made her way back to her desk wondering about the English detective. In many ways he reminded her of her own father, quietly determined and not to be underestimated. She couldn't deny being attracted to him though and she knew from Chief Romano that he had lost his wife in a tragic plane crash only a year or so ago, but there was such a big age gap and anyway he lived in another country she thought. She arrived back at her desk and saw several post it notes attached to her screen. *Stop day dreaming,* she said to herself, and sat down to tackle the mountain of work that never seemed to get any smaller.

CHAPTER 9

He showed the assistant bank manager his driver's licence and the key to his safety deposit box. The manager checked the details against their records and smiled.

'Can't be too careful these days Mr Forretti.'

'Indeed you can't,' said Steve Forretti in reply to the man's banal statement.

'Please follow me,' said the manager and led Steve through some double doors then through another set of doors which he unlocked with a security code. They went through into a room where safety deposit boxes lined the walls.

'The man looked down at the key, let's see... number...?'

'Four three one one six eight,' said Steve Forretti.

'Yep..., check that,' said the man and walked his fingers over the boxes silently mouthing the numbers as he searched for the correct one. 'Here we are,' and he inserted his key in the box, turned it all the way clockwise, then stood back and said, 'I'll wait outside the door here, just tell me when you're through and I'll come back and finish up.'

Steve thanked him, waited until the door had closed behind him then put his own key in the lock, opened it and drew the long box out to reveal a black velvet bag, four neat bundles of hundred dollar notes tied with elastic bands, each measuring just over two inches high, two hundred thousand dollars in total , two memory sticks, a fully loaded Glock compact G19 and a large manila envelope containing his old passport and driving licence, plus another envelope containing his new passport. He took out a bundle of money and peeled off five thousand dollars. He needed to buy some fuel for the boat, pay the dock fees for the quarter, buy some warm clothes and some new waterproofs. The weather was getting colder and there was talk of a potential hurricane brewing out in the Atlantic. He returned the rest of the money to the box, slid it back all the way in, then locked it with his key. He opened the door and told the man he'd finished then waited until he had done his bit, then they both walked out of the vault.

'Goodbye Mr Forretti, keep well and have a nice day now.'

Steve said goodbye and walked out into Kennedy Avenue and the pale autumn sunshine. He was tanned, clean shaven and wore black framed tinted glasses which he still hadn't quite got used to. He parked in the lot just outside Bill & Mary's Marina and strolled through the gate waving at Mary. She was on the phone but waved back through her office window as he walked to his boat, a beautiful white fifty foot Sealine T50, named American Pie. He'd bought her used from the marina in August and paid cash. It was ideal as a comfortable live aboard boat, but big and fast enough for the sea journey, should he wish to visit the Bahamas and the five million dollars in his offshore bank account.

He sat down at his desk and started to sort through his bills, prioritising them and placing appropriate amounts of cash on each one. He had a credit card for emergencies, but he preferred to make as few traceable transactions as he could. Cash was king in Steve Forretti's world.

CHAPTER 10

The plane landed back into Fort Myers on time. Gibson had called ahead from New York and Jack was waiting for him outside arrivals.

'Thanks for coming to meet me Jack.' Gibson got into the passenger seat and threw his bag in the back. Jack looked around then drove out of the car park and said.

'No problem, I couldn't wait to know more about what you found. What's this about a missing picture, tell me more.'

Gibson told Jack how, without prompting, Richard's secretary had recognised her old boss in the CNN report and then how they'd gone to the apartment where Richard's secretary had noticed the missing picture.'

'Yeah, I know the one she means. Rick treasured that picture and always intended to get it copied. He only had a few pictures from when he was a kid and I think that was the only one with him and his dad together. 'Jesus Gibson, I mean that proves it surely, Rick's still alive.'

'I have to admit it's looking more of a possibility.'

'Is that what they call British reserve?' Jack said laughing, 'c'mon what other explanation is there?'

'Well if he is alive, then what was the execution video all about? And if it was a set up, then Richard Boswell was at best a willing participant, or worse, the prime mover behind it, so how does that fit Jack?

'Damned if I know,' said Jack pulling on to the Interstate, 'Damned if I know.'

Back at the apartment Gibson got out of the car and told Jack he was going to take the next day off to go fishing and clear his mind before deciding on the next step. Jack said he understood.

'Look, the way I see this working Gibson, is that we keep business separate to our lives in this community here. We'll only talk about this subject in private and when you tell me it's appropriate, otherwise we keep schtum. So we can still have a beer round the pool and shoot the breeze with the others, and you can relax knowing I'm not going to spoil your stay here, thinking you can't walk down to the pool or the boat dock without me asking you questions, okay?'

'I'm relieved you've said that Jack. I was going to suggest something similar myself, so that arrangement works perfectly for me.'

Gibson went back to his apartment and took a shower. He was mightily relieved at Jack's understanding and put all thoughts of Richard Boswell out of his mind. It was Friday night and he focussed on where he was going to go for dinner. Venetian Village was just a short distance away from the apartment complex and had a variety of restaurants on offer. For no other reason than it being the first restaurant he came to, he stopped at the Mira Mare, sat on a spare stool at the bar and ordered a beer. In the corner stood a crooner providing a modern version of live music singing to computerised karaoke backing tracks which he manipulated on a laptop resting on a music stand in front of him. Despite the strange set up, Gibson thought it worked quite well.

The air was warm and humid and many of the men in the restaurant wore shorts and the women wore thin summer dresses. Gibson had to remind himself it was still early January and back home in Manchester, they'd be freezing. He saw someone being served a pizza at the bar and decided that was for him. He ordered and ate at the bar enjoying the warm friendly atmosphere but it wasn't long before the previous couple of day's travelling caught up with him. He walked back to the apartment, was in bed by ten and slept like the dead.

The following morning dawned bright, sunny and warm. Gibson went for a run along the beach before breakfast, startling flocks of white ibis as he ran along the shoreline. Back at the apartment, he showered, breakfasted then collected his fishing tackle and headed for the fishing pier in downtown Naples. The pier was an impressive wooden structure stretching a thousand yards out into the Gulf of Mexico. He found the other fishermen - and fisherwomen, a friendly lot and spent the rest of the morning and most of the afternoon fishing and listening to tall tales about fish caught and fish that got away.

There was a lavatory block and showers at the entrance to the historical wooden pier, and in the middle, a small wooden booth selling amongst other things, bait, hot dogs and soft drinks, providing all he needed to sustain himself. He caught lots of fish and threw them all back and despite having lathered himself with sun lotion before he left the apartment, by late afternoon he was more than a little burnt so he packed up his tackle and headed back to Park Shore.

A hot bath took most of the sting out of his sunburn but when he looked in the mirror he was reminded of a cooked lobster. He lay on the bed and dozed until five thirty when he decided to get dressed and drive down to Third Avenue Olde Naples and visit the bars to try to get a feel for the places where Richard Boswell socialised.

Olde Naples was aptly named and consisted of low rise buildings giving it a genuine villagy feel. He parked in the car park behind the main street and made his way to Third where he wandered along the street full of expensive looking fashion shops, stylish restaurants and equally stylish people, who were variously window shopping or simply sitting outside restaurants and bars, talking, drinking and laughing in the balmy evening air. It was just turning to dusk and the pretty white fairy lights adorning the trees combined with live music filtering out on to the street to create an atmosphere of sophisticated joie de vivre. Gibson remembered Jack saying that Handsome Harry's was a particular favourite of Richards so he wandered in. The place was packed and he had to excuse himself to get past the crush to order a drink. A smart looking couple at the bar made room for him and he eventually managed to catch the barman's eye.

Gibson ordered a beer, having to raise his voice to make himself heard over the ambient noise. The bar was a modern steel counter affair with a drinks island in the middle and smart black-uniformed serving staff. Two large TV screens hung off the back wall, sound muted, a visual commentary scrolling across the bottom of the respective screens, one tuned to a baseball game and the other showing Fox news. Looking round he noted that everyone was casually but fashionably dressed, expensive watches and glittering jewellery adorned wrists, necks and finger#

'You a Brit or Australian?' said the man from the couple stood next to him.

'Brit,' said Gibson taking a drink of his beer.

'My name's Marty and this here's Debbie,' and both he and the girl shook Gibson's hand. He responded and gave his name. He was getting used to the friendliness of the people but he still found it a little disconcerting at just how readily people would engage him in conversation.

'You here on vacation Gibson?'

'Yes, you?'

'Oh no, we live here, well most of the time. I still have an office in Miami and we have a home in Colorado, but we prefer to spend most of our time down here in Naples, much less hassle, ain't that right honey?' He said turning to Debbie whom Gibson judged to be considerably younger than Marty. 'I'm in real estate, you retired or still working?'

'Retired, well I'm supposed to be retired,' said Gibson.

Debbie spoke, 'just like Marty, he's supposed to be retired but I never seem to see him, always got some big deal on the go.'

Someone who'd just come into the bar shouted a greeting to Marty and he responded with a noisy 'How ya doin' Mel.' There was some banter between the two then then Marty turned back to Debbie who was sucking her drink through a straw, he smiled. 'What were you saying honey? Oh yeah, retired. Well gotta keep the wolf from the door, keep that money rolling in.' He turned back to Gibson. 'And what do you do Gibson, if you don't mind me asking?'

Gibson was thrown at the directness of the question, but he didn't see why he should be less than honest. 'I'm, well I was, a policemen a detective.'

'Wow a real British cop, now ain't that something Debbie?' Marty looked around the bar and shouted for his friend Mel to join them. 'Come over here man and meet my new friend Gibson, a real British cop.' Mel threaded his way through the people crowding the bar, occasionally greeting a friend as he did so.

'Gibson this is Mel, one of the richest people in Naples, maybe the richest.'

'Pleased to meet you Gibson and don't believe this blowhard, if I had his money I'd throw mine away.'

They all laughed heartily and Mel called the bar girl over and insisted on buying them all fresh drinks. Gibson tried to object but he was overruled. By the third drink Gibson was feeling the effects so when his new friend Marty asked him if he'd like to join them for a bite to eat, he readily accepted. They went outside and were seated at an ornate metal table, their server thrusting menus into their hands whilst reeling off details of the evening's specials. Mel turned to Gibson. 'Like steak Gibson?' Gibson said he did. Mel asked the others. 'Steak for you two as well?' They both said yes.

'That keeps it simple,' and turning to the waitress he said 'four fillet steaks. Just show mine the grill then put it on a plate with some fries.' 'The server a made note of how each of the others wanted theirs, then wrote the same information again on the crisp white paper cloth in front of each person as appropriate. A bottle of Chateauneuf du Pape was ordered and talking was resumed. Gibson took the opportunity to introduce Richard Boswell's name into the conversation. He guessed that these wealthy people were likely to be the sort that Richard rubbed shoulders with when he was in Naples.

'Do you happen to have known a Richard Boswell? I believe he used to come in here,' Gibson asked in a rare lull in the conversation. They all stopped talking.

'Rick,' said Marty. 'Sure we knew him, great guy, what a tragedy that was…., but hey, how do you…? I mean why are you asking … ?' Marty put it together. 'Hang on, you said you should be retired, no, supposed to be retired you said, you're still working aren't you… But what's a British cop asking about Rick Boswell for? Don't tell me he was some sort of international criminal?'

The other two were all ears now waiting for Gibson to answer the question.

'No I don't think he was any kind of criminal, it's just that I've been asked to try to find out about the circumstances which led to his…, untimely death, that's all.'

'Oh right, like as in a PI?' said Mel'

'Yes,' replied Gibson and he was saved from any immediate further explanation by the arrival of the steaks. Wine was poured and they all got stuck in to their food, Gibson thought it was one of the best steaks he'd ever tasted. It didn't take long for the questions to begin again.

'So who you working for Gibson, or is it like they say in the movies, you know, confidential client information? 'Asked Marty, while shovelling another mouthful of juicy steak into his mouth.

'No, nothing like that, no big secret, I'm working for his old business partner Jack Otterbein. The company's insurance people would like to have some loose ends tied up that's all so that's it, nothing too exciting or glamorous I'm afraid. I happen to know Jack and he asked me to look into things for him.' Gibson had agreed the cover story with Jack to avoid having to explain the real reason for his enquiries in Naples.

'Insurance companies,' said Mel disdainfully as he cut into the last piece of his steak. 'They'll do anything to avoid paying out.'

'Amen to that Mel' said Marty, drinking the last of his wine. 'Nother bottle Mel?'

Gibson thought he could drink, but he was an amateur compared to this lot. Debbie decided to leave them after the meal. She had things to do she said and gave each of them a big noisy kiss before taking some car keys out of her handbag and walking out on to the street, on rather unsteady legs Gibson thought.

'Great girl that Debbie,' said Mel, 'You're a lucky dog Marty.'

'Yeah well, it took me three goes, but I chose real well this time?' he said, slapping Mel on the back, and they both laughed like drains until tears ran down their faces. Gibson couldn't help laughing along with them, but he wasn't really sure what was so funny. They ordered cognac but Gibson insisted on having just a beer. He brought the conversation back to the subject of Richard Boswell and it was obvious that both Marty and Mel were now well oiled and ready to speak in an unguarded fashion.

'Did Richard have any steady girlfriends you know of?' asked Gibson.

'Steady?' Marty laughed 'He had lots of 'em, that right Mel? All very steady I'm sure,' he said, and laughed again.

'Answer the man properly Marty,' said Mel, 'Marty thinks everything's funny except losing money on a deal.' That made Marty laugh even more.

'There was a girl,' said Mel ignoring Marty's laughter. 'I wouldn't call her Rick's steady girlfriend, I don't think he went in for steady, but there was a girl called Gina he brought in a few times. I saw him with her at some other places too, so I guess you could say she was about as steady a girlfriend as he ever had.'

'I don't suppose you know where I could find this Gina?'

'I think he said he met her when he bought his place in Port Royal, yeah that's right, she worked for that big furniture place on 41, interior designer I think she was, Robb and Stucky, yeah that's where he met her I remember now, she designed his house interior, he spent a small fortune on that place.'

'And what did she look like, this Gina?'

'Tall and thin,' Said Mel, 'with the straightest blond hair you've ever seen, cut in a fringe straight across.' And he made scissors of his fingers to demonstrate a straight line across his forehead. And I don't normally like thin, but she had an unusual beauty that's hard to describe, ain't that right Marty?'

'Yeah a bit weird looking, but like you say, she had something special about her, sorta different.'

Gibson ripped a corner off the paper tablecloth and wrote down Gina. 'Where was it she worked again?' Mel said 'Rob like the name but with two b's I think, and Stucky like Sticky with a u.' Gibson wrote it down, then Marty tapped him on the arm in a conspiratorial manner, waving Gibson closer towards him.

'You know what Gibson? Marty said his voice a little slurry now, 'I wasn't all that surprised when I saw that Rick had been offed, particularly the way he was killed.'

'Oh?' Said Gibson showing his surprise at the remark. Mel was shaking his head as if he'd heard this before. Marty continued. 'He was mixing with some very strange people, that right Mel?'

'Well I don't know Marty, you're the one with the Miami connection, I'm just a simple home boy, don't mix in such circles thank God.'

'What do you mean strange people?' Gibson asked.

Marty lowered his voice and leaned closer to Gibson 'Well he came in here a few times,' Marty looked around to make sure no one was listening. 'With one of the Miami mob's elder statesman. Now they probably thought no one round here would know who the guy was, but I know, and he don't visit to see how your health is, know what I mean?'

'Elder statesman?'

'Keep it down,' said Marty putting his finger to his lips. 'That's what they call the boss, the big boss in the mob. Let me tell you Gibson, these people are more than dangerous. You'd have to be crazy to mix with these guys, the Miami mob is connected to the Russian mafia these days and you have no idea what they're capable of.'

Gibson was about to ask more, but Marty had obviously decided he'd said enough, maybe too much and turned the conversation to how Obama was wrecking the United States with his liberal policies and deflected any further questions by asking Gibson about politics in the UK.

Mel ordered more drinks and persuaded Gibson to try a glass of cognac, then one drink led to another and despite Gibson promising himself an early night, he stayed for another hour. Mel and Marty wanted him to stay longer, but he told them he had work to do the following day so they reluctantly let him go, insisting he promise to meet up with them again soon. Gibson took a taxi back to Park Shore as he judged himself wholly incapable of driving safely, walking a straight line was a challenge.

He rolled over on to his back groaning not wanting to open his eyes. He could see bright sunlight through his closed eyelids and realised he hadn't closed the blinds when he went to bed. Memories of the previous evening came back to him, although he couldn't remember the journey home or getting into the apartment. His last memory was of Mel ordering another cognac. He groaned again as he tried to raise himself off the bed, his sickly throbbing headache increased in intensity with the movement and he lay back down, knowing he was going to feel rough for the rest of the day. He opened his eyes, then closed them, then opened them again and slowly rolled over so he could slide out of bed. He stood up and stumbled to the bathroom.

An hour later, after some toast and coffee and a long hot shower, he felt marginally better. Checking his laptop he found an email message from Bonnie Ledinski, attached to which were two images files. He clicked on the images first. The technicians had done a good job in extracting a full face image from each video clip, the one taken from the execution video showed Richard Boswell with mid grey hair, deep set eyes and a beard, the second one was a bit less distinct and showed a man who looked remarkably similar, but no beard, unshaven and with darker hair. The man in the picture from the CNN report did appear to have a scar over his left eyebrow, but it was too grainy and indistinct to be absolutely certain. Still, Gibson had to admit, the two men's faces did look remarkably similar. He read Bonnie's email.

Hi Gibson, great to meet you the other day. The guys did a great job with the pictures didn't they? We think the area was probably Mantoloking. The date you already know was thirty October. We're, still waiting to talk with our contact at CNN see if we can get a more precise location and if they have any other information they can provide. I'll keep you informed on progress. Anything more you want just let me know.

Best

Bonnie Ledinski

He looked in his laptop case for his memory stick and transferred the two images, then looked on the net for where he could get prints made and found an Office Depot a few miles away. He called the number Jack had given him for Richard's housekeeper and arranged to meet her at Richard's house in an hour's time, calculating that this should give him time to get some prints made on the way.

The house was beautiful but there were even more palatial examples on the other side of the road, backing directly on to Naples beach. Nevertheless, Gibson thought, he wouldn't turn his nose up at the one he was looking at now. Meg the part time housekeeper and cleaner was a smart looking lady despite her casual attire, minimal make up, slim, blond hair, white shorts, pink tee shirt and matching faded baseball hat. She looked as if she worked out. Gibson guessed she was a runner.

'How d'ya like it, some house uh?' said Meg as she and Gibson stood at the front door while she looked for the right key.

'It certainly is, what would a house like this cost?' he asked.

Meg opened the fancy glass front door and they stepped into the hall. 'Well, if you have a spare four million dollars, it's yours.' She picked up a sales leaflet off the hall table and handed it to Gibson.

Distinguished by exceptional detailing, this spectacular elegant Mediterranean-style residence is located close to beach, golf, tennis and boating activities. Enter through custom art glass doors to an open and inviting dining room and bright living room with cathedral ceilings and a gas fireplace. Meander through the wine bar with cooler to a chef's kitchen, breakfast room and cosy family room. A romantic and private outdoor oasis features a shaded sitting area with lanai, summer kitchen, dining space and a gracious sun-splashed pool surrounded by cascading bougainvillea and ivy-draped walls, with the welcoming sound of a gentle fountain. Perfect for entertaining, with a luxurious ground level master suite, private office and three second floor guest suites that open to an entertainment loft with wet bar and sun-filled upper deck. Large garage.

Gibson handed the leaflet back to Meg and said he'd check his bank account to see if he had that much spare cash, and they both laughed. Meg gave Gibson a quick tour of the ground floor and showed him where the lanai had been ripped to give the kidnappers access to the house. It had been repaired so Gibson had to go out of the rear door into the garden to look at it from outside. A high hedge formed a barrier around the perimeter of the garden so Gibson assumed the kidnappers gained access to the property somewhere near the front gate and walked around the house to the rear. He walked back round to the front of the house and saw the security cameras which had now been cleaned. Back inside he had a general look around. Meg allowed him to rummage in drawers, cupboards and generally gave him free reign to poke around wherever he wanted to.

She then showed him the huge garage which housed Richard's small but impressive collection of American classic cars. There was a beautiful turquoise Thunderbird, a cream coloured Chevrolet Corvette, an early Ford Mustang in white, a red convertible Cadillac which Gibson judged to be of late fifties vintage and a mid blue Mercury Marquis Brougham.

They were all in stunning condition and he assumed were either as original or had been lovingly restored. They went back to the main part of the house and Gibson looked around the upstairs. The master bedroom wardrobes contained various items of men's clothing, shoes, socks underpants etc. The bed was now made up neatly, but Meg said that when she showed the police around after Richard had been taken; the bed covers were drawn back as if he had just got up and nipped to the bathroom. The other bedrooms were empty of any personal items.

'The man must be seriously wealthy to have a pad like this, and those cars, I mean?'

'Yep, loads a money round here alright.'

'His business partner Jack, he said Richard might be renting, rather than own it?'

'Could be a long term rental. 'Fraid I don't know that level of detail, I just look after the place for him.'

'Did Richard ever have guests stay over?' he asked.

'Occasionally he'd have what I assumed to be business colleagues staying over, and less often he might have a girl to stay. But I was only here part time, so I couldn't really say how often people stayed.'

'Did you happen to know if a girl called Gina ever stayed here?'

'Gina, now that name rings a bell. I think there was a girl by that name. I only remember because I saw her a couple of times and that was unusual, I mean I never saw any of the others more than once. Not that I was keeping count you understand?' she laughed.

'And when Richard disappeared, what can you tell me about that?'

'Nothing really, he arrived on the Friday from New York. That was August thirty. He'd called ahead and told me he was coming down and to get the pool man in and make sure everything was ready, you know house cleaned etc., then I picked him up from the airport as usual.'

'Did he seem okay when he arrived?

'Yeah, the usual Richard, same as always.'

'So when did you next see him or hear from him?

'I didn't, didn't hear a thing until the cops called and asked me to meet them at the house.'

'So how long was it from when he arrived to when the police called you?'

'Let's see, I think it was the following Wednesday, yeah Wednesday, that would be' Meg counted in her head, 'the fifth of September' Gibson was writing all this down in his notebook.

'When were you due to go back to the house, I mean did you have regular days when you cleaned?'

'No not when Richard was in residence as it were. He said he'd call me when he needed me to clean the place and that was normal.'

'And was it that unusual for him to leave it that long, I mean nearly a week from when he arrived, and he still hadn't called you?'

'No, he didn't have any particular pattern, there was no routine as such, not when he was here anyway. When he wasn't I'd visit three times a week to check on everything, keep the place clean etc., so I wasn't concerned. Sometimes when he was down here, he'd go off on a trip for a few days, never told me where he went, just took off sometimes, so I wasn't concerned that I hadn't heard from him.'

'And when you knew that Richard was missing, I mean abducted, who reported it or raised the alarm or whatever?'

'I think it was his business partner who knew first. I believe he'd been contacted by the kidnappers when he was on his way back from a cruise. The first I knew about it was when the cops called me like I said. They asked me to go to the house and let them in, they wouldn't tell me any more on the phone, so I came down here and the cops were waiting.

They said they needed to look round the house and asked me lots of questions, much the same as you have. When we went in and I saw the hole in the lanai and realised something was seriously wrong. The cops still wouldn't go into detail, just said they had reason to believe Richard had been abducted and I was to keep my mouth shut if I didn't want to put his life in danger. I was scared, it was just like something on the TV, it didn't seem real.'

'Okay well thanks for the information.' Gibson was about to put his pen and notebook away in his pocket, then stopped and said. 'Oh, can I have your number in case I remember anything else I should have asked you?' Meg gave him her cell number.

Then they made their way back down the stairs and he thanked her again for showing him round. Meg smiled said it had been her pleasure and she hoped to see him again sometime. As Gibson drove away, he was left wondering if he'd just missed an opportunity to ask Meg on a date. Then almost immediately he couldn't believe he'd had the thought. If someone had told him a week ago he'd be thinking about dating another woman, he'd have poured scorn on the suggestion and told them he could never even dream of going out with another woman after Jill.

The sheriff's office was situated not very far away on Tamiami Trail east Naples. Gibson parked and entered the functional looking light grey concrete building, and asked for Major Crimes Detective, Rusty Wechsler. He was asked to take a seat in the waiting area and had hardly sat down when a young officer came along, called his name then escorted him along a corridor to Wechsler's office. Once again Gibson was greeted like an old friend.

'Come in Detective Gibson, very pleased to meet you,' The detective stood up and shook Gibson's hand warmly, 'sit down please I'm Detective Wechsler, but just call me Rusty, now what do I call you?'

'Oh Gibson's fine.'

Wechsler asked if he would like some coffee or they could rustle up some tea if he preferred 'you being British and all' he said. Wechsler was paunchy, had fair receding hair, a blond moustache and wore heavy framed glasses. Chief Romano's secretary Betty had called the Collier County Sheriff's office the day before to say that her boss would be grateful if they would give Gibson their full cooperation in relation to the enquiries he was making about the abduction of Richard Boswell. The phone call obviously had the desired effect.

Gibson thanked him for the offer of tea, but said he preferred coffee. Rusty asked him how he knew Chief Romano and Gibson explained about the time he spent on secondment in New York, then one question led to another and Gibson found himself having to tell the story about him catching the serial killer in the UK in 1990. Wechsler said how impressed he was and seemed prepared to chat all day. Eventually Gibson was able to turn the conversation to the matter in hand and asked about their investigation into Richard Boswell's abduction and murder.

He learnt little more than he knew already, just the same information from a different perspective.

'We did our best to assist Jack Otterbein but he was stubborn as a mule and wouldn't listen to us. We even got a hostage specialist over from Miami, but he wouldn't take any advice, so he lost his two mill in diamonds and they still killed his partner.'

'Were you able to trace the taxi driver and the pilot?'

'Yeah that didn't prove too much of a problem, but they were both in the clear. They knew there was something hinky about what they'd been asked to do, but they hadn't broken the law in any way, and weren't implicated in the set up. All the arrangements had been managed by phone and at arm's length.'

He asked Wechsler what he thought about Jack Otterbein's claim that he'd seen Richard on a CNN news report helping to pull someone out of a collapsed building in New Jersey nearly four months after his apparent execution. Wechsler waved his hand in a manner of dismissal saying that they'd looked at the tape of the CNN report and didn't think there was enough to go on to re-open the investigation.

'Some of our guys thought it could be Boswell, some didn't but I couldn't start sending men to look for a guy who just happened to look similar to his partner, when we had all the evidence we needed to convince us Boswell was dead. No siree, it all seemed fairly conclusive to us and we can't spend our limited resources on looking into these sorts of wild claims. Must be the same in the UK, yeah? You have to cut your cloth these days. Having said that, if something more concrete were to be presented to us then we'd certainly look into it, but I'd bet my last dime on that execution video being genuine. As far as the Sheriff's department of Collier County's concerned, Richard Boswell was shot to death on or around October ninth, and is well and truly dead.'

CHAPTER 11

THE PREVIOUS OCTOBER - 2012

Steve Forretti sat in the saloon looking out over the windswept marina. He switched his attention back to watching latest television reports on Hurricane Sandy's progress as it gathered strength out in the Atlantic Ocean. The aerial pictures had a strange and terrifying beauty about them. As he listened to the reports, he realised he was going to be no match for this raging freak of nature that not only threatened to destroy his boat, and therefore his home, but by doing do so could derail his carefully thought out plans. His only consolation being that he chose to store his stash in the bank's safety deposit box rather than hiding it on his boat.

Mary had told everyone in the marina to leave their vessels and find shelter inland. She said the coastguard had warned that they could all be about to experience one of the worst storms in history, predicted to land on the coast of New Jersey with devastating force, and that it would hit sometime within the next twenty four hours. For one of the few times in his life Steve felt helpless and unable to think of a solution.

The main power was out so he was running on batteries. All the other boat owners had left hours ago but he had stayed watching the news, hoping for a miracle, thinking that maybe the main force of the storm would turn and make landfall elsewhere. It still might, but the odds were shortening, so reluctantly he gathered some belongings together took a long and maybe last look around his boat then remembered his Glock. He went back into his bedroom and took the gun, clip and the box of spare ammunition out from his bedside cabinet and put them into his sports bag.

Created in 1982 by Gaston Glock, an Austrian curtain-rod manufacturer, the Glock arrived in the USA during the 1980s crime epidemic. Glock is the single most popular manufacturer of handguns in the United States. Due in no small part to their powerful marketing campaign, the Glock semi-automatic pistols are universally recognized and immortalized. The gun's bare bones ballistic minimalism offers no frills, no extraneous machining. Just the basic things needed to shoot someone, a nice simple lightweight killing machine.

Since Vietnam he'd never had cause to shoot a gun in anger and hoped he never would, but living on a boat and going to foreign ports, not all of them that secure, he always felt better knowing he had a gun to hand if necessary. There was also the chance that he might get some unwelcome visitors one of these days and considered his guns as insurance against such a possibility, however remote a possibility that might be. He went back through the cabin stepped out on to the deck, locked the door, walked up the short gangplank and on to the dock. A sudden and ferocious gust of wind nearly knocked him off his feet, a harbinger of the devastation to come. He looked up at the mottled grey sky, strange semi-circular shafts of sunlight radiated from behind halo shaped clouds in a brooding display that would be the envy of any sci-fi film director.

He drove his car out of the marina and made for County Road, it was deserted. Low lying areas were already flooded as the sea levels had started to rise. He had no real idea where he was going and hoped to find some signs or an official who could tell him where the emergency shelters were. The wind was howling and picking up in intensity blowing debris over the road and he realised he wouldn't be able to drive much further. He drove across the bridge, switched the car radio on and listened to the latest news.

The announcer repeated that at seven that morning Hurricane Sandy had been downgraded to a post tropical cyclone, or super storm but that it was still expected to cause extensive damage and flooding and all persons should find safe shelter. He was lost now and beginning to think he'd left it too late, then he saw a car stopped on the road ahead of him talking to an official of some kind, a man wearing a yellow armband. He seemed to be giving directions to the driver. Steve pulled up behind the car and waited. The vehicle in front drove off. Steve wound his window down and moved forward. The official leaned into his car.

'You looking for any place in particular friend, or just somewhere to get out of the storm?'

'The latter,' said Steve. 'I live on a boat but I obviously can't stay there, so I just need somewhere to stay until this blows over.' They both had to shout to hear each other over the noise of the gusting wind and the man had to hold on to the car to stop being blown over. An empty drinks can blew off the road just missing the man, bouncing noisily but harmlessly off the car windscreen then flying high over the roof eventually landing and skittering along the road some distance behind.

The man told him he could find shelter in St Catherine's School about a mile further on, on the right. Steve thanked him, drove on and found the school situated at the top of a small hill. It was a squat solid looking square red brick building with a distinctive white tower standing proud of the front façade and built slightly higher than the rest of the structure. A clock in the top centre completed the tower's dominance as the building's central feature. Steve parked his car, retrieved his bag from the trunk, went in through the main doors and followed the makeshift signs.

Army style canvas beds with folded grey blankets on top were laid out in a large room. Coffee and some basic food was on offer. The windows had all been battened from the outside and despite the size of the room the sealed windows gave it a claustrophobic feel. The lady in charge had greeted him when he arrived and asked for his name and a contact number, which she then wrote down on a lined paper pad attached to a clipboard.

She said he could choose where to sleep and told him where the bathrooms were. He thanked her, went to a camp bed in the corner, put his bag down on it and walked to the back of the room where a small crowd of people were variously seated and standing around a television set on a wooden table. They were watching and listening to the latest news reports and chatted with each other in the way that strangers do when they're all caught up in such situations, trying to sound casual in their questions to each other, but really seeking the other's opinions to reassure themselves they were safe.

It was too early to sleep, but he decided there was little to be gained by standing around with the others so he went back to his canvas bed, took his jacket and shoes off, places his glasses in his inside jacket pocket folded it neatly, placed them at the foot of the bed and lay down. *It was going to be a long night* he thought and dozed off to the roar of the wind as it increased in intensity, involuntarily remembering a passage about the end of the world from the bible classes he attended as a child. *The heavens will disappear with a roar; the elements will be destroyed by fire, and the earth and everything in it will be laid bare.*

The storm hit with its full force at around eight thirty in the evening. Steve woke with a start and wasn't sure if it was the storm that woke him or the screams of his fellow refugees he wasn't even sure if he hadn't screamed himself. He thought the roof might be torn off such was the force of the storm. Then he felt a tremor and the building shuddered resisting the massive force trying to rip it away from its foundations. The screeching battering wind was followed by driving rain, rain like he'd never experienced before. It felt more like sheets of water being hurled at the building by some demonic force determined to smash it to smithereens, then the lights went out. People gasped, a few screamed. The lights came back on a few long seconds later, courtesy of an emergency generator he assumed, and a low hubbub of conversation began as people tried to reassure each other. The lights were dimmer than before and flickered. He lay back down, pulled the blanket up to his chin and tried to sleep.

He woke up and found himself one of the few people still in the hall. The storm had obviously abated sometime during the night and he guessed that most of the people who'd spent the night in there were locals who'd gone back at first light to see what damage Sandy had done to their properties. After using the bathroom, he went to get some coffee and chatted briefly with one of the other late risers then gathered his things together and went outside. The wind was still blowing hard, and as he looked around, the amount of damage inflicted by the storm became apparent - fallen trees, wrecked houses and roads turned into rivers.

In 2012, hurricane Sandy became the second most costly hurricane in American history. Initial estimates judged the damage as close to seventy five billion dollars, surpassed only by the damage caused by Hurricane Katrina. Nearly three hundred people were killed as the Sandy tore through seven countries before finally making landfall in the United States as a superstorm. After wreaking havoc in the Caribbean, Sandy curved north-northwest and moved ashore as a post-tropical cyclone with hurricane-force, just northeast of Atlantic City on October twenty ninth. Hurricane Sandy affected twenty four states in the USA, including the entire eastern seaboard from Florida to Maine and west across the Appalachian Mountains to Michigan and Wisconsin.

Seaside Heights, New Jersey, where families had walked the boardwalk, eaten fried doughnuts, and ridden amusement park rides for generations, was wiped out by the superstorm. Waterfront rides on Casino Pier on the New Jersey shoreline vanished under the Atlantic Ocean's power, totally destroyed by the storm and swallowed up by the sea. Roads in the immediate area were lined with houses resting on their sides and chocked with debris.

The barrier island home to Seaside Heights and other communities where legions of vacationers from New Jersey and beyond made summer memories became a scene of devastation after superstorm Sandy's surge enveloped it, the boardwalk made famous by MTV's hit reality show "Jersey Shore" was destroyed and a roller coaster from the Funtown Pier sat in the ocean. Throughout New Jersey, roofs were ripped off houses, and utility poles were snapped in two, their power lines tangled like shoelaces after the storm had paid its destructive visit.

His car was undamaged so he threw his bag in the trunk and went up to the crest of the hill to get a better view of the surrounding area. *The word devastation was inadequate* he thought, and stood in awe of what damage Mother Nature can inflict when the mood takes her. He realised there was no way he could get back to his boat in his car, but just then he saw a heavy duty pickup truck in the distance coming towards him.

The vehicle was untroubled by the low lying water and as it came closer he could see the words FEMA stencilled on the front and side. He waved it down and asked if they were going over the bridge and anywhere near Bill and Mary's Marina. The driver turned to consult his colleague.

'Yeah, my buddy Jeb here thinks he knows where you mean, it's not far away from where we're heading so if you want a ride, jump in.'

Steve thanked them and got into the rear cab. 'You had a boat in the marina?' said the man called Jeb turning round in his seat.

Steve noted his use of the past tense. 'Yeah, is it bad down there?'

Jeb laughed without mirth. 'Well let me put it this way buddy, the chances of you still having a boat are between zero and nothing. Sorry to have to say that friend, but you'll see for yourself soon enough.'

As they got nearer to the shore, Steve remained silent as he tried to take in what he was seeing. Boats were littered all over the place, leaning against homes and on top of cars, smashed into pieces, some half submerged in the flood's murky waters. The storm had turned the area into a graveyard of boats. He was to learn later from official reports that more than fourteen hundred vessels, from Jet Skis to forty foot yachts, littered the coastline in the wake of the storm, carried from their docks by the record-breaking storm surge and deposited wherever Sandy saw fit, often hundreds of yards away from where they were moored.

After a mile or so, they saw that the road ahead was blocked by debris, so the driver took a diversion, turning left into a smaller road and as they drove along saw some people gathered round a partially collapsed house, gesturing to each other and it quickly became apparent they were trying to rescue someone from the wreckage of the building. The FEMA driver speeded up then stopped. They all jumped out and ran to help the rescuers. The FEMA driver took charge and quickly assessed the situation while his buddy Jeb called the details in. A woman who Steve guessed to be in her mid-thirties, was trapped in the wreckage.

She was conscious and there was no obvious sign of major injury, no blood at any rate that he could see. The wooden construct house had been pushed over to an angle of forty five degrees and looked in imminent danger of collapsing on top of her, so the rescue had to be handled with some care. The FEMA driver organised them all into a human chain and began to take planks and debris away from the area that blocked access to where the woman was pinned down. They worked steadily for ten minutes and were good making progress when the building moved. It creaked as it threatened to collapse completely and the rescuers ran back a safe distance,

Steve was knocked over in the in the panic and lost his glasses. He was helped up and they quickly re- formed the chain, and continued with their task, then the man from FEMA held his hand up to signal everyone to stop what they were doing and he crawled into the space that the removal of wood and rubble had created. He got to the distressed woman and spent a few seconds talking to her then carefully moved the heavy piece of timber from across her legs to bring it sideways to lie parallel alongside her, his face suffused with blood with the strain of manhandling the heavy object.

She was now free but apparently unable to move. The FEMA man crawled part of the way back out, took the rope given to him by his colleague Jeb, crawled back to the woman and tied it under her arms. He signalled Jeb who started to slowly pull the woman out on her back, the first man trying to clear a pathway on the floor to minimise the pain and damage she would sustain being dragged along the floor.

She yelped and cried as she was dragged over the uneven surface, but better than being crushed to death thought

Steve, as he watched the painful passage of the victim towards the street and to safety. The paramedics arrived just as she was pulled clear. Some people cheered, some clapped and some cried as she was put on to a stretcher and whisked away in the ambulance sirens wailing and lights flashing. Steve wandered back to the FEMA vehicle and leaned against it. It was only then he noticed the television crew filming the incident, presenter in full flow before the camera, looking round for interviewees. He went around the other side of the vehicle and out of sight

.

CHAPTER 12

The previous evening Gibson had gone to see Jack to bring him up to date with details of his visit to Handsome Harry's, his meeting with Richard's housekeeper Meg, and his interview with the Collier County Sheriff, Wechsler. Jack was impressed at the progress Gibson had made and asked him when he thought he could go and try track down the Gina woman.

'Tomorrow Jack. I'll drive over to the furniture place Mel said he thought Gina worked for, and see if I can track her down. I'll let you know what progress I make and we can take it from there, okay?'

'Okay Gibson, sounds good. I'll wait to hear from you.'

That night as he closed his eyes to go to sleep, he talked to Jill. When he'd told the therapist about his conversations with Jill after her death, she warned him that although it was understandable in some respects, it was a sign that he hadn't fully accepted that Jill had died, and he needed to deal with it before it became a serious problem. Gibson said he understood, and he did on one level, but then again he thought, she hasn't gone. I know she's dead, she's not coming back but she's not gone. Tonight when he spoke to her he knew that this time it was out of guilt, but he couldn't help it and told Jill how he had considered asking another woman out on a date. Jill laughed and told him he was silly and now she was where she was, it was okay and he shouldn't worry. He mostly saw her in the time between being awake and going to sleep, when she would be sitting on the sofa in their living room, but sometimes he would talk to her briefly, during the day if he was on his own and saw something that he wanted to tell someone about. He wondered if he was going a bit mad, but thought that if he was, it wasn't something that bothered him that much.

The next day, Gibson rose early and went for a long run along the beach, then showered and had breakfast. It was still too early to go to try to find Gina. He reckoned the furniture place wouldn't open till ten, so he had time for an hour by the pool. He lay there thinking how much better he was feeling, although he had to admit, despite Jill telling him it was okay, he still felt guilty that he was thinking about calling Meg. See if she fancied going for a bite to eat sometime. He dozed off in the sun then woke with a start when a small child screamed and jumped in the pool. He looked at his watch, *time to go Gina hunting* he thought.

Robb & Stucky was a high class furniture retailer and interior designer. They were housed in a huge showroom in Naples on Tamiami Trail, US 41. Gibson wandered around, impressed by the quality of the furniture on offer. He was soon accosted by a smart looking dark haired, female sales assistant, dressed in a black tight fitting skirt and white lace blouse, who insisted on showing him around, asking questions about his taste and what his plans were, telling him she would be happy to come to his home and offer some design ideas, and when would it be convenient for her to visit. When she eventually drew breath, Gibson told her that he wasn't there to buy any furniture but to enquire about someone who may work there, or who may have worked there in the past.

The saleswoman's face changed, smile gone and an altogether different expression took its place.

'You need to speak with HR and they're on the fourth floor, the elevator's over there. Have a nice day now.' Gibson took the elevator and found HR. A pleasant looking young girl sat at a reception desk asked him if she could help. He showed her his PI card and explained who he was looking for. She consulted her PC and said there was a record of a woman called Gina who had worked there for a few years and that she was the only Gina in the system so it was probably the same Gina.

'But,' she continued, 'Rob and Stucky have gone through a change of ownership in the last few months. and Gina's moved on. I'm afraid I don't know where she's gone, but let me make a couple of calls, see if I can find out, okay?'

Gibson thanked her, and asked when she could do that.

'If you can just wait here a minute, I'll make the calls now.'

She picked up the phone and made a couple of internal calls, writing down the information she was give, on a notepad.

'Okay, seems that Gina is now working freelance, and has an office next to Sotheby's International, on Broad Avenue in Olde Naples. Should be easy enough to find.'

Gibson thanked her for the information and went to find Gina.

As predicted, he found the office easily enough. It was simply named, Naples Interior Design Inc. He parked and walked up to the office door. He could see one woman sitting at a large desk talking on the phone and the back of another woman on a high stool working at a draughtsman's drawing easel. Although he couldn't see her face, he recognised Gina immediately from the description given by Mel the previous night. He could also now see what they meant. She was thin with almost white blond hair that swished like heavy silk when she turned round to see who had entered the office. She smiled and spoke.

'Hi, can we help you?'

'Yes, I'm looking for someone called Gina, would that be you by any chance?'

She got up off the stool and Gibson could only think elegant.

'Yes I'm Gina, and you are…?'

'My Name's Gibson,' and he took out the ID card given to him by Margie, It was only the second time he'd used it and he still felt a bit self conscious. She took the card off him, studied it and handed it back.

'Not in trouble am I?' she said smiling again.

'No, no I just wanted to ask you some questions, that's all,' Gina raised her eyebrows questioningly, Gibson carried on, 'about Richard Boswell, I assume you know he was abducted and…'

'Yes I know all about what happened, I should think everyone in the country knows, hard to have missed that horrible video clip on the news. But why do you think I can help, I mean I knew Richard, we were friends, more than friends really, but I hadn't seen him for a while so I don't think I can be of any help. And anyway why is a private investigator asking questions, surely it's a police matter?'

The other woman had finished on the phone and was now listening in to the conversation.

'Look it won't take long,' said Gibson 'I'll explain, just a few questions and then I'll be out of your hair. Is there anywhere we could talk in private?'

Gina looked at him deciding. 'Okay come in the back. Would you like a coffee? I'm going to have one' Gibson gratefully accepted. They went into a back room and she gestured for him to take a seat at a shiny white dining table. She served coffee and sat down opposite him. 'Okay ask away, but I'm pretty busy so I'd appreciate it if you could be quick.'

'Okay, I'm working for Richard's business partner Jack Otterbein and the firm's insurance company have insisted that Jack tries to find out more about the circumstances of

Richard's death. They're looking at a big pay-out and they're being difficult, so Jack has employed me to poke around and ask questions so he can tell the insurance company he's looked into everything and force them to pay up.'

'So this Jack employs a British PI? Weird, and I don't see what the insurance company hope to find out, I mean the poor guy's dead, that video, what more do they want?'

Gina was obviously suspicious about Gibson's cover story and he was wondering what he could say next to make it sound more credible, but she saved him from any further explanation.

'Look, like I say, I'm busy and all this sounds a bit odd to me, but go ahead, ask your questions, then I can get back to my work.'

'Right okay, so how well did you know Richard Boswell?'

'Pretty well, we went out a lot and we were getting close, very close, I think too close for Richard. We got on well but Richard made it clear at the start that he didn't want any serious commitment and that suited me to begin with, and anyway I thought he might have another relationship going on in the background, I don't know, but then, well I think we both changed and things got more serious. We went on some short trips together and we got on really well. I thought maybe this was going somewhere but then I think Richard got scared, frightened he might getting in over his head, so he called it a draw and we each went our own way.'

'When was that, when did you spilt up?'

'July last year, so over a month, maybe six weeks before he was killed.'

'And did you see him again, after you split up?'

'Nope, I kept away from the places I knew Rick went to. I didn't want to bump into him. I was quite upset about the whole thing.'

'Okay, now you might think this a strange question but I'm trying not to take up too much of your time, so can you tell me if Richard ever said anything about having another place, somewhere else?'

'A place, you mean like a home?'

'Yes, sort of, I mean anything, a condo, a caravan, sorry trailer you call them, or an RV, anything like that?'

'You're right it is a strange question, but no he never mentioned having a home anywhere else.'

'Right okay, well thanks for your time. May I have your telephone number in case I think of any more questions I need to ask you?'

'That's it?'

'Yes,' said Gibson and stood up as she rooted in her handbag. She found a business card and gave it to him. He went to the door and held it open for her, but Gina remained seated at the table, deep in thought.

'You think he's not dead don't you?' she said

Gibson couldn't lie. He walked back and sat down again. 'Well I don't think anything, but Jack, his business partner, he thinks Richard might still be alive.'

'Wow, is that really possible?'

'I suppose it's possible, unlikely in my opinion, but yes, possible.'

'So all that stuff about the insurance company, was....bullshit?'

'Yes I'm sorry about that.'

'It's okay, look, you know what you were asking about, about Rick having another place, a home somewhere?'

Gibson nodded.

'Well I wasn't lying when I said I didn't think he had a home somewhere else, but one night we'd been out to Campiello's on third, then we'd gone back to Rick's house and carried on drinking champagne. We were dancing to some of his old music and Rick was very romantic. It's probably the only time he really opened up to me. He told me he loved me, a first, and then told me he was going to take me away with him on his boat.

I wasn't sure if he was kidding around, because he'd never mentioned having a boat before, so I asked if this boat had a name and he said he'd forgotten, said he'd only just bought it and whatever it was called he'd rename it Gina, and we could run away on it together. So I guess it was a big boat, big enough to run away on anyway. So the next morning, over coffee, I asked him about the boat again and he flat out denied he had one, said his friend had just bought one and he been kidding around, but I felt he'd been telling the truth the night before and for some reason had regretted it. Things went south from then on and a week later he told me our relationship was getting too serious for him and we split up.'

Gibson had been making notes as she spoke.

'And did he give you any clue as to where this boat, that he didn't have, where it was moored?'

'Not precisely, but I think he said it was somewhere in New Jersey.'

CHAPTER 13

Jack could hardly contain himself at the news that Gibson might have found where Richard had gone to hide and he had to remind Jack that this was only a possibility and that they still had no conclusive proof that Richard was still alive.

'Yeah but the fact that he had a boat and kept it a secret, I mean that proves he was intending to disappear don't it?'

'It would if it were true that he had a boat, but we don't know for sure. He told Gina the next day he was only kidding so let's keep some level of scepticism about this Jack.'

'C'mon Gibson it all fits, boat in New Jersey, then Rick on that CNN report in New Jersey, I mean I thought you cops didn't believe in coincidences?'

'Yes well that's true, but still, I think we shouldn't jump to conclusions.'

'Yeah, maybe you're right, and anyway I'm getting carried away. I mean New Jersey's a big place, how the hell would you find where he kept his boat, there must be hundreds of marinas.'

'There are, but my contact in NYPD got her colleagues to try to identify where CNN filmed the rescue that Richard may or may not have been involved in, and they think it's in the Mantoloking district. So I did some research on the net before I came here and there are only eight or nine marinas in that immediate area, so in theory, finding him and his boat might be possible.'

'Well what are we waiting for?'

'That was the good news Jack, the bad is that virtually all the boats and the marinas around there were badly smashed up in superstorm Sandy, and I'm not sure any of them remained intact after that. You should see the pictures, the place was devastated, looks like a war zone.'

'Oh shit.'

'Yes, but from what I've read on the net, they're all busy now, rebuilding the marinas so if I can find the one his boat was moored at, even if his boat is now gone, then maybe I can still get a line on him? That's assuming of course that Richard is still alive and he had a boat.'

'Great, so when can you go?'

'I'd l get on it first thing tomorrow Jack. Get an early start. I'd already booked a little fishing trip for this afternoon anyway.

'Okay Gibson. Well have fun, and good luck. Promise me you'll let me know as soon as you have any more information, no matter how small or insignificant I seems.'

'I will Jack.'

Gibson said he would, and went back to his apartment to make preparations for his trip to New Jersey.

Including Larry the captain, there were six of them in total on the fishing boat, aptly named Speedy Gonzales by its colourful owner. The other four fishermen were all friends, but they made Gibson welcome. Before long they were all chatting and joking as the boat left the Dock, moving slowly through Naples Bay in accordance with the warnings, 'No Wake' and 'Idle Speed only'. It was a different matter once they were clear of the bay and into the Gulf of Mexico. 'Hold on guys,' the captain said, and opened up the two huge outboards. The engines roared and the boat dug its back end deep into the water, reared up and lunged forward, the noise making it necessary to shout to be heard. All conversation slowly ceased and Gibson looked back at the deep swathe created by the boat as it sped through the clear blue Gulf waters.

They spent the afternoon fishing over various reefs and then did some backwater fishing up against mangroves. Gibson had never caught so many fish in his life and discovered varieties of fish he didn't know existed. They caught Grouper, Snook, Pompano, Jacks, Spanish Mackerel and other fish types that Gibson forgot the names of. By the time he got back to his apartment he was exhausted but happy. He had been given two huge Pompano fillets and instruction to simply grill them with some paprika, oil, salt, pepper and garlic. There was far too much food for one.

Meg's phone rang out for quite a long time and he was just about to give up when a breathless voice answered.

'Hello Meg here, who's this?'

'Oh it's Gibson, the detective, we met the other day.'

'Hi, you thought of some more questions?'

Just two really, and I hope you'll forgive me if I'm out of order, but the first question is - are you involved, I mean are you..?' Gibson ran out of words. Meg laughed. 'I know what you mean and don't worry I'm not offended, just the opposite And no, I'm not involved, as you put it, so what's the second question?'

'Just well, have you eaten yet?'

'Sorry?'

'I've been out fishing this afternoon and I have some beautiful fish here I'm about to cook. There's far too much for me so I wondered, well, if you'd like to come round maybe join me for some supper. I could come and collect you if you like?'

There was silence at the other end and Gibson started to feel foolish. 'You know, that's the nicest thing that's happened to me for a while, and yes I'd love to come round for supper. Just tell me where you are and what time you want me and don't worry I can there drive myself.'

Meg turned up with a bottle of chilled chardonnay. Gibson served the fish with some green beans sautéed in butter and garlic, plus a green salad.

'I'm impressed' said Meg, 'a man who can cook, where have you been all my life?'

They had a great time and never stopped talking all evening. At eleven o'clock Meg said she had to go as she had to be up early in the morning and thanked Gibson for a wonderful evening, and said the next time he had to come to hers. Once she'd gone Gibson cleared up then went to his bedroom, set his alarm for six, collapsed into bed with a smile on his face.

He was on the road early the following morning to make sure he had plenty of time to get to Fort Myers for the flight to Philadelphia International. He'd booked an early departure and arranged to collect a rental car from Hertz on arrival. He'd requested a car with a satnav and as part of his preparations he'd written down the addresses and zip codes for all the marinas in the Mantoloking area.

There were nine in total and he reckoned it could take him the best part of two days to get round them all, but then again he could strike lucky and find the right one first time, assuming that Richard was alive and that he'd had had a boat moored in the area. He tried to push any doubts aside and focussed on the map he had printed off from Google which showed the locations of the marinas and tried to decide which order he would visit them in, north to south or the other way round. The captain announced that they would shortly be landing so he put the map away and belted up.

The eighty odd mile drive to the coast would take him just short of two hours he reckoned so he estimated arriving at the first marina around midday. He made good time, arriving at Cove Marina, the northernmost one and found the owner, a man named Charlie McBride. Gibson asked if a Richard Boswell had ever had a boat moored at his marina and showed him the two postcard size pictures of Richard. Charlie scratched his head and asked Gibson to wait while he checked with someone else. The marina still showed some signs of the damage inflicted on it by the storm and Gibson could see piles of wood stacked up on some adjacent land along with the remnants of boats.

The remains of recent snow were still evident and he was cold even with the jumper and jacket he was wearing. He reckoned it was at least forty degrees colder than Naples and everyone else up here was wrapped up in warm winter clothing. Charlie came back with a negative and wished Gibson luck as he bid him goodbye.

His second visit to Sunset View marina produced the same result. Gibson was hungry so he stopped at a MacDonald's, then continued to Bill and Mary's Marina. He parked, went to the white clapboard marina office and knocked. A woman's voice told him to come in. The lady on the phone held up her finger to indicate she wouldn't be long and continued her conversation then put the phone down.

'Yes sir, can I help you?'

'Maybe,' said Gibson. 'Is this your place?'

'For my sins yeah. I'm Mary in the Bill and Mary, why?' She was a woman for sure but she looked as tough and strong as any man.

'I wonder, could you tell me if a man called Richard Boswell had a boat moored in your marina at any time? These are two pictures of him, one with a beard as you can see, and one without.' She remained seated and Gibson put the two photos on the desk in front of her. She studied them for a while then handed them back.

'And who might you be?' Gibson showed her his PI ID card. She looked him up and down.

'And why do you want to find this man, he in trouble?'

'It's complicated and he could be in trouble yes, it depends. I'm working for his business partner and this man may have gone missing, that's why I'm making enquiries.'

'I see.' She said.

'So do you know this man?'

'Sit down why don't you?' Gibson sat. 'You know we've had a rough time around here, Sandy caused huge damage to everyone on the coast and the insurance companies are playing their usual games, act of God and all that. More like an act of the devil if you ask me.'

'Yes, I sympathise,' Gibson said wondering where this was going.

'I'm sure you do, but sympathy don't pay the bills my friend. D'you know that Obama guy came down here after everything was smashed up. Big entourage, camera crew the works. He told a friend of mine, a woman who owns a marina down the coast from here, that FEMA would help her and he hugged her on TV, promised she'd be back in business soon and all that sort of stuff. Guess what? It was bullshit, just all about the publicity, she never heard diddly from him after that, never got any help, nothing. What I'm saying is that we're on our own, we've had to beg borrow and steal to put this boatyard back together, so anything I have of value is for sale, get my drift?'

Gibson got the drift and pulled out his wallet. He had no idea how much she was talking about, nor for that matter how good her information might be. He slid out two one hundred dollar notes, one at a time, watching her face as he did so. She looked him in the eyes and shook her head. He pulled out another three notes. She held out her hand and Gibson passed the notes over. She held one of the notes up to the light, and snapped it from each end. Satisfied, she folded the notes and put them in her jeans pocket.

'How many of those pictures you got?'

'Enough,' he replied, 'why?'

Give one back to me, the one without the beard.'

He handed her the photograph and she rooted in her desk for a pencil, then started to draw on the photo. She turned it round so it was the right way up for Gibson. Richard, if it was he, was now wearing a pair of heavy framed tinted glasses which she had quite expertly drawn on the picture.

'The guy with the beard, same guy I assume, but I've never seen him, not looking like that anyway, though for some reason he looks familiar. But this guy,' she tapped her pencil on the picture of Richard without the beard and with darker hair - and now wearing glasses. 'This guy I do know, but he ain't called Richard, what was it Boswell? No, this guy is Steve Forretti.'

'You're sure?'

'I'm as certain as I am that you're standing there in front of me.'

'And where is this Steve Forretti? I assume he has a boat here?

She laughed derisively. 'Had a boat you mean? But yeah he did *have* a boat here, sold it to him myself, but like everything else round here, Superstorm Sandy took it away. As for where he is now, I don't know. I do know that he intended to buy another boat and come back here when we've finished fixing the place up. He called only last week to see when we thought we might be open, asked me to look out for something similar to the boat he had before, it was a beaut.'

Gibson had his notebook out now. 'When did he buy the boat and can you remember how he paid for it?'

She pulled a ledger of the shelf behind her and thumbed through it. 'August first last year and he paid cash.'

'Is that unusual, cash I mean?

'No honey, I mean what else can a man buy with undeclared cash? Lots of boat buyers pay cash, although there was something unusual about the way he paid.'

'Oh?'

'Yeah, we did the deal over the phone and then he sent a courier round with the cash the next day. I never set eyes on the guy until he came down here, middle of September if I recall correctly.'

'Do you have any idea where he's living now?'

'Nope he didn't say, somewhere temporary I guess, until he gets a boat to live on.'

'You say he called you, do you have his number?'

'That wallet of yours looked pretty full to me Mr private detective.'

Gibson wondered if Jack expected to pay out such sums for information but he couldn't give up now. He took his wallet out and slid another hundred out.

'Look buster, let's not play games, another five hundred okay?' Gibson grimaced, took out four more notes and handed them over.

'You're a hard one,' he said.

'It's a hard road pilgrim,' she replied and rooted once again in her desk drawer and pulled out a notebook. She asked for the picture back and wrote a number on the bottom.

'It's his cell,' she said, and handed it back to Gibson. 'Now if you're finished asking me questions I've got work to do.'

He thanked her for the information, handed her a card with his cell phone number on and said goodbye. As he walked out of the door he heard her say, more to herself than to Gibson. 'Why do I feel like I've just pocketed thirty pieces of silver?'

CHAPTER 14

Gibson was sitting in his rental car, cell in hand. Bonnie Ledinski answered on the third ring. 'Yo Gibson, how's it goin'?'

'Hello Bonnie, I'm in New Jersey.'

'My you do get around Gibson, so what can I do for you, you get my email okay?

'Yes, got the email thanks, by the way did you manage to get a more precise fix on where that CNN report was filmed?'

'No I haven't, there was so much going on at the time and CNN have so much stuff they recorded after the superstorm, it's going to be a while before we can get a more precise location. I talked to my contact at CNN but the team that filmed that report are out in Afghanistan now so I'm not able to make any real progress.'

'Well it might not matter. The guy in the news clip may well be Richard Boswell after all, but it seems he may have a new identity?'

'Go on Gibson, this is getting interesting.' He told Bonnie what had happened since he'd left New York and brought her right up to date. She listened without interruption, then spoke.

'So you now have a name and a number but nothing else?'

'That about sums it up. Other than he's probably staying somewhere in New Jersey, perhaps not too far away from here, if he's planning to get another boat and keep it in the same marina. Then it looks as if he intends to put his original plan back on track, and why wouldn't he?'

'Okay, that sounds logical. I can do some checks based on his new name and geographical area, which might pull up some information on the guy, depends how careful he's being. He paid cash for the boat so he's probably using cash for everything else as well, in which case, he may not have a lot of traceable activity; however the cell number is a different matter.'

'How soon can you put a trace on it?' asked Gibson.

'It'll take me an hour or so to set up the triangulation, so later today we'll be able to start, but before we go any further, how certain are you that this Steve Forretti really is Richard Boswell?'

Gibson considered his reply 'Ninety five per cent I suppose.'

'Okay well we're going to have to factor in that five per cent doubt, we can do without any embarrassing publicity so we need to moderate the way we make the final approach.'

'Agreed, and what about jurisdiction, I mean do we have to tell the local police or the Collier County Sheriff's department?'

'Strictly speaking, we do, but we'll play on the doubt you have, increase it a bit so we can say we weren't confident enough, anyway all that will go away if we let them have some of the glory.'

'Right, same the world over, politics,' said Gibson

'Amen to that. Listen, I suggest we monitor the phone overnight to establish he's at wherever he calls home at the moment, then when we're satisfied, we choose our time and go in with adequate resource, maybe early tomorrow morning?'

'You've done this before haven't you?'

'A few times, and I messed up once by being too impatient so now I'm a bit more methodical. Give me an hour or so and I'll call you back.' She rang off.

Gibson called Jack, he picked up right away. 'Hi Gibson, good news?'

'Maybe.'

'So c'mon Gibson what've you found out?'

Gibson brought Jack up to date, telling him about having to pay the marina owner a thousand dollars for information and how she told him that the man in the photo was called Steve Forretti, then how they were going to use triangulation of his cell to locate him.

'Steve Forretti? a new identity, are you sure I mean?... I just can't believe what I'm hearing...'

'It is all a bit bizarre I admit, but it looks as though you were right about Richard still being alive.'

'Sounds pretty certain from what you say, so what did a thousand bucks buy us, his new address?'

'Fraid not, just conformation of his new name and his cell.'

'But I could have given you his cell number?'

'I don't think he'd be stupid enough to use his old one Jack.'

'You never know Gibson, sometimes people slip up, I mean what number did she give you, If it is his old number that would clinch it wouldn't it?' Gibson looked at his notes and told Jack the number.

'Nope, you're right, that's not Ricks cell, so when do you think you'll go in and... what, arrest him?'

'Tomorrow morning, don't have a time yet, but if it is Richard, then yes he'd be arrested, I can think of a few crimes he's probably committed, extortion for one, but let's not worry about that, let's see if its him first, then worry about the details.'

'You're right Gibson and well done, keep me informed and let me know when you plan to go in, call me anytime, day or night, anytime okay?'

'Will do Jack,' and he rang off. Gibson drove around looking for a place he could get a coffee and ended up in a town called Brick. True to its name, the town had streets of houses built of red brick. Some of the streets reminded Gibson of London mews architecture. The old was mixed with the new with some impressive Georgian buildings interposed between clapboard houses. He was inadequately dressed for the cold of New Jersey and stopped at a Wal-Mart to buy a more substantial winter jacket and some gloves, then drove around the centre of the town until he saw a place called the Brick Street Café & Tavern.

He parked and went in. It was warm and cosy he ordered a coffee and was asked the usual questions about his accent, was he from South Africa, or Australia or was he a Brit? He was in the process of explaining when his cell rang. Excusing himself, he asked the caller to hang on and found a table in the far corner of the room, put his coffee down. It was Bonnie.

'Okay, we have an initial fix. It looks like our friend may be living in a mobile home in a place called Cedarwood Park near somewhere called Toms River. Where are you at the moment?'

'In a café in a town called Brick.'

'Right, let me see how far away you are' there was a brief silence, 'it looks like it's about twelve miles from where you are, so you could go and have a look at the place and let me know what access looks like, that sort of thing. It'll be getting dark soon so maybe go and have a look and call me back?'

'Okay, give me the zip code.'

Cedarwood Park was just off Lakewood Road. Gibson drove through the entrance, looking at the various types of homes. There were the traditional metal trailers interspersed with more elaborate faux clapboard mobile homes set in tree lined avenues. The park had been thoughtfully landscaped and it looked a very pleasant and peaceful place to live. He had no idea which home was Richard's, or Steve as he might now be called. Tomorrow they would have a more precise fix. He drove back out of the park and started to look for a motel. Bonnie Ledinski called him at nine that evening and they discussed tactics.

They dismissed the idea of waiting for the trailer park office to open, he might have left by then and anyway, they couldn't be sure he would have rented under any of the two names they had for him, so they decided that surprise would work best. Bonnie was confident they had the right location within acceptable parameters to be able to identify the right mobile home. She went on to say that it would take her and her assistant about two hours to drive down from New York so they agreed to rendezvous at Gibson's motel at five the next morning.

Bonnie brought two flasks of coffee and some Danish pastries for breakfast and the three of them sat in Gibson's room going over the plan. Bonnie's assistant was Officer

Dan Mitchell, and he could see why she'd chosen him. He was well over six foot, broad shouldered and athletic looking. The plan was simple. They would arrive before dawn, wait until it began to get light then they would move quietly towards the trailer. Bonnie and Gibson would flatten themselves either side of the mobile home door, Bonnie with gun drawn and Dan would knock and shout Forretti's name. The rest of it they agreed, would be played by ear and according to how Forretti aka Boswell reacted.

They all travelled together in Bonnie's unmarked police car. It took them just over fifteen minutes to get to the area where Cedarwood Park was situated, but as they approached, an ambulance raced past in the opposite direction, sirens screaming. It was immediately followed by two police cars in full cry. Bonnie put her foot down and screeched to a skidding halt at the entrance to the trailer park. The immediate area was illuminated by two spotlights on tripods. Two police cruisers flanked each side of the entrance, roof lights flashing. Six uniformed officers stood guard, one with a shotgun cradled in his arms, another holding an AR15 assault rifle. The other four were vetting anyone going in or out of the trailer park.

'What the fuck...? said Bonnie as she slid to a halt. 'Jesus' responded Dan.

She looked briefly at Gibson then all three of them piled out of the car and walked quickly over to the police manning the entrance, Bonnie Ledinski took out her police badge as she approached, holding it high in the air .

'Officer Ledinski NYPD,' she shouted clearly as they got nearer to the gate. The policeman nearest to them nodded for them to approach. He put out his hand for Ledinski's badge and checked it out.

'To what do we owe the honour of a visit from NYPD?' he said smiling, and handing her badge back.

'We're here to check out a Steve Forretti who may be renting a trailer here, we have reason to believe he may have committed several crimes including extortion. So tell me, what's going on?'

'I don't know the details, but there was a shoot-out about an hour or so ago, one guy dead, the rest got away, I don't know any more, we're just minding the gate, you need to see detective Dwyer, he's over there in the Crown Vic.' He pointed at a mid grey saloon parked at the edge of the entrance.

They walked over to the car where a man in the driver's seat was busy speaking on a cell phone. He looked at them as they approached and finished his conversation, then wound his window down.

'Can I help you folks?'

Bonnie showed him her credentials and he invited them to get into the car. Bonnie sat in the front passenger seat, Gibson and Dan in the rear, the warmth of the car a relief after their brief exposure to the pre dawn cold. Formal introductions were completed and Bonnie asked what had happened. But Dwyer, or just call me Joe, insisted that Bonnie tell him her story first, especially, as he pointed out with some justification, that she was well out of her jurisdiction. Bonnie suggested Gibson tell the story and Joe Dwyer listened intently, making notes now and then as Gibson spoke, occasionally asking Gibson to repeat some detail of the story or for clarification on a particular point, especially when Gibson used a English expression he didn't understand.

'Uh-Oh,' he said and pointed as Gibson finished speaking. 'Here come the vultures.' They all looked over at the van, complete with a large dish on its roof, arriving at the gates of the park, 'So let me fill you in on what happened here,' detective Dwyer continued. 'Or at any rate, what we think happened. Three men, we think it was three maybe more, arrived here two or three hours ago and tried to either take or kill a guy living on his own in a rented trailer. We checked with the owner, and you won't be surprised to learn that the guy was called Steve Forretti. As for what happened, we can only assume that this Forretti guy heard the men approaching or whatever, and took pre-emptive action. The neighbours' recollection of events is sketchy but there were a number of gunshots and a lot of yelling, then one guy screamed and the old biddy who lives opposite peeped out and took a look at the action.

She said that two men went down outside the trailer, and that one of the men that'd been hurt was dragged away by another man who appeared to be okay. Then she saw the guy from the trailer come out with a bag and gun in his hand, then he went over to the guy on the ground she said, and looked through his pockets, cool customer your Mr Forretti. The old lady says he then went to a car and drove off. That's it so far. We're waiting for forensics and an autopsy on the deceased. The body had no ID on it, all very professional, other than of course they bungled the hit.'

'Any idea who the three guys were?' asked Ledinski.

'None at all,' replied Dwyer.

'Do we have a tag plate for any of the vehicles?'

'Not for the vehicle that brought the three guys. They must've parked well out of the way of security cameras so we don't even have a make and model to look for. We might get lucky on that score, but don't hold your breath. However, we do have a tag number for Mr Forretti's car, registered to a Natalie Greenberg in Tennessee. So we have a licence number, a false one, but a make and model, so we've put out an APB and who knows?'

'How much driving time would he have had before the APB kicked in?' Gibson asked

Dwyer looked at his watch, 'I guess one to two hours depending.'

'So we don't know which direction he went in, and he'd probably gone at least fifty miles by the time the APB was in play, plus the time that's passed since then, presumably without being apprehended, so he'll either be a hundred miles away, or holed up somewhere.'

'Sounds like a reasonable guess.'

Bonnie spoke. 'We still have his cell number so I'll call my guys and see if we can get a fix, see where he is now?'

'Worth a try, but he might have figured that's how he was located by the mob. Everyone knows about triangulation these days,' Dwyer replied.

Bonnie made her call and gave instructions for them to call her back as soon as they had any information. She closed her cell and addressed Dwyer again. 'So what do you think went down here detective Dwyer?'

'Joe please,' he looked back at Gibson. 'What did this Forretti guy, or what's the other name, yeah this Boswell guy, if they're one and the same, what did he do for a living?'

'He was in the travel business and foreign exchange, a bit of currency speculation from what I was told, and he handled transfers of money for third parties, like a bank.'

'Sending money abroad, overseas, that kinda thing?' asked Dwyer.

'Yes, that was what I was told, it was quite a big business.'

'So this same guy who deals in payments overseas, fakes his own death, buys a boat, gets a new identity, and then some very professional hit men try to either capture him or kill him. Is that a fair summary?'

Gibson thought for a few seconds. 'I'd say that was it in a nutshell, yes.'

He turned back to Bonnie. 'You thinkin' what I'm thinkin'?'

'The mob?'

'The mob.'

CHAPTER 15

S teve Forretti calculated he probably had an hour or so before the cops put out an APB on his car. He was tempted to put his foot down, but he couldn't risk being pulled over. He stuck to the smaller roads which had few if any cameras on them but he had to drive slowly and be careful of black ice. By now he was over the initial shock of being visited by what was undoubtedly the mob, and he was now trying to figure out how they had tracked him down. He racked his brains trying to think of anyone who could have possibly known where he was.

His plan had been fool proof, or so he thought. He analysed and analysed and thought back but he couldn't think of anyone who could have known where he was. He simply hadn't told anyone. He remembered telling Gina he was buying a boat and he thought maybe he told her it was in New Jersey, but not where in New Jersey *and New Jersey's a big place, half as big again as Florida, so the chances of getting a fix on me from that meagre piece of information was simply not possible, especially as I definitely didn't tell her about my new identity.*

He then realised they could have located him by tracking his cell, but again, no one knew his cell number, *except for who?* Apart from ordering the odd pizza, the only person he'd called on it was Mary at the marina, *but how would the mob, or anyone else know he'd had a boat at that marina?* He'd paid cash for everything, no one knew his old name, he just couldn't figure it out, so he pushed it to one side and tried to think about his next move.

He needed to get rid of the phone and he was about to throw it out of the car window, but then realised it could tell someone which direction he was heading in, so maybe there was a better way. He continued driving looking for a suitable opportunity then saw an all night garage in the distance. He drove in and waited. A few minutes later another car drove in and filled up at the pump, then went to pay at the cash window. The car had at least one other passenger in it, so Richard had to wait.

Ten long minutes later, just as Richard was about to give up and move on, another car drove in. The driver was on his own, so he put his cell on silent mode, drove over to the adjacent pump. The driver of the other car finished filling up and went to the cash window to pay. Richard walked quickly round the other side of his car until he was near enough to try the rear door of the other car, it opened, so he threw the phone down into the rear floor well and closed the door. He waited until the other car had gone, then drove out of the garage and went in the opposite direction.

He realised that he still needed to dump his car and find somewhere to hole up while he thought about what to do next. He checked his watch again; it had been an hour and twenty minutes since he'd left the park, so he was running out of time. He'd headed in the direction of Philadelphia reasoning that it would be easier to hide in a more densely populated area and he was now entering the city outskirts. His mind turned to his stash, *would the cops put his picture on the news, but where would they get his picture from, the security cameras in the park maybe, but that would take a lot of time? No, they wouldn't have one unless they figured out that Richard Boswell and Steve Forretti were one and the same person, as the mob obviously had. If that happened then the bank might call the cops?* He was in a bind and he knew it.

He banged his hand on the steering wheel again and again. 'Shit, shit, shit!' He said out loud. 'How did such a great plan get so fucked up?'

He was approaching Fairview about eight miles east of Philadelphia and spotted a rundown looking motel called The Step Back Inn. He drove into the car park and found a spot in the back where he thought it unlikely anyone would see the car, took his bag out of the trunk, went to reception and booked a room for one night. He paid cash in advance and used the name Peter Hammond. The room was pretty poor, but the place in general suited his needs for now. He dumped his bag in the room and went out to find somewhere to eat. He dined in a nearby Dunkin Doughnuts then went back to his hotel room.

He lay down and the bed creaked every time he moved, but he was too tired to care and fell asleep almost immediately. He woke with a start at quarter to midnight and he knew what he had to do. He needed sanctuary, a safe place for a while until he could figure a way out of the mess. He closed his eyes and slept fitfully until morning when he awoke again feeling drained. The room had a coffee maker with capsules of coffee and sachets of dried creamer. He made and drank two cups of the plastic tasting brown liquid, then went out to find a shop selling cell phones. He bought three prepaid phones and went back to his hotel room. He put two of the phones in his bag and used the other one to call directory assistance, and asked for the number of the FBI in Washington.

Agent Vogel was courteous and listened patiently as Richard Boswell explained that he had information on the Miami mafia including names and details of where substantial amounts of laundered money had been deposited in off shore accounts over the past three years.

'And you know where this money is because?'

'I helped them put it there.'

'I see, and you are again?'

'John Doe, c'mon don't play the fool, you think I'm kidding around here? The mob tried to rub me out today. If you're not going to take me seriously you'd better put me on to your boss.'

'Have you any idea how many crank calls we get like this Mr Doe?'

'No and I don't want to fucking know how many crank calls you get, look just put me on to someone who knows the difference between a crank call and the genuine article.'

'Okay, keep your shirt on. Now I assume you want something in return for giving us this information?'

'Correct, and as I've just told you, they tried to off me today so you can make an intelligent guess what it is I want, but in case you can't, here's the deal. I tell you who I know and what I know, which should be plenty enough for you to make some serious moves against the Miami mob. In return I want protection, a safe house, a new identity, all the usual things that people need if they're to survive ratting out the mob.'

'Well that will depend on the quality of your information, but if it's something we can use to nail any of the mob guys, then you probably have a deal. So where and when do we meet?'

'I'll call you back.' Richard said and closed the phone, took it to the bathroom dropped it on the tiled floor and stamped on it until it was smashed into little pieces, then went out. He needed to walk, get some fresh air and consider his options. He had to think things through and try not make any panicky decision he might regret later. He decided there was no reason to think the cops would know he wasn't Steve Forretti, although they would know by now that his licence plates weren't legit.

As far as the cops at the trailer park are concerned, surely they'd think I was just a guy who'd been attacked by three men and ran away. But it was now obvious to him that the mob knew that he, Richard Boswell, wasn't dead and they knew he was using another identity, so he assumed it was only a matter of time before they found him again. He hadn't planned on them finding him before he'd had a chance to put his insurance plan in place. It could still be done but he needed to buy some time. *Adapt and survive* he said to himself, and went to the motel to call Agent Vogel back and arrange a meet.

Special agent Dale Vogel said he would need to consult his boss, Section Chief Lazaro Arbus and kept Richard waiting for a few minutes. He came back on the phone said the chief thought the safest thing was for him to stay put and they would come to him and escort him to Washington. Richard told him where he was staying and what name he was registered under. Vogel said they could be on the lunchtime flight which would take an hour to get to Philly, then another forty five minutes give or take to get to his motel, then factor in at least half an hour for whatever, he said,

'So, we should be with you by late afternoon. Sit tight and we'll be along as soon as we can.' Richard suddenly realised how hungry he was and went to find some breakfast. He found a local place called Big Albert's Diner and had a ten ounce steak with fried eggs and all the trimmings, then walked back to the motel to wait for the FBI.

He was snoozing when there was a knock on the door. He had his Glock under the pillow and took it out.

'Who is it?'

'Agent Vogel.' He put the gun back under the pillow and let them in. They introduced themselves and Vogel asked

'So what do we call you?'

'My real name's Richard Boswell, but I've been using the name Steve Forretti for a while now. I'll explain all that as we go along.'

Vogel was a little younger than Richard; he guessed late fifties, dyed light brown, reddish hair, medium height, blue eyes, ruddy face and a tight smile. Arbus was obviously of Hispanic stock, late forties, squat compact body, dark brown eyes and slicked back black hair. Richard sat back down on the bed. Arbus took the only chair in the room and sat down. Vogel folded his arms and leaned back against the wall.

'Richard Bowell, I know that name' said Vogel.

'Yeah, I was famous for a while, executed on CNN.'

Vogel pushed himself away from the wall and pointed at Richard, 'I knew I recognised you, you're the guy, in the video, millions paid in ransom and they still killed you, Jesus so it was staged… you clever motherfucker.'

'Thanks' said Richard, 'I think.'

'Okay waddya got?' said Arbus.

Richard reached under the bed and pulled out his sports bag. He unzipped it, took out his laptop, placed it on the bed and switched it on. He clicked on the Excel spread sheet icon and then on a specific spreadsheet.

'This is a sample,' he said, Arbus took his time looking at it with Vogel looking over his shoulder.

'How much of a sample?'

'About a quarter of the total value of the transfers I made for them,' said Richard.

'And the rest of it?'

'In a safe place.' said Richard.

'Suppose these are just meaningless figures, made up stuff?'

'Don't be stupid, why would I give you made up stuff? It's my life we're talking about here.'

Section Chief Lazaro Arbus took a small tape machine out of his jacket pocket, switched it on and put it on the bed. 'Okay, let's have the whole story and don't leave anything out.'

Richard told how JARIC had expanded their hotel booking business to include making overseas payments on behalf of third parties. Richard's experience in dealing in foreign currency transactions and his ability to predict the rise and fall of currencies made him able to do great deals for companies paying large sums of money for goods or services abroad. He'd even handled transactions that involved buying players from Europe for American soccer clubs. He either worked on a consultancy basis, charging a monthly fee to advise companies when it would be favourable to make payment involving foreign currency, or he charged a commission on individual transactions. It was a good business he told them.

Then a company in Miami had approached JARIC to make some foreign transfers on their behalf, fairly normal stuff purchasing goods from abroad, all legit, then one day he got a phone call from one of the bosses asking for a meeting. They met in the Caravaggio an expensive fifth avenue restaurant and as the meal progressed, Richard realised what they were asking for and initially backed off But they convinced him that there was no risk to him or JARIC, and anyway they would pay well for his services. He'd told them he'd think about it and get back to them. He decided to leave out the fact that he'd consulted his business partner Jack as he realised that might get Jack into trouble for aiding and abetting and he saw no point in that, so he left that detail out of his story.

He went on to say that he decided to accept their proposition and described how easy it was for him to launder the money, creating false bookings and false hotel invoices for large groups of non-existent customers going to expensive hotels and on luxury cruises. Some of the offshore accounts were set up as hotel or cruise agents. In any event, JARIC was making so many legitimate overseas transactions in such large volumes that it was easy to hide the movement of the mob's money in amongst the straight deals.

He finished telling his story and said. 'That's it, that's what I did.'

'Names, you didn't give us any names yet.'

'And I'm not going to, not until I'm convinced you're going to hold up your end of the deal.'

'Okay, but what made you decide to stop washing their money?'

'Well I figured out that at some point, the mob would consider I knew too much and that I'd served my purpose, and at that point they would terminate our arrangement - and me into the bargain. I don't think the mob go in for long term relationships, so I made a decision to get out and started making my plans, which included creaming off a little bit on each of their transactions. I set up an offshore account for myself in Grand Cayman, and whenever I made a transfer of funds for them I'd take a little bit for me.

'And how much did you cream off into your own offshore account?' asked Arbus

'About two million bucks all told,' said Richard

'You realise you won't be able to keep any of that money don't you?'

'I guess, but maybe we could negotiate around that?' said Richard not wishing to appear to be prepared to give up this decoy account too easily.

Arbus gave him a look. 'I don't think so my friend.' Richard shrugged.

'Okay, well put that to one side and let's have the rest of your story.

Richard went on to tell them in more detail about his staged execution and how his escape plan got seriously derailed due to hurricane Sandy and then about the mob finding him and how he decided he only had one way out, and this was it.

Arbus sat there saying nothing, absorbing what he'd been told, then he spoke.

'Okay, now neither I nor Vogel here is financially competent enough to tell if the information you've shown us is genuine, the smart guys back at the ranch can do all the checking on that. Your story's very convincing, and if this stuff,' he said pointing at the laptop, 'if it's crap, it's good enough looking crap for me not to look like a complete asshole for taking things to the next stage.' Turning to Vogel he said, 'Let's get some reservations for the three of us to fly back to Washington and we can take things on from there, that okay with you Boswell?'

'I'm in your hands, say, what do I call you?'

'Agent Arbus will do for the time being.'

'Okay then Agent Arbus, that's fine by me. By the way, I have a gun, so maybe you'd better take charge of that.' He was reaching under the pillow and Vogel shouted.

'Stop… don't do that, if you don't mind I'll get the gun, okay, just move away?' Richard moved away and let Vogel retrieve the gun.

'Any more weapons?' Vogel asked.

'No that's the only gun I own,' lied Richard, 'and while we're on the subject of guns, what about the guy I killed back in the trailer park?'

'If it went down the way you said it did, then that's okay,' said Arbus. We'll check through back channels to see what the local cops are doing about the shootout and play it by ear, but that's not our main concern at the moment. C'mon let's get this show on the road, Dale, you got those reservations sorted?'

Vogel who was speaking on his cell nodded and took it away from his ear momentarily.

'The flight's in an hour and a half,' he said and went back to talking on his cell giving his credit card number to pay for the flights.

'What about my car?' said Richard, 'it's parked round the back.'

'Leave it,' said Arbus, 'Dale, call a cab and let's get out of here.'

During the hour's flight to Washington, the FBI men asked Richard about his life in general, was he married, any kids, girlfriends, long term relationships? The questions seemed innocent, casual, but Richard knew they were really trying to build a background picture to identify any weak points in his personal circumstances. He was able to tell them he had no kids or long term relationships and he was married, but was now divorced. They lapsed into silence for the remainder of the short flight. They deplaned and were met outside the terminal by someone Richard assumed was another agent. He drove them to FBI headquarters on Pennsylvania Avenue.

*

The Witness Protection Program was created in nineteen seventy by Gerald Shur. He realised that witnesses were often too scared to come forward, due to the repercussions they might suffer at the hands of the accused. The first criterion that must be met is that the individual's testimony must be considered credible and be deemed absolutely essential to the case in order for Witness Protection to take place. The witness must also be considered reliable and all doubt that they will back out of providing their testimony must be removed.

There are three different federal organizations involved in placing a witness into the witness protection programme. The U.S. Attorney General has the final say on whether or not a witness can be placed into the program. Once a person has been deemed in need of the Witness Protection program, the Marshals Service will then go about trying to make that person 'fall off the face of the earth.' This includes things such as creating a new identity for the witness. Since the program began in 1970, Witness Protection has gotten a conviction rate of 89%

*

At FBI headquarters Richard was escorted to an office on the twenty ninth floor where he was left while Vogel and Arbus went to brief their superiors on the situation. They had shown him where the restrooms were and said to just pick up the phone and dial one to order some coffee or a soft drink. They also told him that he should not try to leave the floor he was on, as it would cause a security alert and that would have consequences.

When they left, Richard put his bag down and wandered round the room gazing out over Washington from the large windows. He turned back and took in the room. Light grey painted walls, dark grey and light grey carpet tiles, a large plain oak coloured functional looking desk and six office chairs tucked in around it. On the desk were yellow legal pads and pencils, bottles of water with glasses, plus two microphones on stalks. In one corner of the room was a podium and a screen, in the opposite corner, a video camera mounted on a tripod, a microphone sticking out of it pointing at the desk.

He sat down and waited. After forty five minutes, Vogel came back into the room with three other people, two preppy looking men who Richard guessed to be in their late thirties and a slightly older smartly dressed woman who had the air of being in charge, at least over the two younger men. Vogel introduced Richard to them all and they sat down except for one of the men who went to the video camera and fiddled with the controls. The woman took charge of the meeting.

'Okay Mr Boswell, my name is Marilyn Young, and these men are Frank and Ken,' she said, pointing to each of them in turn. 'We're the team who will vet and initially evaluate the information you provide. I assume you have no objection to us recording this session.'

Richard shrugged his shoulders in assent and the red light blinked as the man started the video camera.

After this initial evaluation and assuming the results are satisfactory from our perspective, you will be transferred to our New York Field office as they have an existing specialist team looking at the Miami mafia operations. Agent Vogel will accompany you and continue to be in charge of your security while you're there and is assigned to you until you testify at the Grand Jury. After that, new arrangements may be put in place, we'll see at that time, okay?'

'Okay,' Richard replied thinking *what choice did he have?* He was their hostage now.

'I understand you will withhold certain information until you have been assured about the deal you will be offered, a perfectly rational decision, so here's a formal document outlining the details of the deal on offer.' She slid a manila folder over the desk to Richard, then carried on talking, 'however as with all contracts and negotiations, there has to be a significant element of mutual trust, otherwise the agreement isn't worth the paper it's written on, okay?' she looked directly at Richard. He looked briefly at the folder and said, 'agreed.'

'Okay, you can read the formal agreement at your leisure but to paraphrase, what is says, is that in return for you providing information of appropriate quality, and which the FBI believes sufficient to be able secure a conviction against a person or persons involved in organised crime, The FBI in return, will offer you temporary accommodation, funds to live a reasonable life and protection until you appear as a witness in any hearings or trails relating to the information you have provided. Subsequent to these trails or hearings, whether or not a conviction is secured, you will be offered a new life, new identity, a secure job and a place to live. There will be choices involved in the final package, and these can be discussed in more detail at a later stage, but those are the basics. Any problems with that Mr Boswell?'

Richard looked at the folder then back to Marilyn Young, 'No, I don't think so. Where do you want to start?

'At the beginning, tell us the story you told to agents Arbus and Vogel, then afterwards we'll ask some questions okay, begin please.'

Richard told the story again. He told them about his assumption that the mob would eventually consider his knowledge about their financial dealings to be a risk at some point and he decided to pre-empt the possibility of them eliminating that risk by staging his own execution, and how everything was going to plan until he was attacked in the trailer park. He told them he still didn't understand how the mob had found him, but they had, so he had then decided the only safe haven would be the FBI and here he was. He went on to tell them in broad terms how he had met the mob and how he had distributed money for them into offshore bank accounts. They all listened intently, making notes as he spoke. When he'd finished, Marilyn Young told Ken to go first and he asked how funds were paid into JARIC from the mob.

'Some came in as raw cash, huge amounts. JARIC had many bank accounts and so I spread the incoming cash payments over multiple bank accounts and over long periods to avoid any unusual spikes in cash receipts that might cause anyone to raise a query, but remember we dealt with many organisations with huge numbers of members and they would often pay for their trips in cash collected over long periods and we would set up bank accounts local to their area to facilitate these incoming payments, so I was able to integrate the mob's cash and filter it, if you like, through these channels. It was tedious and hard work and I often worked long hours making the arrangements and not the least, keeping an accurate record of the cash amounts paid and distributed. Other funds came in as pre-washed from mob set up companies, so those were easier to deal with.'

Ken nodded his satisfaction with the answer and Marilyn signalled for Frank to ask his questions next. 'When you staged the execution video, which I think we all saw extracts of on the news at the time. Good production by the way, very convincing.' they all laughed including Richard.

Frank continued, 'it was reported at the time that a ransom of "millions" was paid. How many millions was it, the precise amount, and what happened to those "millions"?'

Richard realised they would probably check with the cops on how much was paid and find out that it was paid in diamonds, *but maybe they wouldn't, at least not for a while, so what's to lose by not being entirely truthful. Maybe they'd be more inclined to let me keep a lesser amount?*

'It was the usual thing,' he said, 'you know, the news people, why spoil a good story with the facts?'

'You saying it wasn't millions?' said Frank

'That's what I'm saying yes, not millions, just the one million,' lied Richard, 'less what I've already spent of course.'

'And what is your estimate of the value of what's left?' asked Frank

'I'd guess somewhere about eight hundred and change.'

'And where is this money now?'

'In a safe place,' said Richard smiling

Frank said 'No other questions at this time.'

Marilyn said, 'okay I have three questions, one, when are you going to give us the names of the companies used by the Miami mafia to channel money to you for laundering, two, when are you going to give us the names of the people you dealt with in the Miami Mafia and three, when do you plan to provide the rest of the data showing deposits and transfers. In other words, the complete financial picture of all the business you conducted on behalf of the mob, including locations, account numbers etc?'

Richard doodled with his pencil as he considered his answer. 'The answer to the first two questions is now, I'm prepared to give you the names of the individuals and the names of the companies now, the answer to the third question, is later, that leaves me a little leverage, just in case we have some problems agreeing details of the final terms.'

Marilyn looked round at each of the people round the table in turn seeking there agreement or otherwise. Vogel put his hand up in agreement, Frank did the same and Ken nodded. 'Okay unanimous. Agent Vogel and I will leave now, Frank and Ken will stay and take details of the people and companies involved, then we can check if we have a file or any current surveillance activity on these organisations or individuals. When you've finished, Dale here will take you to your temporary accommodation. He will be responsible for your safety and security until further notice, so I hope you get along well. You'll be spending some time together.

Richard took his laptop out of his bag and started it up. He clicked on the file he wanted.

'Okay, these are the companies I dealt with. I don't know anything about their activities, just the names of the company, their bank account numbers and the names of the people who represented them in our transactions.'

Frank and Ken scribbled away on their pads as Richard spoke. 'The process was simple, I would tell them the account numbers to transfer money into and I'd process it from there on. Money would be moved into JARIC's account by bank transfer. So the companies were; Universal Solutions Inc, Summit Security, Apex Merchant Services, Chainbox and Jets Inc. All Miami based companies.'

Richard carried on. 'All matters and conversations relating to the offshore accounts, transfers made, amounts etc., were conducted person to person, no phone calls, no emails no traceable types of communication. We'd meet outside my office as I assume they didn't trust me not to make recordings, so it was always a public place, the same ones rotated each week, but they would choose the venue an hour or so before, and call me as though they were arranging a social lunch or a drink. Cash was also given to me at these meetings and I would bring it back to the office for processing as I described previously.

The individuals I dealt with were Enrico Graziano,' Richard stopped talking and asked. 'Do you want their nicknames as well? They all had 'em.'

'Yes we do,' said Ken, 'it's all useful stuff.'

'Okay, well Graziano was known as Caesar or sometimes referred to as The Emperor. He was the big boss, at least the biggest one I ever met, scary guy. He actually came to Naples to check me out early on, wanted to see where I socialised and so on.

Then there was Giuseppe Azzerelli, or Pooch as he was sometimes called, then Anthony Russo aka Baby Fat Tony,' the two men laughed shaking their heads as they wrote it down. '

Another one was Joe Garabed, a mean looking guy, never smiled, they called him Jolly Joe. Then there were a couple of Ruskies by the name of Anatoly Dumanovsky who for some reason was nicknamed Uncle Yoyo and the last guy, Roman Budnikov, called Cyberman by the Italian guys, and that's it. Those are all the people I ever had dealings with. They didn't represent any of the companies exclusively as far as I was concerned anyway.'

Gibson noticed how Frank and Ken had looked at each other at the mention of Budnikov's nickname Cyberman.

'Okay well I think that's enough for today, we'll leave now',' said Frank, 'we'll get agent Vogel to come and collect you shortly.

Frank went over to the VCR, took out the flash card and switched it off. 'Nice meeting you Richard, I'm sure we'll meet again,' said Ken and they both left. Richard blew out a long breath closed his eyes, leaned back and wondered if his plan could still work.

CHAPTER 16

Jack was deeply shocked when Gibson called him to tell him of the debacle at the trailer park. 'I just can't believe what I'm hearing. The mob, I mean what the fuck are the mob looking for Rick for, trying to kill him an all? Man this is way beyond me, I just don't understand. Why would the mob be after him for Chrissakes?'

The usual I should think, money. He either owes them bigtime or he's crossed them in some way, or maybe it's Steve Forretti they're after and it's not Richard at all, or maybe Richard chose the wrong identity, I honestly don't know what's going on and the only person who does is Richard and or Steve Forretti, if they're one and the same person, the real mystery is, how they found him before we got there.'

'Would they have been able to use his cell to find out where he was?'

'They would, it's not such a big deal these days, but how they knew his number, is what mystifies me?

'Jesus Gibson, I still can't believe it, my partner, my lifelong buddy, why would he stage that execution video, demand that ransom, I mean why?'

'I'm afraid I can't answer that one Jack. But what do you want me to do now, do I stand down or carry on trying to find Richard?'

'Where would you start?'

'I can honestly say, I haven't got the foggiest idea Jack.'

'What about his phone, why can't you track it now?'

'We did and we found it in the back of a car driving through the outskirts of Baltimore. Forretti or Richard, must have realised he'd been tracked using his cell and somehow managed to put it in someone's car after he left the trailer park.' There was a silence. 'You still there Jack?'

'Yeah, just thinking sorry. Look I know you said you had no idea where to look, but is there anything you can think of? I mean we've come this far…'

'Well I'd guess he's not going to fly anywhere, he'll have worked out that he might be spotted at an airport, and he'll also want to dump his car as soon as possible, but he can always find another car, maybe even steal one, so wherever he goes, it'll be by road I think. We don't know how much money he's got with him, so we don't know if that's a limiting factor or not. But suppose it isn't, I mean he's got all those diamonds, so if he's well-funded, then he has virtually the whole of the USA to hide in.'

'Yeah, so, what do we do?'

I think I might as well come back to Naples and wait, see if my contacts in NYPD come up with anything. But as of now, I don't think I'm serving any useful purpose hanging around here, kicking my heels.'

'Yeah, I guess you're right Gibson, have a safe flight and maybe I'll see you tomorrow?'

'Goodbye Jack.'

When he returned from New Jersey, Gibson met with Jack, and told him, that reluctantly, he'd have to shelve the hunt for Richard Boswell,

'At least until I hear from Bonnie.'

Jack understood. Gibson felt frustrated at not being able to make progress, but decided to use the time to try to get to know Meg better. She'd told Gibson, that when he had the time, there was an open invitation for a return dinner at her place. He called and told her he was back in Naples, and asked if the invite was still valid. She'd laughed and told him it was.

'So, Gibson, when are you thinking of taking me up on my generous offer?'

'Is tonight too soon?' he asked

'Not for me,' she replied, and gave him her address.

'Shall we say seven?'

'Perfect,' said Gibson, 'see you then.

He arrived at Meg's house on Ninth Avenue South bang on time and parked on the driveway. He got out of the car and looked around. There was a mixture of house styles and sizes on the avenue. Looking south, he could see a beach entrance in the distance. Meg's house was a traditional Naples single story clapboard building, painted robin eggshell blue, edged in white, with a light grey roof. The front garden was laid to lawn.

She opened the door as he approached and welcomed him with a hug and a kiss on the cheek, then gave him a quick tour of the house. After the tour, they went outside to a small back garden, where they drank a couple of Blue Moon beers, with slices of orange dunked in. Dinner was baby back ribs cooked on the barbeque. The evening flew by, the conversation never flagged. Although Meg was originally from Indiana, she'd lived in Naples for many years and told Gibson how she'd come to the area on a two week vacation in 1980, and when the vacation was over, she went back home packed her things and came back down to Naples and had stayed ever since.

She was very knowledgeable about the history of Naples and told Gibson about some of the famous people who used to vacation there, like Gary Cooper, Hedy Lamarr and even Greta Garbo. Then over coffee they told each other of their previous marriages. Meg said her story was as old as the hills, but with a twist. She and her husband had built a business in Naples, Property Master, which arranged house inspections for house buyers. The business grew steadily and they ended up employing more than twenty staff, Meg looking after the office and admin, George her husband managing the work force and the day to day arrangements for scheduling the inspections and trouble shooting.

'Over the years, we'd developed close working relationships with many of the realtors in Naples but unfortunately for me' said Meg, 'George had developed another kind of relationship with one particular realtor, and ran off with him.'

'Him?' exclaimed Gibson.'

'Yeah him, it happens, anyway he came crawling home two weeks later begging for forgiveness.' She said she showed him the door and served papers two days later. They hadn't got any kids she said, so it wasn't that bad, a lot of hurt pride but she told Gibson she was over it.

It was his turn. He told her about where he'd been brought up, and about being an adopted child and about his sister Sophie who was also adopted.

'Did you ever find out who your real parents were?' Meg asked.

'No,' he replied, 'I never really felt that curious about it. I had a great Mum and Dad and that was good enough for me, but Sophie, once she knew she was adopted, she felt she had to find her real mother, and she did, but it was a bit of a disaster. She found her biological mother in a sort of refuge, a home for down and outs. It transpired that her mother had come over from Ireland as a girl and ended up as a prostitute, then as she got older and her looks went, she took to drugs and drink, ended up living on the streets. She couldn't even tell Sophie who her father was.'

'How sad is that?' said Meg.

'It was, she was never the same afterwards, and soon after Mum died, our adopted Mum that is, she left home and went to London. The last time I heard she was working as a high class 'escort' as they euphemistically call it.

'How tragic, like mother like daughter,' said Meg.

'So it seems. Haven't seen her for years now but I really must try to find her again. We were very close as kids. Anyway moving on, I'd always wanted to be in the police and so I joined the force. Then I got married, quite young, too young really and it just didn't work out, but then I met Jill who was my wife until….' Gibson had to stop talking and take a deep breath.

Meg waited. Gibson got his composure back and carried on, but it was an awkward moment. He told Meg how they'd met, both on the rebound from previous failed relationships, but how it all worked out okay. He couldn't lie to Meg about how much he'd loved Jill and still loved her.

He told her how it had been Jill's long time wish to visit the Giza pyramids in Cairo so she went on a short break to Egypt with her friend April as he was busy with an important case. Jill and April had arranged to stay in Luxor for four nights and on the second day they went from

Luxor airport on a day trip excursion by plane to see the pyramids.'

Gibson stopped talking again and took a drink of water, then carried on his voice faltering a little as he continued. 'They arrived safely and had the day seeing the sites but then on the way back the plane flew into a sandstorm on its final approach into Luxor airport,' Gibson had to stop again briefly before continuing. 'And the plane crash landed, killing everyone on board.'

Gibson bowed his head then lifted it up and looked at Meg, tears were running down her face. They said little after that and Meg started to clear up, and refusing Gibson's offer to help saying she could manage, adding that it was way past her bedtime she needed all the beauty sleep she could get at her age. Gibson took the hint and left.

On his way home, he wondered if his grief had spoilt an opportunity to get close to someone again, but the following afternoon, when he returned from fishing, a case of Blue Moon with an orange plonked on top had been left outside his apartment door with a note attached.

'Call me if you need someone help you to drink these, Love Meg.'

He took the beers' into his condo and was just putting some of them in the fridge, when his cell bleeped to tell him had a message. He brought the phone to his ear and listened to Bonnie's voice.

Hi Gibson, I'm calling to let you know that Steve Forretti's car had been found parked behind a motel called The Step Back Inn, on the outskirts of Philadelphia. She said it had actually been found some days ago, but it had taken some time for it to be identified as the car that the NYPD were looking for, in connection with the shooting at the trailer park.

Bonnie asked Gibson to call her back as soon as he got the message. He phoned her straight away.

'Hi Gibson thanks for calling back, you got my message about the car?'

'I did thanks Bonnie, is there any more?'

'Well it looks like he used the name Peter Hammond to check in and paid cash in advance for one night, then left with a couple of guys the next afternoon.' 'From the description the manager gave us of the guys he left with, they don't sound like the mob, but who knows?'

'Why do you think they weren't the mob?'

'Just the general description, suits, ties smart clean shaven, didn't fit somehow. But like I say, you can never tell.'

'Anything else at all?' asked Gibson

'Not really. It's hard to trace where he got the car as he was using someone else's licence tags. We got some prints, no matches, but maybe they'll be useful if and when we catch up with this Steve or Richard guy. Maybe we can ask the cops in Naples if they have a sample of Boswell's prints to compare. Anyway, we checked Philly airport and as far as we can tell, no one has flown out of there under the name of Richard Boswell, Steve Forretti or Peter Hammond. In the meantime I'm working on a couple of angles, I don't want to say anything just yet but something's come across my radar so I've put some feelers out, I'll let you know.'

'Sounds intriguing, call me as soon as you know anything.'

'Will do,' she said and rang off leaving Gibson a little deflated. Jack had been good as his word and hadn't pestered Gibson, but he could appreciate Jack's frustration and felt a little guilty at not being able to move things forwards. But sometimes, as he'd learnt in the past, you just have to wait, be patient, and you usually get a break eventually. Meg was now a regular visitor to Gibson's apartment, and she and Gibson would spend time together round the pool. He introduced her to Jack, who had met her before briefly, when he visited Richard's house. The next time Jack saw them at the pool together he suggested they all go out to dinner, 'on my tab,' he said and despite their objections Jack insisted.

'I choose the restaurant, so I pay. It's an old tradition,' he claimed winking at them as he said it. They all went out the following evening at six. Gibson felt underdressed when he saw the others. Mary Lou wore a green silk blouse with cream trousers, the colours contrasting with her red hair to great effect. Jack wore a bright red and white Hawaiian style beach shirt outside of some grey slacks, while Meg wore a white sundress that showed off her tanned shoulders.

Jack took them to his favourite restaurant, the Cibao Grill in the Neapolitan Plaza just a few minutes away from Bay View. It was a family run restaurant, the family being from The Dominican Republic. The place was packed and the food was delicious. Over dinner Gibson got to know Mary Lou a little better, she was obviously quite sophisticated and refreshingly for Gibson, she seemed to have a good grip on European affairs. The conversation ranged over many subjects, including the comparison of politics in the USA and the UK, finding that many of the problems were similar in nature.

They also discussed religion, and Gibson told them how he'd become a convert to Catholicism late in life.

'You Americans,' said Gibson, 'are much less inhibited about discussing religion or God.'

At one point in the conversation, Mary Lou put her hand on Gibson's arm, and said that Jack had told her about his sad loss, and how sorry she was. It was a sincere moment and could have made him feel awkward in other company. But somehow, Gibson felt anything but awkward. He told her, he was appreciative of the gesture.

Jack told some hilarious stories about politicians who had been caught with their fingers in the till, or with their pants down. Gibson assured them that things weren't that much different in the UK on that score. Wine was drunk and the conversation turned to less weighty matters and Gibson was asked why he was known only by his last name. He explained there was no mystery and that his first name was John, but as far back as he could remember, people had just called him Gibson. He took the opportunity to ask Mary Lou about her name and if she'd been named after the song.

She told him the question had been asked many times, but that she had been born in fifty eight and the song had been written by Gene Pitney in sixty so if anything it was the other way round. Meg, whose pre-marital surname name was Fairbrother could trace her ancestors all the way back to the Mayflower, whilst Jack on the other hand, hadn't got a clue about his ancestors other than the Otterbein's had come from Germany and at least one of them had been a bishop.

In view of the amount of wine they'd consumed they decided to walk back to Bay View, the girls walked arm in arm chatting and the men walked behind, Jack taking the opportunity to ask Gibson if there's been any progress since Rchard's car had been found.

'Sorry Jack, we seem to have reached a dead end. I'll talk to my contact at NYPD tomorrow, but maybe you have to face the prospect that Richard may never be found now. Maybe the mob got him, maybe he's on the run, but as it stands, he's what your American detectives describe as being in the wind.'

CHAPTER 17

The fourth floor apartment in an anonymous looking building in downtown New York was adequate and well equipped, although far from the standard that Richard was used to. The adjacent apartment was occupied by agent Dale Vogel and another agent, Paul Brunner. They alternated every two days and were directly responsible for Richard's security and wellbeing. They also acted as chauffeurs, taking Richard to the FBI office.

Richard was allowed out but only if accompanied by one of the agents. They went to movies and restaurants, walks in the parks, pretty well wherever Richard wanted to go. The regime was relatively unrestricted but nevertheless he found it mind numbingly boring and claustrophobic, the debriefing sessions at the FBI became the high point of his days in many ways. The New York FBI division had active open files on most of the people Richard had named, the exception being Anatoly Dumanovsky aka Uncle Yoyo, but based on the information Richard had provided, Uncle Yoyo was added to their serious interest list.

On his first visit to the New York FBI offices, Richard was introduced to the new team of interrogators. Two of them, Larry Roorda and Dave Ramsey could have been clones of Frank and Ken, but for their names. There were two other investigators who attended the meetings, a woman named Anne Bryant and another man by the name of Mathew Klinowski, who was obviously in charge. At this first meeting with the new team, agent Klinowski explained unsurprisingly, that their division in particular, had been monitoring the activities of the Miami mob for many years, but that it was relatively complicated as the 'families' considered Miami and southern Florida as open territory as against the jealously guarded territories that existed in other major cities where one family would generally control the action.

He told Richard that the Mafia's traditions in South Florida dated as far back as the thirties and the gambling heydays in Broward, when Meyer Lansky and his associates came south to claim a piece of the action in dozens of "carpet joints" - classy casinos that operated around Hallandale under the beneficial eye of a crooked sheriff. At that time the mobs owned the casinos in Havana and were alleged to have close links with President Batista, who was said to be happy to take the mob's money in return for favours.

'Mobs in Miami go as far back as the 1920's,' said Larry Roorda. When Al Capone had a house on Palm Island. He used his stay there as his alibi for the St. Valentine's Day Massacre, but all that sort of stuff's small beer compared to what we have now,' he said. 'The Russians moved in over the last few years and they've brought a new dimension to the level of violence and crime, taking the game to a whole new level.'

He went on to say that the mob's influence had grown continuously over the years and they were able to wield undue influence over the economy of the whole of Florida with their "bought in" political power, and it had far reaching consequences for the stability of the entire country if their activities were not curtailed. 'But,' he said, 'as serious as the criminal activities these people are involved in, political corruption, prostitution, gambling, murder, protection rackets, I could go on, but all these crimes are nothing compared to the activities now being funded by offshore mob money.

Cybercrime is the Holy Grail for the mob and they're in it up to their necks. And believe me, this activity is a serious game changer. It's hard to imagine the extent and scale of the damage they can inflict on the rest of us, whole economies are at risk, to say nothing of the risk to our national security, so cutting off their money supply is a bit more serious than simply stopping them having a luxury lifestyle.'

He went on to tell Richard that in the previous year, the FBI uncovered a Mafia funded operation that had successfully hijacked over four million computers in a hundred countries, including half a million computers in the United States, rerouting Internet traffic and generating over fifty million dollars in illegitimate income, and that they were currently working in conjunction with other federal authorities and counterparts from other nations in an effort to dismantle a number of enormous similar botnet operations. He went on to list a number of examples of other similarly funded scams including Cyber-attacks on NASA, defence satellites, credit card companies, music companies, banks. 'The list goes on,' he said. 'So you can see why we need to get these activities stopped, and hitting their finances is probably the most effective thing we can do. Stop the funding, stop the crime.'

Richard was surprised at the level of passion displayed by Klinowski when he spoke about these matters and didn't doubt their resolve to act against the mob's activities in this area. He now understood why Frank and Ken had given each other the meaningful look when he mentioned Budnikov's nickname Cyberman during that first interview. He also realised that these activities had escalated far beyond the criminal, and that as far as the FBI were concerned they were now at war with the mob, and their cybercrime activity in particular. Soon, they would demand that Richard give them the rest of the information he had on his dealings with them.

The session ended and agent Vogel drove him back to the apartment, but suggested they stop for a coffee on the way. Richard said he would prefer to go straight back but Vogel insisted. They found a parking space not far from a Starbucks about a mile from the apartment block. Vogel found them a table in the corner, away from the other customers and they ordered.

'So why the stop, what's this all about agent Vogel?'

'Nothing really, just thought it would be nice to stop and have a coffee and a chat, that's all.'

Richard waited until the waitress had brought their coffee, then turned to Vogel.

'Don't fuck about Vogel, do you think I'm dumb, why are we having a coffee and a chat, why bring me here?'

'Please call me Dale, I mean we've known each other long enough now.' Vogel sipped his coffee.

'Okay *Dale,* I'll ask you again, what's this all about?'

'Well I just wanted a word in private, and well, maybe the apartment isn't so private?'

'Yeah, well I assumed the apartment was bugged, but as you're the ones bugging it, why should you care?'

'Well let's just say I needed a confidential word, that's all.'

'If you don't cut the bullshit then I'm walking out of here, so you have ten seconds to get to the point.'

'Okay keep your shirt on, it's just that I'm a little short of money at the moment, and I thought maybe you could help me out, that's all?'

'Help you out, what the fuck are you talking about?'

'Just that I thought you could help me out and I could do you a little favour in return.'

'Oh yeah, and what favour would that be?'

'Well I was at the initial interview you had with Marilyn's team and you weren't exactly truthful about the ransom, were you?'

'Go on.'

'Well I did some checking and according to my information, you got a little more than you told them.'

'And?'

'Well I thought you could maybe extend me a loan of say, half a mill?'

'And what happens when your buddies check and find out that I lied to them about how much the ransom was?'

'Yes I've been thinking about that and I reckon if they do check, and there's no real reason why they would, you could say it's none of their business and you only took it from a company you owned half of. Anyway, they're not that interested in the ransom or what you did, even though technically you broke the law. No, what they want is to nail the mob, get their hands on the information you have about the offshore accounts. They couldn't give a rat's ass about a couple of million dollars you might have swindled out of your own company. So what do you say?'

Richard thought about what Vogel had said and he couldn't fault his logic.

'Suppose I just tell you to go fuck yourself agent Vogel? Or suppose I just tell your buddies you've tried to rip me off, for five hundred grand, end of your career I should think don't you?'

'You think I haven't thought of that? Think I'm some sort of moron Boswell, I've been around the block a few times pal so please don't make the mistake of underestimating me. For starters, my buddies, as you call them, wouldn't believe you, and secondly if you don't play nice, the mob just might get to know where you live these days, I'm sure they'd pay plenty to know where you are, so all I'm doing is looking after you, see?' You won't miss a few grand and it will be much better for both of us. If I'm happy then you're safe, just look on it as insurance.' Richard said nothing, Vogel continued, 'Look I'm not an impatient man; I'll give you till tomorrow at noon to make up your mind. C'mon we'd better go, agent Brunner is due to take over the babysitting in an hour.'

Richard phoned for a pizza then opened a beer as he waited for delivery. He sat at his kitchen table drinking his beer and considered his options. *Report Vogel to Section Chief Lazaro Arbus or Marilyn Young? Vogel would just deny it and he could be right, they probably wouldn't believe me. Give him the money? He'll be back for more, blackmailers always come back for more, then once he's got as much as he thinks he can get he'll probably drop the dime on me with the mob anyway.* The doorbell rang and he went to answer it. He sat down at the table again and picked up a slice of pizza. As he ate, an idea began to form in his mind, but he needed time to think it through.

At ten the next morning, he heard the doorbell, then agent Brunner knocking and shouting through the door.

'Time to go Boswell, don't want to be late, I'll be outside in the car.' Richard shouted he'd be down presently and picked up his bag with his laptop in and went downstairs. The two men didn't talk on the way to the FBI headquarters. Brunner was not a talker and carried out his duties of looking after Richard, with the minimum of social interaction. He obviously despises me thought Richard, either as a snitch or because I'm going to be getting a nice life paid for by the American tax payer. Either way Richard didn't care and concentrated on thinking his plan through.

The de-briefing session covered lots of stuff they had already covered previously, but Richard was getting used to the process and just went along with it. He assumed they were looking for inconsistencies or just nailing down the detail. They also explained that part of this process prepped him for his appearance in front of a Grand Jury and they had to be confident that his testimony would be consistent and that he and the story he told could stand up to the most detailed cross examination. The session broke up at twelve thirty and was due to resume an hour later. Richard was always accompanied by either Vogel or Brunner when he went out for lunch and it should have been Brunner waiting to escort him out of the building, but he wasn't too surprised to find Vogel waiting for him in the lobby.

'I told agent Brunner I'd take over early and you won't be surprised to learn that he was only too happy to accept. You've probably already sussed that you're not exactly his favourite person.'

As they walked past the security guard and through the doors on to the street, Richard replied, 'I should care. Is he in on your little scam?'

Vogel laughed 'Paul Brunner. No he's far too, too straight. Man, he's the original boy scout, doesn't drink doesn't smoke. As for his sexual preferences I wouldn't know, but I've never seen him with a woman. So no he doesn't know anything. No one else does, this is just between you and me okay?'

It was the reply Richard was hoping for. 'Yeah, just you and me agent Vogel.'

'So have you decided?'

'What choice do I have? But we're going to have to take a trip to New Jersey, so how are you going to arrange that?'

'Where in New Jersey?'

'Lakewood Township.'

'And where exactly are the diamonds stashed?'

'A safety deposit box. A bank safety deposit box'

'Which bank?' Richard looked at Vogel and didn't reply. 'yeah okay, whatever. So where's this Lakewood Township place, as far south as Atlantic City?'

'No, well north of there,' said Richard.

'Okay I'll check the distance, but let's guess about an hour and a half drive, no big deal. We can go in the morning. You have no meeting tomorrow so I'll say you want to get out of New York get some fresh air, walk along a beach, so I'm taking you to Long Island for a few hours, that should do it.'

Richard shrugged again.' Okay, whatever. What time do we leave?'

'Let's say ten, no point in losing any beauty sleep is there, I'll knock on your door at ten, okay?'

'Yeah sure, now can we get some food, I'm hungry after all that talking in there.'

The next day dawned sunny, breezy and cold. Richard looked out of the window and thought how in previous years he'd take a few days off when he got fed up with the cold in New York and fly down to Florida, where unlike here, the weather now would be warm sunshine with temperatures in the high seventies to low eighties. He sighed and dressed in some warm clothes. Over breakfast he thought through his plan again.

There were risks and imponderables, but he had to take the chance, faced with the demands of agent Dale Vogel he was left with little choice. *Adapt and survive,* he kept saying to himself, *adapt and survive.* Richard checked his pocket again for the safety deposit key and one of his unused cell phones. He still had his driving licence in the name of Steve Forretti.

The FBI hadn't bothered to take it off him so that helped in case there was someone new at the bank who needed to see some ID. He also knew he would need it ultimately, to be able to claim his money from his offshore account in that name.

At ten on the dot, Vogel knocked on his door 'Rise and shine, all aboard for our day out to the seaside, and bring a warm coat. It's colder than a witch's tit out there.'

Richard gritted his teeth and opened the door. They rode most of the way in silence. Vogel had the radio tuned to a right wing talk show and occasionally shouted at the show's host when he made a comment he didn't agree with. The roads were clear and they arrived in Lakewood Township in just over an hour. Richard directed Vogel to the bank and pointed to a parking place on Kennedy Avenue about two hundred yards from the bank entrance. Richard made to open the door and said

'Okay, you wait here and I'll go get the diamonds.'

'Not so fast buster, I'll come in with you.'

They walked side by side to the bank and went inside. Richard was nervous on a few counts, but tried to stay calm. Vogel stayed back, reading some leaflets on a shelf. Richard walked towards one of the desks and spotted the assistant manager who saw Richard at the same time. He came over and greeted Richard.

'Well hello Mr Forretti, I've been wondering what happened to you, you know with the storm and all, I was concerned when we hadn't seen you for so long. It's good to know you're okay. Now what can I do for you today?'

Richard explained he would like to access his safety deposit box and they went through the routine of signing in. The manager went away and came back with his key.

'Follow me please Mr Forretti.' The man said and they made their way to the vault. As usual the assistant manager used his own key, then left Richard in the vault and went to wait outside.

He turned the key and drew out the long metal box. He was still undecided as to whether he should take everything or leave some diamonds behind. He didn't know how much he would need in the immediate future or when he might be able to get back to this place. One thing he would need was his gun. He took out the Glock and pushed it down his belt at the back of his jeans, then took his old passport and driving licence in the name of Richard Boswell and put them in his inside pocket.

He took the velvet bag out and poured a small pile of diamonds into his palm, looking at them briefly before putting them back, deciding at the last minute to leave them along with the memory sticks. He took what cash he had in the box and stuffed it in his jeans pocket, pushed the drawer back and locked it. He went outside the door of the vault, thanked the assistant manager and walked out through the next set of doors and then out through the main doors of the bank followed closely by agent Vogel. Vogel moved to his side as they walked towards the car.'

'You get the diamonds okay?'

'Yes,'

They got in the car and Vogel said 'show me the diamonds.'

'No, are you crazy, let's find somewhere a bit less public. Drive.' Vogel looked as if he was about to object at being told what to do by Richard, but he drove off nevertheless. Once they were out of town Richard said 'Keep going,' then 'down there,' pointing towards a slip road by a bridge that spanned one of the many inlets. They drove down by the side of the bridge where there were some abandoned wooden buildings.

'This private enough for you?' said Vogel a little sarcastically as he brought the car to a stop next to a large partially demolished wooden structure 'Boy that storm did some damage round here,' he added as he took in the scale of the devastation. 'Now the diamonds,' he said holding his hand out. Richard made as if to root in his pocket with his right hand and leaned towards Vogel as he did so, but at the same time used his left hand to grab his Glock out of the back of his jeans, and poked the muzzle of the gun in Vogel's face.

Vogel's mouth dropped open, his eyes blinked several times, then he started to raise his hands in mock surrender. He found his voice.

'Whoa, what's this?'

Richard moved the gun and poked it into Vogel's ribs. 'Shut up, put your hands straight in front of you, palms on the dash and don't move a muscle,' said Richard sounding much tougher than he felt. Then he reached beneath Vogel's jacket, unclipped his holster clip, removed his gun and stuffed it in his belt. It was a standard issue Glock 22.

'Okay I'm going to get out of the car and when I tell you, you get out your side. Any funny stuff and I shoot.' Vogel stayed silent and nodded just once. Richard backed out of the passenger door keeping his gun trained on Vogel. Once he was out, he told Vogel to get out, then moved round the back still keeping his gun trained on the FBI agent.

'It might be a cliché Boswell, but you'll never get away with this.'

'I told you to shut up. Now get the car keys and throw them on the ground at my feet.' Vogel did as he was told. 'Now lean into the car and pop the trunk lid.' Vogel looked at Richard and realised what he was going to do.

'No, look I suffer from claustrophobia you can't lock me in there, I can't....'

'Shut the fuck up and do as you're told or we do it another way.' Vogel gave Richard a hard look then leaned into the car, popped the trunk and the lid stated to rise, but as he came back out of the car he suddenly lurched sideways and down towards the bottom of his leg and with a speed that caught Richard by surprise. Vogel suddenly had a small revolver in his hand. He pulled the trigger twice before Richard could react, the first bullet went wild but Richard felt the second one grazed his cheek at the same time as he finally managed to pull the trigger on his Glock. Vogel's face briefly registered surprise then he fell down into a heap.

Richard looked at the gun in his hand, which was now shaking. He felt nauseous but made himself walk over to the body. The driver's door was still ajar so he put his gun and the one he'd taken off Vogel on the driver's seat then leaned over to examine Vogel's prone form. He turned him over on to his back, he was stone dead, blood leaking from his empty eye, blood and other matter from the back of his head where the bullet had passed through.

Richard found the small pistol a few feet away and added it to the arsenal on the driver's seat, then looked around to see if the noise had alerted anyone. There was no one in sight, no police sirens, nothing. He felt weak and shaky but needed to recover his strength, and quickly. He got the guns and put them in the trunk then sat in the driver's seat, closed his eyes and took some deep breaths.

He began to feel better and after a couple of minutes he stood up and went about the task of getting Vogel's body into the trunk. The dead weight wasn't easy to move but he finally managed it and closed the trunk lid. He was sweating now despite the low temperature and cold wind. He retrieved the keys, got into the driver's seat started the car and was about to drive off when he remembered the near miss with the bullet. He pulled down the visor and looked in the vanity mirror. There was the slightest graze on the side of his forehead.

He looked round and saw some tissues on the back seat, wetting one with his spit he cleaned the small amount of blood from the graze, checked the mirror again, then turned the car round and got back on to the highway. *Another plan fucked up*, he thought as he drove along aimlessly, trying to gather his thoughts. He pulled into a rest area, took out the cell and dialled. It was answered on the third ring.

'Hello?'

'Rick here, plan B is seriously messed up, but be patient and I'll be in touch, okay?'

'Okay,' she said.

CHAPTER 18

Meg and Gibson had been to Captiva Island for the day and taken a picnic lunch. They visited the Ding Darling wildlife refuge where Gibson did some fishing in the morning while Meg read her book. After lunch they went shelling on one of the island's many beaches and went swimming in the beautiful clear blue waters, then spent the rest of the day sunbathing, reading and snoozing on the beach. By late afternoon, they felt they'd had enough sun and Meg drove them back to Naples. Richard Boswell had receded to the furthest corner of Gibson's mind and it came as a rude shock when Bonnie called his cell during the journey and told Gibson she had some news on the situation.

'Remember I said something had come across my radar, well it's a bit unofficial, but an ex colleague from NYPD, let's just call him David, joined the FBI IT division, he's a top technical guy which is why the FBI poached him from us. We still keep in touch and we were chatting the other day and he was saying that they had a new lead on some mafia funded operations and that the info had come from a guy running from the mob, so my ears pricked up and I asked him to find out more. He refused of course, but I worked on him over a couple of days and eventually David, shall we say, succumbed to my charms.'

Gibson could imagine how Bonnie's charms would be irresistible.

'So,' she carried on, 'he told me they had a real find, a guy who'd been helping the mob move money off shore, but he'd crossed them somehow and the mob tried to kill him so he went to the feds and asked for protection. The time line fits your man Boswell.

'That's interesting, so where does that get us?'

'Yeah, well it depends. The problem is if the feds place a really high value on his intel then they'll wipe the slate clean for him regarding previous stuff, providing it wasn't too serious. But at least you might be able to tell your client you've found him. What was your client going to do anyway, I mean if you found this Richard Boswell?'

'Good question, well I guess for starters he'd want the two mill in diamonds back, then after that I don't know, but presumably the police would want to file charges of, I don't know the law here, but deception, fraud, etc.'

'Right, well I don't think you can say anything to him yet, but I'll poke around a bit more and see what I can dig up. I'm due to meet with David tomorrow for a coffee so I'll pump him for more information and let you know.'

'Thanks Bonnie,' said Gibson, trying to remove the image from his mind of Bonnie pumping Dave.

Jack showed Gibson into his den and insisted on making them some coffee before Gibson told him anything. Once they were seated and Jack had had a sip of his coffee, he spoke.

'You've probably realised by now Gibson that I'm a coffee addict, my doctor tells me I drink far too much of it, but what the hell, so you got good news for me, or the other type?'

'Depends, we might have located Richard, and before you jump to any conclusions it's still a might, okay, not definite, not yet anyway, but I thought it only fair to tell you.'

'Okay I hear ya, so where *might* Richard be?'

'With the FBI.'

Jacks face drained of colour and he put his coffee down on the table. 'The feds, what the fuck is he doing with the feds?'

'Look this is all supposition at the moment, and strictly off the record, just that a lot of things match, the timing, the man's story of being attacked by the mob. This man who might be Richard, has gone to the FBI for protection and claims he's been helping the mob move their money around. So could Richard have been involved with the mob or Mafia or whatever they're called. You said the division of your company that Richard looked after operated like a bank, so could he have been involved in moving mafia money offshore?'

Jack sat motionless absorbing what Gibson had told him. 'Jack, you okay?' asked Gibson after a minute or so. Jack seemed in a daze.

'What, oh yeah, just a bit surprised that's all, so when do you think you'll find out for definite?'

'Hopefully in the next couple of days, are you alright Jack?'

'Sorry I was just thinking. So what does this mean, the diamonds, Richard?'

'Difficult to say, but my contact says that if the FBI place a high value on what this man has to give them, then that will be their priority and anything else he's done will be much less important as far as they're concerned.'

'You mean we may not get the diamonds back, Richard'll walk?'

'I'm sorry Jack I just don't know how it works over here. Let's see if it is Richard first and then look at what the consequences are. But you never answered my question.'

'What question?'

'Could Richard have been involved with the mafia?'

Jack looked up at Gibson and said. 'No, no way,' and shook his head. Gibson had the feeling he wasn't being entirely honest with him

CHAPTER 19

Putting the phone back in his pocket, he suddenly realised how exhausted he was, he needed to rest, if only for a few minutes. He closed his eyes, then woke with a start to the noise of an emergency vehicle tearing along the highway. He looked at his watch and realised he'd been out for over half an hour. *What to do now, how long will it be before Vogel is missed, how often does he report in? I've probably got until this evening or possibly till tomorrow morning before the balloon goes up, so I've got the use of his car until then.* Richard drove out of the rest area and on to the highway, did a U turn and headed back to Lakewood Township and the bank. The assistant manager was still there and spotted Richard as he walked through the bank's door.

'Hello again Mr Forretti, don't see you for weeks and now twice in one day.'

'Yes, I forgot something, can I get into my box again, sorry for this, head like a sieve these days.'

'No problem, I don' think we need to go through the signing in again, just let me get the key and we'll get you down there straight away.'

This time Richard emptied the box completely, the diamonds, the cash, the memory sticks and his passport in the name of Steve Forretti. He thanked the manager and left, got to the car and thought about his next moves. He had to get rid of the car and the body, but first he had to go back to New York and get his laptop, *without that and the data on it I'm well and truly fucked* he thought. Going back would be risky but he had no choice. The shift changes between Vogel and Brunner almost always took place in the mornings, so he calculated he should have enough time to get to the apartment pick up his laptop and get back out of New York by this evening, he just hoped that Vogel wasn't due to report in any time before the next morning's shift change.

The roads were busy and it took longer to get back than the journey down. The slow traffic added to Richard's anxiety, making him unusually careless and he had two near accidents before managing to calm himself down. He found a parking space near to the apartment and as he walked away from the car, a traffic cop approached him.

'That your vehicle sir?' said the policeman pointing at Vogel's car.

'Something wrong officer?' replied Richard.

'No, just that we've had quite a few car break ins round here lately so please don't leave anything on view, okay?'

'No there's nothing on view, but thanks for the warning.' The officer saluted him and moved on. Richard's legs felt like jelly as he walked towards the apartment doors. He was back out with his sports bag containing the laptop and on his way out of New York within less than half an hour. *Next, get rid of this car and the body, but how and where?* He couldn't imagine where he would dispose of both the car and Vogel's remains without them ever being found, then he realised it would be better if they were found, he just needed to create a situation that would lead the cops to think in a particular way.

He drove south, back down towards Toms River where he had some knowledge of the local area and where he knew there were a number of country areas, the sort of deserted areas he needed to carry out the first part of his plan. An hour and fifteen minutes later he parked down a dirt road deep in a pine forest just a few miles west of Toms River. He got out of his car and looked around. Apart from some birdsong and occasional animal screeches, it was completely quiet. He waited, then decided he had to make his move, *Just be my luck for a ranger to come round the corner just as I'm dragging the body out of the trunk.*

Richard opened the trunk and heaved the body out on to the ground, then dragged it by the feet into the long grass at the side of the road. Vogel's shoes came off in the process so he went back, picked up the shoes and threw them into the grass near the body. Then he went back to the trunk and took out the three guns. He put his own Glock down the waistband of his jeans, put the ankle pistol in his pocket, then took Vogel's Glock, which hadn't been fired and went over to stand by the body.

He turned Vogel over on to his back and pointed Vogel's gun at the eye socket where the bullet from his own gun had passed through previously. He looked around then back at Vogel's face and fired one shot into the empty eye socket, bent down and picked up the brass casing ejected from the gun and put it in his pocket, then dragged the body a few yards away so they wouldn't see any corresponding holes in the ground behind his head.

The noise of the gunshot had sounded louder than normal in the silence. He hoped if anyone had heard it, they'd think it was someone out hunting. He went back to the car, took a bunch of tissues from the box and wiped Vogel's Glock clean, then still holding the gun by the tissues, went back to where the body lay and dropped the gun into the grass nearby. He then took the ankle pistol out of the other pocket and repeated the process, wiping it clean and still using the tissues, held the gun by the barrel, took it over to Vogel's body, leant down, laid the pistol in Vogel's open palm, then pressed Vogel's hand on to the gun to get some of the agent's prints on it.

He stood up and breathed in deeply to try to quell the nausea, then bent down again, took the pistol out of Vogel's hand and threw that into the grass as well. Taking a final look round, making sure he'd set the scene as he wanted it, he got into the car and drove off, hoping he could find his way back to the highway without too much trouble.

He now needed to get rid of the car. Someone would eventually find Vogel's body and then the car some miles away, wherever he could find to dump it. He hoped they would assume that the mob had followed them, and killed Vogel in the process of kidnapping him, then slung Vogel in the trunk, and driven out into the wilderness to dump his body. He hoped the way he'd laid things out would indicate that the kidnappers took Vogel's Glock away from him, but then Vogel tried to shoot them using his hidden ankle gun, the kidnappers then using Vogel's own gun to kill him. To reinforce the scenario, when he dumped the car, he would wipe his prints off the steering wheel, as the kidnappers would have done to wipe their prints off, but leave his own prints in the rest of the car.

He felt confident the cops would read it in the way he intended, and felt pleased with himself. It was a nice neat outcome from a very messy situation thought Richard. His pleasure at having potentially contained the situation was short lived though, replaced with doubt and regret. Killing anyone hadn't remotely been part of his plan and he had now killed two people.

He tried to shake the feeling of guilt and concentrate on where to dispose of the car. Once he'd dumped it, he needed to buy another car, but as he had plenty of cash left, *that shouldn't be a problem* he thought, *but first I need to steal a licence tag, and for that, the outskirts of a big city would be best, so I either go back to New York or on to Philadelphia.* An hour later he was crossing the Brooklyn Bridge into lower Manhattan.

Richard found a multi story car park, went up to the fifth floor and parked next to a car that had been reversed into its parking place. He'd already taken the screwdrivers from the toolkit in Vogel's car trunk, so he went to the back of the car he'd parked next to, ducked down and removed the licence plate. He then drove Vogel's car, down three floors found a vacant place and parked. A woman came out of the lift and went to her car three spaces down so he waited until she'd gone then used his jacket to wipe the steering wheel and handles clean. He checked around and made sure he hadn't left anything behind and that he had everything he needed in his sports bag, including the car licence plate, then he hid the keys under the driver's seat, got out, closed the door using his jacket, and walked away.

Five blocks and twenty minutes later he found what he was looking for, a used car lot with some fairly low grade looking vehicles for sale, garish neon yellow plastic signs attached to the windscreens of the cars 'Bargain', 'Low Miles', 'One Careful owner' etc. He started to look at the stock and very soon was joined by a flashy looking black man in a bright blue blazer, black jeans, white shirt opened to the navel and a straw hat jauntily set on the man's head.

'Hey man you lookin' for anything special? My name's Max, that's max for maximum value, and max for maximum quality.'

'Something reliable I guess,' replied Richard ignoring the outstretched hand. The man shrugged and smiled a big smile, 'Man, everything I sell is reliable. My reputation is, as they say, beyond reproach.'

Richard couldn't help smiling. 'Fancy words for a car salesman.'

'Fancy words, fancy cars, I can do fancy all day long,' he said, and laughed a screeching infectious laugh. He stopped laughing and slapped the bonnet of the car Richard was looking at. 'Now this here 2004 Pontiac Grand Am GT1 is a case in point, low miles, two careful owners, silver colour, match any clothes, good tires, a steal at six grand and worth every cent.'

'I'll give you four grand cash now,' said Richard. And I don't want any paperwork, okay?'

'Come into the office my friend and I'll get the keys.'

They walked over to a wooden hut. Richard counted out four thousand dollars and the man handed the keys over. Richard asked Max for some screws, then went over to the Pontiac, put his bag on the passenger seat, went around the back, attached the stolen licence tag to the car then got in, started it and drove off. He stopped at the first gas station he came to and filled up, visited the restrooms, bought some coffee, diet cokes, water and some snacks, then made his way the to the interstate 95 for the long drive south

.

CHAPTER 20

His cell rang just as he was nodding off after lunch. 'Hello Gibson, you sound a bit out of it, have I called at a bad time?'

'No, not at all Bonnie, I was just napping, any news?'

'Well yes, good and not so good. The good is we found your guy, the bad is that we've lost him again, you couldn't make this up, really…'

'Oh, tell me more.'

'Right, well it turns out your guy *was* the one helping the feds with their investigations into one of the Miami mobs. It seems he had lots of information on movements of money offshore, it's all a bit sketchy but you get the picture. Anyway, one of the special agents assigned to look after him failed to report in three days ago and that set the alarms off. The agent, a guy named Vogel, and your guy, Boswell, disappeared. The last thing they know is that this Vogel, an experienced man apparently, said he was taking Boswell for a day out in the fresh air to Long Island, but they never returned to their respective apartments in New York and Vogel missed his call in that evening.'

'That's it?'

'No, and this is why I know so much. Remember Joe Dwyer, the detective we met outside the trailer Park, near Toms River?'

'I do yes, why?'

'He called me. Some men out hunting found a body two days ago in a state park just south of there. One of their dogs picked up the scent and the short story is that it was the FBI agent Vogel, shot through the eye. No attempt to hide the body other then it was off the road and in some long grass, all his identification was still in his pockets, his wallet untouched.'

'Dwyer got on to the feds and they asked him to close the scene down until they got there, but he refused and insisted they tell him what was going on. That's how I know about the dead guy being Boswell's minder.'

'Any sign of Richard Boswell?'

'No, nothing. The current thinking is that someone knew Boswell was talking to the feds and they were watching him and decided to kidnap him, killing Vogel in the process.'

'Are we to assume it's the same people who attempted to capture or kill Boswell aka Forretti at the trailer park?'

'Seems the most likely scenario.'

'If it is the same people, the mob as you call them, is there any clue as to where they might take him or what they'll do with him?'

'My guess would be Miami to answer the first part of your question, but as to what they'll do with him, I wouldn't know. They'll certainly want to know what he's told the feds and then, well I think your guess is as good as mine.'

'You think they'll kill him?'

'I'd be surprised if they didn't.'

'Am I allowed to tell my client all this?'

Bonnie was silent, obviously considering the question. 'Yeah, why not, but tell him it's sort of confidential. Maybe not mention the speculation about what they might do to him. It's going to be public knowledge at some stage, but the Feds'll get the spin guys on it to give it a different slant, they won't want to look fools for losing an agent and a witness.'

'Okay well let me know if anything else turns up, but apart from satisfying my natural curiosity, I can't see the point of me pursuing this case anymore, so I'll tell my client what you've told me and call it a day.'

'Okay Gibson, maybe we'll speak again but if we don't, it's been a real pleasure working with you.'

'The same goes for me Bonnie and thanks for everything.'

'No sweat Gibson, keep well.'

Gibson put the phone down. *No point in hanging around, he thought, might as well get this over with so I can get on with what's left of my holiday.* He walked over to Jack's apartment. Jack greeted him enthusiastically.

'I have an update for you Jack,'

'Great' said Jack and ushered Gibson into the living room and sat him down, then poured each of them a generous slug of Four Roses Bourbon.

Jack handed Gibson his drink and sat down 'Okay, shoot,' he said.

Gibson repeated the story Bonnie had told him. Jack stopped Gibson at the point where he said the thinking was that the mob had kidnapped Richard.

'Whoa, just hang on, the mob now have Rick?'

'That's the assumption, why, you seem doubtful?'

Jack seemed flustered. 'No, no it's just all a bit, I don't know; confusing I suppose, carry on.'

When he'd finished telling the story he said to Jack. 'Look the original assignment was for me to find out if Richard Boswell was still alive, and if he was, why he staged his own execution. Well I think I've established he's alive, or… was anyway, as for why he staged his own execution, It seems beyond doubt now that he was somehow involved with the mafia, moving money around for them, and he wanted to convince everyone, maybe the mafia in particular, that he was dead. I can only guess that the two million he demanded from you as a ransom, was to fund a new life or something.'

Jack said nothing and sipped at his bourbon. 'Yeah, I suppose you're right, but suppose it isn't the mob that've got him?'

'I just can't see it any other way Jack, so I think I've done as much as I can, which isn't a lot really, but look, just pay my expenses and five hundred dollars and we'll call it quits, how about it Jack?'

'No, I know we never discussed exactly what I'd pay you, but I suppose we thought maybe the insurance people would be paying you something, as it's turned out I don't know what the situation will be with them now, and if what you say is true then there may be implications for JARIC, the feds, the cops, investigations, who knows? But anyway I'll pay you five grand for your trouble Gibson, plus expenses of course. That should at least make a contribution to your holiday spending money.'

'Well if you're sure Jack, that's very kind. I'll add up my expenses and give you back anything I have left from the cash you gave me and we can settle up over the next couple of days.'

'Yeah sure,' said Jack still looking thoughtful, 'look,' he continued, 'I'm just thinking, what you say about Rick being kidnapped by the mob, I mean that's speculation isn't it, I mean it's not definite is it?'

'Well it's not definite, no, but it seems to be reasonable speculation. I'd say personally, it was a racing certainty that they killed the FBI agent and kidnapped Richard to find out what he's told the authorities, and then, well, what they do with him after that is anyone's guess I suppose, but …?'

'It's okay Gibson I know what you're saying, they'll kill Rick, but suppose, just suppose the mob, haven't got Rick?' Gibson opened his mouth to protest, but Jack waved him down, 'hear me out, suppose they haven't got Rick, then Rick's still out there somewhere and he owes me two million bucks, well one million at least, so if it turns out that the mob haven't got him, would you still be prepared to go look for him?'

Gibson was becoming mildly annoyed at Jack's apparent reluctance to accept the obvious, but he decided it couldn't do any harm to indulge him. 'Okay, Jack, if it turns out that somehow the situation isn't as it seems, I'll consider it, okay?'

'That's good enough for me Gibson,' said Jack smiling again. They shook hands and Gibson left.

Meg came round that evening and they went out for a few beers and some take-away fish and chips from the pub in Venetian Village. He told Meg he was through with the investigation into Richard Boswell and that they should make the best of the time they had left together before he had to go back to the UK. Meg suggested that the next day they should leave early and go to Marco Island and book an escorted canoeing tour of the ten thousand islands, 'not all of them,' she added, laughing.

She picked him up at eight thirty the next morning and an hour and a half later they were clambering into their canoe in the Collier-Seminole State Park, having first sprayed themselves all over with some sickly smelling mosquito repellent. They followed the convoy of canoes and pretty soon they got into the rhythm of paddling and steering.

They made their way along the Black Water River and the guide told them that there were over a hundred and forty five species of birds that lived in the islands including owls, bald eagles, cranes, ospreys and roseate spoonbills. As they made their way through islands of mangroves Gibson was startled to see a huge brown whale-looking creature just a few yards away, which then disappeared below the brown murky water. He shouted his alarm, but Meg laughed and told him he'd just encountered a manatee, one of the gentlest creatures on earth, and that they were in no danger.

The guide had warned them that they may see some alligators and water moccasins and that they should just steer clear of them, and they would leave them alone, Gibson thought this was probably an exaggeration just to make the trip more exciting, but changed his mind when Meg pointed out an alligator, that looked to be at least five feet long, lurking in a nearby clump of mangroves they were passing. They paddled past, without it moving a muscle, much to Gibson's relief.

The day was a great success and they drove back to Naples recounting to each other the highlights of the trip and laughing at some of the larger than life characters they'd met. Gibson said he was constantly amazed at how many Americans seemed to be eccentric caricatures, uninhibited in what they wore and how loud they were, he loved it.

Meg dropped him off at Bay View and told him to ring her tomorrow and they could make plans for the evening. He'd had no reason to think anyone would call his cell so he'd left it behind on his bedside cabinet but when he went into the bedroom after his shower he saw it was showing a missed message and a voicemail, he picked it up, it was Bonnie. The messages said simply, *call me on my cell when you get this.*

CHAPTER 21

Richard found a shop selling sunglasses and went in. He eventually found some lightly tinted ones with black frames and bought two pairs. He thought it would be wise to assume another identity for the time being. He then found a general store and bought four packs of the smallest freezer bags, forty in all. Depending on what he had to pay a lawyer to do what he wanted, he wanted to be in a position to cash in some of the diamonds if necessary and he knew that he would be ripped off selling them for cash, so he needed, at the very least, to know how much he was being ripped off by.

He had very little knowledge of how diamonds were valued, other than some vague idea that the cut was important, the weight in carats and the lack of any flaws, but as he hadn't got a clue how to apply these criteria, he decided he had to improvise so he walked back to the Purple Parrot Inn, went up to his room, locked the door, took his sports bag from out of the wardrobe and put it on the bed, then took out the velvet bag containing the four hundred and ten diamonds and poured them on to the counterpane. He put ten diamonds each in thirty of the bags, and eleven in each of the remaining ten bags. Having had no means of checking the true worth of the diamonds, he relied instead on Jack complying with the demands of the 'kidnappers'.

Accordingly, he now had forty bags worth approximately fifty thousand dollars each. He didn't expect to get anything like their true value when he cashed them in, especially as he'd be asking for cash for the first few bags, but at least he now had the means to negotiate a piecemeal price. He put the plastic bags containing the diamonds into the velvet bag and put the velvet bag back into his sports bag.

He needed to hire a lawyer for the next stage of his plan and logged on to the internet. Choosing the right lawyer would be critical. He needed a well-established firm, one that was likely to be around for a long time, but one that wasn't too big. He also needed a lawyer with the right attitude, reliable but not too straight laced. He researched as much as he could on line and chose three possible firms, all within walking distance of the Purple Parrot.

The first one he looked at was Arnold & Foley on Truman Avenue. They advertised as Experienced and respected lawyers, specialities; criminal, litigation, estate planning and mediation. The attorney profiles showed a choice of four, Arnold Whiting, Waino Kango, Rodney Chang and Marilyn Pickering. Their pictures were very influential in him making his choice of who to go and see, as Richard always thought himself capable of judging someone's personality by how they looked, even in a photograph.

He looked several times at each of the four lawyers, then dismissed them. He went through the same process with the next firm of lawyers, Fox, Greenfield and Breakstone. This time there were three possibilities, but after looking at each of their bios and photographs, he couldn't see anyone who looked right for the job and moved on to his third selection, a firm called Shaffer Passimodo, They had a range of practice areas including criminal law. He looked at the bio of each of the partners and their pictures and made an appointment for three thirty with a lawyer and public Notary called Michael Hoffman.

Their offices were on South Street, a two story wooden structure painted white, with a dark green roof. Richard was asked to wait in the reception area. After a few minutes a man came out of a door and went over to the girl on reception, she pointed and he came over, introduced himself and asked Richard to follow him. Hoffman was a slimmish smartly dressed man in his mid-fifties, dark curly hair, blue striped suit, five o'clock shadow, confident eyes. Once in the office, they shook hands and Hoffman walked behind his large wooden desk, sat down and gestured for Richard to sit down on the chair opposite.'

'Now what can we do for you, Mr er, Forretti, that is your name yes?'

Richard liked the look of the man in the flesh, not too straight laced, his body language implied a no nonsense attitude. 'It'll do for now,' he replied. Hoffman raised his eyebrows a little and frowned.

'You don't look like a nut job but let me make it clear. I don't do games, so you'd better convince me very quickly that I'm not wasting my time here, bogus names are not a good start to any conversation, especially with a lawyer, this lawyer anyway.'

'Okay I understand, but hear me out, I just need to know if you're interested in my proposition. If you're not then it won't matter that you don't know my real name, will it?'

Hoffman looked at his watch. 'You've got three minutes left before I kick you out.'

'Okay,' said Richard, 'I have information on a certain organisation, confidential money matters, information that they know I have and they will kill me to stop it falling onto the wrong hands, namely the FBI. So I need to set up an insurance plan, for want of a better description.' Richard stopped and looked at Hoffman, 'should I go on?'

'Please do,' said Hoffman, leaning back in his chair hands laced over his middle, obviously intrigued.

'The way I figure it, is that if I can lodge this information with a lawyer, together with signed affidavits, which can be used in a Court of Law if necessary, then I can tell the party in question that if anything untoward happens to me, then the papers will be sent to the appropriate authorities. Those are the basics of my proposition. I can give you more detail but there's little point in my going any further if you're not interested, so…?'

'Why not just give the information to the FBI now?'

'A number of reasons, but the main one being that this organisation would subsequently find me and kill me.'

'Surely the FBI would protect you?'

'They would, but for how long, and I don't want to live my life in a witness protection program, I have other plans, plus I've sort of burnt my boats with the FBI anyway.'

'You've already talked to them?'

'It's a long story, but yes I have spoken to them and gave them a certain amount of information, but not enough for them to take any action against this organisation, not without me telling more and testifying. Look it's all a bit complicated, but the point is, are you interested in my proposition or not?'

'Hmm, well that depends I suppose.' said Hoffman stroking his chin, 'on what you expect to pay for this service, or insurance as you describe it?'

'A hundred thousand up front in cash, plus an annual fee of twenty five thousand dollars.'

'And how long do you think this *arrangement* will need to stay in place?'

'Minimum of five years, depends.'

'So, two hundred and twenty five thousand bucks in total for the five years?'

'No, two hundred thousand, the initial year's payment includes the first year's annual fee.'

Hoffman laughed. 'And what's to stop this organisation finding out who's holding this information and killing yours truly?'

'How would they ever know, I'm not going to tell them am I?'

'Not willingly but suppose they find you and torture you?'

'That's a risk, I suppose but they could only go so far, because if they kill me without me telling them, then the threat will be carried out and they lose.'

Suppose they don't kill you but you blab anyway?'

'Then your get out of jail card is to simply give them the package.'

'How do I convince them I haven't peeked?'

'That's up to you but why would you, the deal is just the deal? Anyway, there has to be some risk, no reward without risk as the saying goes. So do I walk away and find someone else or shall we discuss the details?'

'One hundred and fifty up front, okay.'

'A hundred up front, in cash, then thirty grand a year. I reckon that's enough to make it worthwhile to keep the deal going for the term.'

Hoffman stood up, leaned across the desk and offered his hand. 'You got yourself a deal mister.'

Richard told him his real name and told him a version of the story, sufficient for Hoffman to understand what it was all about, but vague enough so that Hoffman couldn't be accused later of withholding information that he should have given up to a law enforcement agency, then they discussed the mechanics of how the arrangement would work.

'For the first year,' Richard said, 'I'll call you in the first week of each month with a password we'll agree on later, then in the following years I'll call you every three months. If I don't call you as arranged, you can assume I'm dead and you send the documents to the FBI, anonymously.'

'What if you've died from natural causes?'

If you can establish that I've genuinely died a natural death, then, I'll leave it up to you to do what you want, I'll be past caring by then.'

'And how do you know you can trust me?'

'I don't but there will be another person who will know about our deal, so if you welch on it then....' Richard shrugged his shoulders.

'Is that a threat?'

'No, I'm merely stating a fact. I don't know what that person could do anyway, but why should you worry if you're going to stick to the deal?'

'You're right I guess,' said Hoffman laughing. You've really though this through haven't you?'

'You can bet your life on it, I've certainly bet mine.'

Hoffman smiled, 'Okay on the practical front what do you need. Where is this information?'

'Well you'll need to prepare an affidavit suitable for me to sign, for use in a Court of law. I'll swear whatever is necessary, in relation to the information I'm providing. And state that I arranged for the release of this information, only in the event of my death, by means other than natural. Something like that. I'll leave the legal jargon to you. Plus I'll need a couple of hours use of an office with a printer and that's about it.

I'll give you all the information on a memory stick, and a hard copy in a sealed envelope. I'll leave it up to you where you keep it. Maybe a bank safety deposit box? And I'll need you to make some sort of provision for passing on the responsibility of continuing with the deal, should you be incapacitated in any way, and unable to fulfil your obligations.'

'Hoffman nodded. 'Okay, we can do all that. Tomorrow morning okay with you?'

'That's fine, say ten?'

'I'll be here,' said Hoffman showing Richard the door. 'And don't forget the deposit will you?'

Richard smiled and they shook hands. 'See you tomorrow,' he said and walked out into the bright warm sunshine. He felt a little more relaxed as he strolled along, the horror of killing agent Vogel was fading and once his carefully planned *insurance policy* was in place, he would feel safer.

He was also pleased with the arrangement in that it meant he had easily enough funds left to do the deal, without having to cash any of the diamonds in. And he could now think about resuming his disrupted plans. But before that, he needed to communicate the existence of his insurance policy to his old friends in Miami, *maybe a simple phone call was the answer* he thought. He still had one of the three cells phones left that he'd bought in New Jersey.

CHAPTER 22

G ibson called and got her voicemail.

'Hi Bonnie I didn't think we'd be speaking again so soon, something happened? Call me.'

No sooner had he put the phone down than it rang.

'Hello Gibson, just got your message, listen there's been a development and I thought you should know.' Gibson tensed assuming he was going to be told that Richard Boswell had been found dead. Bonnie continued, 'Vogel, you know, the FBI agent who was killed, his car's been found in a multi story car park in lower Manhattan. Now I wouldn't have bothered to tell you that, his car was bound to turn up sometime.

The thing is though, where it was found is in my general jurisdiction so I was able to dig into things a bit more deeply. To get into this car park you have to take a ticket at the barrier, and a camera automatically records the licence plate of the car as it passes through, so we know the time and date that Vogel's car entered the car park, okay?'

'Yes, I see,' said Gibson not seeing at all and not sure where this was going.

'So, I asked if there were any more security cameras, continued Bonnie, 'and there were, so I requested the tapes for the date and time in question and fortunately they were still current. They have quite a sophisticated system that keeps records three month's rolling data. Now, this is where it gets interesting. I started checking the tapes from the time that Vogel's car was recorded going into the car park and about twenty minutes after the car went through the barrier, a man, on his own, toting a sports bag is shown on the tape walking towards the first floor exit and although I couldn't swear it's the same guy, he bears more than a passing resemblance to your guy in those videos.'

Gibson sat down on the bed.

'Are you still there Gibson?'

'Yes, sorry just trying to think what the implications are, I mean if it was Boswell who dumped Vogel's car then…..'

'Boswell killed Vogel,' said Bonnie, 'hard to see it any other way.'

'Jesus Christ.' Said Gibson

'But having said that, we're still only working on suspicions, speculation rather than facts. We have no direct evidence, and hand on heart, I couldn't swear for sure that it's the same guy as on the tape.'

'Have you told anyone else about this?'

'Not yet, but I guess I'll have to tell the feds eventually, although I haven't finished yet?'

'There's more?'

'Not yet, what I mean is, I haven't finished investigating. See, it strikes me that if it is your guy on the tape, then he dumped Vogel's car and he's now on foot, but he's hardly likely to hang around, so I guess he's going to get the bus, or a train or more likely get some new wheels, but for sure he'd do something to put distance between him and Vogel's car.'

'I can see that, so what's your thinking?'

'Well, I've asked for reports of any car thefts around the immediate area on that day, see what that brings up. But like I say, it could be that he hops on a bus or a train and gets clear of the area before he buys or steals a car, who knows, but we'll see. I'll let you know.'

'Okay, but when I said have you told anyone else, I meant any of your colleagues?'

'Well as it happens, I haven't, why?'

'Nothing really, and please don't take this the wrong way, but I still have this niggle in the back of my mind about those people turning up at the trailer park just before we did.'

Bonnie was silent for a brief moment, then said 'Are you suggesting what I think you're suggesting? That I've got some sort of leak in my department?'

'No I'm not suggesting that, just, I don't know, I can't get rid of this niggle, like I say, those people turning up, bit of a coincidence don't you think?'

'I suppose these things happen sometimes, I mean we now know that the mob had good reason to shut the man up, so they would have been actively looking for him.'

'Yes you're right, probably just my suspicious mind working overtime.'

'Okay, I'll call you, if and when I turn up anything else, and just for your peace of mind, we'll keep this strictly between ourselves for the time being, okay?'

'Thanks Bonnie,' he said and she rang off.

Indecision wasn't part of his makeup. He'd always known what to do and rarely dithered about anything. Not that he'd always been right, far from it, but this time he was torn. He'd told Jack he was off the case. He'd done what Jack had asked and established, pretty well beyond doubt, that Richard Boswell was alive, if not necessarily alive and well. But now, now it looked as if Jack might have been right, maybe Richard Boswell wasn't in the clutches of the mob, but if he wasn't Gibson thought, where the hell was he?'

He decided not to tell Jack about his conversation with Bonnie, after all, as she said, there were no facts, just speculation at this stage. He decided to sleep on it.

Gibson slept fitfully, then was woken by a huge explosion which shook the building. The event coincided with his dream and he shouted out loud in fright as he woke to shadows dancing on the walls as the next bolt of lightning lit up the sky, flashing through the bedroom blinds. Then another huge clap of thunder caused a shock wave so powerful it made the bed judder. He swept the covers to one side, went to the window and peered through the blinds. Another flash of lightning traversed through the sky and lit up the bay, followed closely by another clap of thunder, diminished now as the storm started to move away, then came the rain, hard sheets of water in waves, bouncing off the concrete pathways, spray illuminated in the glow of the low garden lights, huge volumes of rain clattering on the windows as though some malignant force wanted to smash them in.

The wind howled and the palm trees thrashed about in distress as if trying to shake off the assault. He watched fascinated at the raw power Mother Nature could conjure up when the mood took her. As he watched he began to feel calm and safe in his warm dry space, his clouded mind cleared and he made up his mind.

I'm going to find Richard Boswell, not for Jack but for myself. I'm hooked and it's now a matter of what, professional pride? Maybe, maybe, I do know that whatever the reason, I'm going to get to the bottom of what's going on, and the only way to find that out, is to find Richard Boswell. His mind made up, Gibson went back to bed, falling asleep as soon as his head hit the pillow.

The next morning after breakfast he took out his notebook and read everything he'd written in relation to the missing Boswell. He needed some indication of where Richard might go to hide. His old boss had once told him that when looking for a missing person, a runaway, you had to change the emphasis in your mind, and that no one ever really runs away, they always run to somewhere. At the time, it had taken Gibson a while to see that his boss was right, but as usual he was. So what you had to do was focus on where a person would go to and why he or she would go there. He'd also learnt that people who run away usually run to somewhere they're familiar with, at least to some extent, or think they're familiar with, as in somewhere they might have studied for some reason. They need to know the territory, the escape possibilities, somewhere they know they can blend in. Knowledge of a place gives them an edge over anyone looking for them.

He didn't want to ask Jack, so he tried to think who else might know where Richard went to get away from things, other than, in Richard's case, his boat in New Jersey. As he looked through his notes, he came across the details of his meeting with Gina. *Yes here it is "we went on some short trips together".* He looked at his watch. He reckoned she'd be an early starter so he checked the number she'd given him and dialled. She answered the call as Naples Interior Design.

'Hello, Gibson here, I called to see you a while ago, I'm investigating....'

She cut him off saying, 'yes I remember, did you find Rick, is he still alive?'

He hesitated. 'Well it looks as if he could be yes, I'd say it's almost certain.'

'So you haven't actually seen him, spoken to him?'

'No I haven't, but that's what I'm calling you about. You see we did know where Richard was for a while then he disappeared again, so I thought I'd give you a call, see if you can think where he might have gone?'

'Me, how the hell would I know where he's gone? Anyway I thought you were going to look for him on his boat?'

'Sorry, I phrased that badly, I mean, look perhaps it's be better if we met rather than speak over the phone.'

'Yes it might be, but I'm just about to get in my car to drive to Fort Myers. A new client, quite a big contract, and I'll be away for the rest of the day, so if it can wait..?'

'No, not really, so maybe we can do this over the phone now?'

'Okay ask your questions, but please be quick I'm late leaving already.'

'Right, well at our last meeting you said that you went away on some short trips with Richard.'

'Yes, and?'

'Well, when I said I wondered if you could think where Richard might have gone, I was wondering if the places he took you to, I mean were they places he'd been before?'

'Yes, but what about the boat, did you find it, surely that's an obvious place to look for him?'

'Yes we did find his boat, but it was wrecked in the hurricane, super storm Sandy, so that's why I'm looking at other possibilities. So where did you go with Richard on these trips?'

'Jesus, sounds like Rick's having a rough time. Well he only took me to two places, two times to Key West and once to The Bahamas, and yes I'm sure he'd been to both places before. I remember being impressed that the manager at reception at the hotel we stayed at in Nassau knew Richard and greeted him like an old friend, the Hilton I think it was, but it had some other names tagged on as well.'

'And what about Key West, where did you stay there?'

'I don't remember the names, but they were really small places, quaint you know, not Hiltons or Ramadas', just small Mom and Pop type places, family owned. If I do remember the names of any of them I could let you know if it's important. Listen I really am going to have to go, is there anything else?'

'No, not for the moment, but if you do remember anything else please call me. You have my number. So, thanks for your time. And, I may call you again if I need to, if that's alright?'

'Yes, please do. And let me know if you find Rick. I still have a soft spot for him, despite him dumping me.'

Gibson promised to let her know and they said goodbye. Having been to neither the Bahamas nor Key West, he decided to do some research on both places, on the net. The Bahamas was much nearer than he thought, just a couple of hundred miles south east of Florida, with regular flights from Miami. He also found out that visitors from the USA were obliged to go through customs and must possess a valid passport to enter the Bahamas, *so that would be a negative for Richard Boswell thought Gibson*, assuming he hadn't changed his identity again.

Further research revealed that there were instances of illegal boat journeys between the Bahamas and Florida. Gibson pondered, *Would Richard Boswell take the risk of his entry into a place like the Bahamas being recorded, assuming that he had a passport that is? Why would he? Also, would he risk an illegal boat trip to gain entry? Possible but unlikely.*

Gibson abandoned the Bahamas and started his research on Key West, which, said the official tourist information website, was the most southerly point of the USA. *So why not Key South?* He carried on reading, The Keys, or Cays as they were originally called by the Spanish, were a string of separate islands just south of Miami, linked together by a single road called the Overseas Highway, the last section of US1, a road that runs from Fort Kent on the Canadian - United Sates border, all the way south to Key West, some two thousand and seventy miles.

He whistled in awe at the sheer scale of the distances involved. He further noted that it was home in the thirties to one Ernest Hemingway and where, it was claimed,

Hemingway wrote Farewell to Arms while living over a Ford dealership on the island. He looked at a map of Key West, it was quite a small place, just three miles by five, and with a population of around twenty five thousand souls. *Was such a small place ideal as somewhere to hide, thought Gibson? Depends if anyone knows you're there I suppose.*

Key West fascinated him and he decided it would be a bit of a bonus if he could persuade himself that this was where Richard Boswell might have run to. A trip to Key West was on the cards now anyway and the more he considered it, the more he convinced himself that Boswell would favour Key West over the Bahamas, if for nothing else than he could drive there without any immigration or customs issues. It was a long shot, too long really, thought Gibson. He then brought up a map of the whole of the continental United States and gazed at it for a while. *Who am I kidding, he could be anywhere in this enormous country.* He closed his laptop down and started to think about lunch.

Gibson spent the afternoon by the pool variously snoozing, swimming and chatting with some of the other residents. Meg was busy opening up a house for one of her clients who was coming down for a few weeks' vacation, so he was at a loose end for a couple of days. He decided he would go fishing the following day, *the distraction will do me good* he thought.

Since Bonnie's last phone call he felt restless and no matter how hard he tried, his mind kept returning to the subject of Richard Boswell. He'd built up a picture of the man and it didn't chime with him being a murderer, but if Bonnie's suspicions were correct, then it was hard to come to any other conclusion. *Yes he'd killed a man at the trailer park, but that was in self-defence. Killing an FBI agent and disposing of the body was another matter entirely.*

He tried to put a different interpretation on what Bonnie thought she'd seen, but Boswell dumping Vogel's car in the car park could only mean that he had killed Vogel. There was no other way to see it, assuming it was Richard Boswell. During one of his snoozes by the pool, Gibson had talked the situation through with Jill. She told him to follow his instinct and he woke feeling a little more confident. Gibson had seen Jack around the pool a couple of times since the latest call from Bonnie and Jack had said he would be sending him a cheque for the five grand he'd promised Gibson, and apologised for the delay. This made Gibson feel even worse about not telling Jack the latest information, but he didn't want to start Jack off again asking him to find Richard. This time Gibson decided he was going to find Boswell first and then tell Jack. Without the company of Meg to distract him, Gibson found he was becoming obsessed with speculating on the whereabouts of Richard Boswell and decided to call Bonnie to see if there were any developments.

'Hi Gibson, you must be psychic, I was just about to call you.'

'Hi Bonnie, something happened?'

'Yeah, I'm not sure where it gets us, but it's interesting for sure. You know I said I was going to continue investigating, see if there were any cars stolen near to where Vogel's car was dumped?'

'Yes I remember, and did you? I mean find any cars stolen?'

'Yeah, too many really, but that's not the interesting bit. No, in amongst the reports for incidents that day was an index tag being stolen from a car in that same car park.

'So if it was Boswell who dumped the car, then you're saying he could be the one who stole the tag? Why would he do that?'

'I think you Brits licence the vehicle, but over here we don't, we issue a licence tag to the person who buys the car. So the way I figure it is, that the guy has three choices. One, he buys a car legit, provides ID etc., but for obvious reasons, he ain't going to do that. Two, he steals a car which involves certain skills and risks. Or three, if you have dollars, you can buy a car with cash, no questions asked, and drive it away. But to avoid paperwork, you'll need to already have a tag, so steal a tag, no big risk, no big deal, and no record of the type, colour of vehicle etc, see?

'Yes I see,' said Gibson, taking the information in. So let's just think about this Bonnie. If Boswell was the one who dumped Vogel's car in that car park, and he then steals a tag with the intention of buying a car to get away, then he's thought this through in some detail. This isn't a spur of the moment thing, so that being the case, it seems fairly certain that he killed Vogel then set things up to look as though what? Someone else, the mob maybe, killed Vogel and kidnapped him?'

'I guess that's the way we were supposed to read it from the way things were left.'

'Hmm', said Gibson, 'our Mr Boswell is one clever man Bonnie, but luckily for us, not infallible. I almost feel sorry for him, being caught on tape like that.'

'Yeah, but even so, we can't scour the whole of the United States looking for one stolen licence tag, no car type, colour etc., I mean we're good at tracking anything and everything these days, but there are limitations.'

He didn't answer. 'Gibson, you still there?'

'Yes, just thinking. Suppose you had a date range of a couple of days or so, and an area, one road to look at for instance, would that make a difference?'

'It might yes, depends on where, which road, a main highway then probably. C'mon Gibson give, what's your clever British detective mind thinking?'

'I'm not sure about the clever mind, more like a good old fashioned hunch, not even that maybe?'

'C'mon, don't keep me in suspense.'

'This may sound a bit weak, but our man Richard took this girl away a couple of times, once to the Bahamas and once to Key West. From what she was able to tell me, he'd been to both places before, maybe more than once, so I figure that maybe, just maybe, he might choose to hole up in one of these two places, for a while anyway. My old boss told me people never run away, they always run to. To somewhere they know that is. I realise it sounds a bit obvious in one sense, but anyway, I think that the Bahamas is out because he'd have to fly there, then go through immigration and why take a risk of leaving a trail, even if he was travelling under a new identity, so my guess is that he'd head for Key West. On the other hand of course, he could go somewhere completely different.'

'You've really put some thought into this Gibson. You getting a little obsessed maybe?'

'No, not a little, a lot. For some reason this whole thing has really got under my skin and I know I won't settle until I find out what's going on and why.'

'What about your client, what's his view on this, you discussed it with him?'

'No I haven't as it happens, not said anything to him since I told him I was off the case. This time I'll see if I can get the answers before I go back to him, that is if you're still willing to help me find Boswell?'

'I need to think about this, I mean the situation's changed now. As far as the Feds are concerned, Boswell's been kidnapped by the mob and is a possible witness to Vogel's murder, but if I'm right about him being the man walking out of that car park, then that makes him potentially a fugitive from justice, a suspect himself, in the murder, or killing at any rate of one FBI agent, Dale Vogel.'

'Yes I see what you mean, but suppose you hold back on the basis that you don't have anything definite, and all you're really doing at this stage is helping me to locate Boswell, which is in the general interests of the police anyway, even though strictly speaking, I'm acting for a private client? I mean you're not certain about the man you saw coming out of that car park, and neither do we know where he's gone, if indeed it is him. Also, my theories about Key West might be complete rubbish so you'd potentially be wasting a lot of police time looking for him there. Whereas, if I do it, and it turns out to be a wild goose chase, then no consequences, just leaves me looking foolish.'

Bonnie laughed. 'You've got a point when you put it like that Gibson.'

'Look Bonnie, suppose we go about it this way? You check to see if you can trace the vehicle with that licence plate travelling to Key West in the days following the dumping of the car, and if you get a result, I'll go down there and see if I can find the man. If I do, then I hand everything over to you, you call out the cavalry and pick him up? What do you say Bonnie?'

'Jesus Gibson, you're asking a lot. I should say no way Jose, but…. well, as Chief Romano thinks so highly of you, and he did tell me to offer you any assistance you asked for, well, what the hell. Okay, so from what I know about Key West, there's just the one road in and out, that right?'

'Yes, the US1, it goes all the way from Homestead, right down to Key West. Looking at the map, he would have taken the Interstate-95 from Manhattan for most of the journey south, then linked up with the US-1 at Homestead. So, if he has gone to Key West, then it would probably be within, say two or three days of him leaving Manhattan, depending how many stops he makes, and then there's just the one road as you say, so that narrows down the search considerably. Are we on?'

'Yeah okay, we're on, as you say. Let me talk to my colleagues down in Florida, see what they can do to trace a tag in given those parameters. We'll focus on the US1 as it goes into Key West and I'll ask if they can cover seven days after the date that Vogel's car was dumped, that should be enough to see if you're right about his destination. I'll come back to you soon as I hear something, okay?'

'Thanks Bonnie.'

'Don't mention it, I must be crazy but..... I'll call you.'

The next day, after his morning run, he showered, had breakfast and tried to relax by the pool, but he found himself checking his cell every few minutes and becoming anxious, waiting for Bonnie's call. This was ridiculous, he told himself, it's going to take a few days to get the information on the licence tag, if I go on like this I'll be a nervous wreck by the end of the week. He decided the best remedy was to go fishing, so after lunch he packed his fishing tackle into the trunk of his car and set off for Naples pier, making sure he took his cell phone along with him.

He quickly relaxed in the company of the characters on the pier and had soon forgotten all about Richard Boswell. There was a huge school of Spanish Mackerel in the bay and nearly all the anglers on the pier were pulling some out of the sea, the big fish flapping and bouncing on the wooden floorboards, much to the delight of the tourists who got busy with their cameras. Some other fishers like himself, returned most of their catch to the sea.

Then Gibson caught a particularly large specimen, which he struggled to bring on to the pier, but then clubbed it to death and put into a plastic bag to take back to Bay View. It was a beauty, about three or four pounds he reckoned, silver with a dark blue green shiny back and bright yellow elliptical spots along the length of its body.

Meg was coming round for dinner later and the mackerel would make a nice feast, he thought. He would barbeque it on the communal Webber near the pool and regale the Bay View residents with an exaggerated story of how he struggled with the creature, finally bringing it in after a worthy fight.

He asked for recommendations from his fellow anglers on the best way to barbeque the fish and was deluged with suggestions, but the best seemed to be to simply wrap it in foil, put some butter and herbs inside the stomach cavity, season with salt and pepper, then bake it on the barbeque for ten minutes or so, making sure to drink lots of beer during the cooking process. *Sounds like a proper recipe to me* he thought.

Shortly after catching the fish he left the pier, not wishing to let the heat spoil the fish. His new friends bade him farewell and he arrived home with the afterglow of the sun on his skin and a feeling of bonhomie towards his pier friends. *My very own pier group*, and laughed to himself at his feeble witticism.

Gibson gutted the fish in the sink and prepared it for barbequing before taking his shower. Meg arrived at six thirty and they set the dining table, put some fingerling potatoes in a pan of water and set them on low, then took some tins of beer down to the pool along with two plastic tumblers and the prize fish on a plate wrapped in foil.

Compliments were plenty as Gibson cooked the fish while he and Meg drank beer and chatted with a few of the other residents who were left over from an informal pool cocktail party. When the fish was cooked, he and Meg made their way back to his apartment and they ate the fish with the fingerlings and some mango salsa that Gibson had bought at the Naples farmers market the previous Saturday.

Gibson slowly woke the following morning and felt the comforting warmth of another body against his, then fell asleep again. He woke up again and found himself alone in bed and started to wonder if he'd imagined it. Meg gently opened the bedroom door with her shoulder and elbow, careful not to spill any of the coffee, a cup in each hand.

'You're awake?' she said cheerfully as she put one of the cups down on Gibson's bedside table.

'I think so, although I could still be dreaming,' he replied sleepily, a big smile on his face.

'I borrowed your dressing gown, hope you don't mind.' Meg said.

'It's not mine it was here when I arrived, and I don't mind, but maybe you'd look better with it off.'

Meg stood by her side of the bed and put her coffee down, struck a coquettish pose and looked at Gibson with a mock shocked expression.

'Oh Mr Gibson sir, I hope you're not trying to take advantage of a poor defenceless woman?'

'I certainly am, now put that coffee down and get in this bed immediately and lets do some more of that advantage taking.'

Meg laughed, took the gown off and got into bed.

Gibson had just got out of the shower and was making more coffee when the phone rang. He answered it and recognised the voice immediately.

'You always this lucky Gibson?' said Bonnie.

'I try my best, have we got a trace?'

'We do, three days after Vogel's car was dumped in the car park in Brooklyn, a car with the stolen licence tag was recorded on a road traffic camera at mile marker sixteen, fourteen and nine on US1 approaching Key West. The tag didn't match the car it was registered to, so I think we can say it's the one. The car bearing the tag is a silver coloured Pontiac Grand Am.'

He sat down on the kitchen stool, the excitement made him feel dizzy.

'That's great Bonnie, fantastic result, what can I say?'

'You can say that you're going to find this guy and somehow we can bring this to a conclusion that doesn't end up with me being horse whipped for not telling my superiors or the Feds the information I've given you.'

'I promise we'll do that, but remember, we don't know for certain this is Boswell, though it looks like it. See, l don't figure him as a killer and that confuses me. Maybe the mob did kill Vogel and somehow Boswell got away in Vogel's car?'

'If that was the case then why didn't he contact the Feds for help, come rescue him?'

'Yes good point. Well I suppose the only person who can provide the answers is Richard Boswell so I'd better go and find him.'

'That you had Gibson, that you had. Keep in touch and if or when you find him let me know, and don't go in on your own, okay? Whatever your feelings about this guy not being a killer, we know he already killed one person when he was cornered and may well have killed Dale Vogel, so no big hero stuff okay?'

'Okay understood.'

CHAPTER 23

'I couldn't help overhearing Richard's name being mentioned. I thought you'd finished that, I thought you'd told Jack you were off the case?'

Gibson hadn't seen Meg since Bonnie had given him the new information on possibly seeing Richard Boswell leaving the car park in Brooklyn.

'Well as far as Jack's concerned I am off the case, but some new information's come up so I may have to go away for a few days.'

He'd kept Meg up to date about the Richard Boswell situation but only in general terms and Meg had never asked for details. Gibson wanted to keep Meg separate from his investigation into the circumstances surrounding the disappearance of Richard Boswell, but it was unrealistic not to tell her anything, after all he'd thought, she worked for the man for a couple of years as a house keeper.

'Soon?' Meg asked.

'Yes, tomorrow probably, said Richard

'Is he on the run or something?' asked Meg

'Yes sort of, it's a bit complicated, but he may be hiding out somewhere and I'm going to try and find him, talk to him, find out what'd been going on.'

'And Jack doesn't know?'

'No, so I'd appreciate it if you'd keep this to yourself Meg.'

'No problem Gibson, but if you're not doing this for Jack, then who are you doing it for?'

'Well, me if I'm honest. This whole thing has got me....., drawn in somehow, and I need to bring it to a conclusion, it's difficult to say why, but once I have the answers I will tell Jack. It's just that I want to do this my way and I don't want Jack on my back, so let's just keep this to ourselves for now, okay?'

'Yeah sure, none of my business anyway, but Richard was a nice guy, so I hope he's not in too much trouble.'

Gibson couldn't think of a suitable answer so he changed the subject. 'How about we go for a nice lunch at the Crab shack? Sit out on the deck in the sun, watch the boats go by, have a couple of beers, a bottle of crisp cool Chardonnay and some crab legs?' Then we can go to sleep by the pool this afternoon, and I can get an early night and be up with the lark for my trip tomorrow?'

'Gibson, you know they say the way to a man's heart is through his stomach, well you've just proved it's the same for women, this woman anyway. C'mon let's go I'm starving now you've mentioned food.'

After lunch, and a lazy afternoon by the pool, Meg went home and Gibson made his preparations for his journey the next day and got an early night. He woke before dawn, having set his alarm for six o'clock. He was breakfasted and ready for the road by seven. It was warm and humid, an early morning mist obscuring the sun. *The sun would win through,* he thought idly as he went down the steps through the door to the outside to get his rental car which he'd parked under the smart white wooden awning.

He'd studied the route the previous night before retiring. Google maps told him the journey to Key West would take just short of five hours. *That would give him plenty of time to think of just how he was going to find Richard Boswell,* he thought. Key West had a fluctuating population of around twenty five thousand people, depending to the time of year. There were an assortment of hotels, mostly small establishments, but from his research on the internet, he reckoned there were somewhere around seventy five possible places where Boswell might choose to stay.

He had a choice of two roads for the journey from Naples to Key West, both of them just short of a five hours drive. The US41 also called the Tamiami Trail, which was a more direct route, travelling south east through the Everglades then to Homestead below Miami where it joined the 997, then the US1 for the journey south through the Keys, or the faster Interstate I-75, referred to as Alligator Alley, which would take him east, straight across Florida and to the north of Miami where he would join the 821 and down to the US1. He chose the slightly slower, but he assumed, more scenic route, the US41 through the Everglades.

Once he was out of the suburbs of Naples, traffic was light and he settled in for the long drive. The road had now turned into a single lane highway each way. Meg had warned him to fill up with petrol, or gas as she called it, before he left Naples as there were very few filling stations along the way. The Everglades started almost as soon as he left Naples.

A canal ran alongside to his left, both sides of the road bordered by low shrubs and trees. Where a break in the trees occurred Gibson could see to his left, vast swathes of grassland stretching as far as the eye could see, and to his right, more grassland interspersed with large areas of low lying water. White clouds hung over the everglades suspended in a solid blue sky, telegraph poles lined the road and on top of virtually every pole sat a huge bird of one sort or another. As he drove along he caught glimpses of herons, some white, some blue grey standing in the reeds at the side of the canal.

He passed a junction and saw a road on the right, a signpost to Everglades City. *This must be the junction that Jack had mentioned in his account of when he dropped off the ransom* he thought. As Gibson drove on he came to another sign warning him of panthers crossing. Everywhere he looked there were birds of various sizes, and types. It was all he could do to concentrate on his driving.

After just over two hours the scenery changed as he left the Everglades behind and passed through Homestead, just north of the keys then joined the US1 Overseas Highway and came to the legendary Key Largo. Due to his father's influence, Gibson had been introduced to the films of Humphrey Bogart and was a lifelong fan. To be in Key Largo seemed unreal to him, even though he knew that most of the film had been shot in a studio in Hollywood, with just a few of the opening scenes filmed in Key Largo itself.

He travelled on to the next key, driving over bridges that connected the narrow strips of land, all with beautiful turquoise water on each side, to the left the Atlantic Ocean and to the right the Gulf of Mexico. Groups of motorcyclists riding Harley Davidsons, occasionally drove past him, others going the opposite way, ten, twenty at a time. All indistinguishable from each other, sporting remarkably similar body shapes, ranging from big, to big and fat, some of them with girls sat on the rear seat, hardly any of the bikers or passengers wearing helmets, most of the girls wearing very little at all.

The men invariably had beards, long red hair turning grey, tied in a ponytail, burnt red suntans, leather trousers, or jeans and an assortment of chains adorning their bodies and clothes. The site of the bikers further reinforced Gibson's impression that being in America was like being on a permanent movie set and nothing was real, it was all much larger than life, certainly for a relatively reserved Englishman. He loved it.

The further he drove the more the buildings and scenery changed, becoming reminiscent of the pictures he'd seen of the Caribbean. He stopped at the next key, Islamorada, to fill up and to use the rest rooms, then bought some snacks and bottled water and carried on through, down to Marathon and over the famous Seven Mile Bridge, connecting Marathon to Little Duck Key.

Gibson felt a sense of awe and admiration at such a feat of engineering. The views were spectacular and the whole experience of driving over the bridge exhilarating, he wished he could share it with someone and he found himself talking to Jill, describing the drive up to the top of the bridge then the views as he descended. Suddenly without warning, he felt a deep ache inside his whole being and came close to tears for a few moments, then managed to get a hold of his feelings. He apologised to Jill, then laughed at himself, knowing she'd be telling him to pull himself together and stop being so sentimental, but not meaning it really.

He drove on through Big Pine Key, then several more keys with names he tried to remember but there were so many, then an hour later he saw his first sign for Key West.

Laid back was his first impression, warm sunny weather, palm trees, low rise wooden buildings in the main, some quite handsome buildings too. He drove around aimlessly getting an impression of the place, flashy shops, lots of jewellery stores, lots of small bars and restaurants, the place had a jolly atmosphere, plus some strange looking ageing hippy types strolling around. It also had its share of artists' studios and Gibson had the impression that you might find people here who still advocated flower power.

He needed somewhere to stay and remembered passing the Key West Visitor Centre on Roosevelt Avenue, so he made his way back to where he thought it would be and went round in circles for a while but finally found the office and a car parking space nearby.

Wendy, who dealt with him was extremely friendly and helpful. She was small and fat, dressed in a yellow smock type dress, had pigtails, although she must have been well over seventy Gibson guessed, and wore thick bottle bottom wire glasses and a big wide smile. She insisted on knowing his full name before they started with his enquiry and further insisted on calling him John which he found disconcerting.

'Now John, budget deals for just two nights are hard to come by, time of year and all that, however you just might be lucky. I have a single room, shared facilities, but I know the place personally and it's real cute. It's a B&B called Hemingway's Hideaway, run by Mr and Mrs Hemingway, no relation to you know who though, least I don't think so,' she said smiling her big smile. 'And you can park nearby on the street, not usually a problem,' she added.

It was seventy five dollars a night for three nights and by far the cheapest thing on offer. Gibson took it. As Wendy had promised, there was parking to be had on the street outside Hemingway's Hideaway. He had just the one small bag and was greeted by a man who was holding the door open as he walked up the path. Hemingway's Hideaway was a large clapboard building, a two story house, painted deep pink with a grey metallic roof, and a bright yellow front door with matching window frames. Only in Florida, thought Gibson.

'Welcome to our humble home Mr Gibson. Wendy called to say you were on your way round, come in and follow me, your room is all ready for you.'

Gibson thanked him and briefly shook the extended hand, then followed his host up some wide wooden stairs.

'Now would you like a coffee or anything? Oh, by the way I'm Robert Hemingway, but please call me Bob, everyone else does, and before you ask, no I'm not a descendent, but I am related, distantly.'

'Oh really,' said Gibson.

'Yes it's all a bit complicated, Here we are, please go in and make yourself comfortable. Just dial one on the telephone there if you need anything, breakfast is between seven and ten, oh and the shower room and rest rooms are just along the hall there. Enjoy your stay Mr Gibson.'

Gibson tried the bed, *not bad* he thought. He unpacked his things, stuffed his underwear in a draw and hung up the one jacket he'd brought with him. He went to the window and looked out on to the street, dark shadows from the building contrasted the blinding bright sunlight splitting the street in half. He went back to the bed and lay down. It was a relief after all that driving. *Okay, I'm here in Key West now, but how do I find Richard Boswell, it might only be a small place, but it's still big enough for one man to hide in.*

He'd been thinking about how he might find Boswell for most of the journey down to Key West and an idea had formed in his mind. He sat up and took his notebook out of his bag, leafed through it and found the number he wanted. He looked at his watch, three thirty in the afternoon. He dialled. It was answered almost immediately.

'Hi, Naples Interior Design, Gina speaking how can I help?'

'Hello Gina, Gibson the detective here.'

'Hello Gibson the detective,' she replied a hint of humour in her voice, 'ringing back so soon. What can I do for you today?'

'I'm really sorry to bother you again, but when you went to Key West with Richard Boswell, did he take you anywhere that he'd been before? I mean like a favourite bar or restaurant, anything like that?'

'No, we never went to anywhere like that, not a favourite place, or anything from the past. Although, he did take me to one particular fish restaurant which he really liked. It had just opened I think. Rick thought it was really something special. He loved his fish, but me, I can take it or leave it. All fish tastes a bit bland to me, if I'm honest. Anyway he insisted we go back again two nights later. He was still raving about the place on the journey home.'

'And what was the place called?'

'Hmm, now that's something I can't remember, but it was a really short name, so let me think…..I remember Oceana, that's it, and you can see the sea from the dining room windows. It's above a parade of shops on…hmm, nope can't remember the street. Are you calling from Key West now?'

'I am yes, why?'

'Nothing, just envious that's all I suppose. You should have asked me to come with you detective Gibson, I could have helped you with all that detecting, especially if involves going to nice restaurants.'

'I thought you didn't like fish?'

'No, but I like wine, and good company.'

Gibson laughed, wondering if he was being chatted up.

'Okay I'll remember next time.'

'You do detective. Now, if there's nothing else I can do for you today, I must get some work done, but don't forget, next time, okay?'

'Yes thanks. And I won't forget.'

'You're welcome, I'm sure,' she said and cut the line.

Gibson sat a while wondering at his new found animal magnetism. He looked around for a local telephone directory and found Yellow Pages in the bedside cabinet drawer, along with a Gideon's Bible. He called the Oceana restaurant to establish the opening times. They were open all day from ten in the morning 'until whenever,' said the man.

Gibson scribbled the address in his notepad, went downstairs and wandered around until he heard voices, then knocked on what he assumed to be the kitchen door. Bob popped his head out.

'Do I need a key, I'm just popping out for a while?' Asked Gibson

'You can have one if you want, if I can find it, but generally guests don't bother, up to you,' he said kindly.

'No, just thought I'd ask, by the way could you tell me which direction I walk in to get to South Street, the Oceana restaurant?'

'Right, that's just near South Beach, turn left out of here two blocks and you'll come to South street, turn right until you can't go any further and you'll see the restaurant on your left.'

Gibson thanked him and went on his way. The restaurant was empty other than one table of very late lunchtime diners. Gibson assumed from the state of the table and the number of glasses and bottles left on it. The restaurant was big and airy, light blue painted walls, wicker chairs and simple wooden tables. Shells and nets adorned the walls. Large slider windows ran all the way along the front of the room, with more tables and chairs out on the veranda.

The place would have looked tacky without the stunning view of south beach, the near white sand and blue ocean beyond. He went to the bar, sat on a stool and ordered a beer. The barman served him and asked him if he was eating.

'No, just looking for a friend of mine, I'm pretty sure he's down here on vacation but I don't know where he's staying. I know this is one of his favourite restaurants though, so I thought, if he's been coming here I might be able to find him through you.'

'Well I'd be happy to try and help, what's your buddy's name?'

Gibson had anticipated the question. He didn't know what name Boswell might be using, though he assumed it wouldn't be Richard Boswell in view of the coverage the execution video had got only months previously, so he'd come prepared.

'Better than that,' he said, 'I have a picture of him.' He showed the barman a picture of Boswell, the one without his beard.

The barman looked at him suspiciously, then back at the photograph. 'I think he might have been in a couple of nights ago, sat on his own if I remember right, hang on.'

Then the barman shouted at a small swarthy looking waiter who was starting to clear the table that the late diners had just vacated. Gibson tried to stay calm but he was elated at having possibly, found Richard Boswell.

'Charlie, put that down and come over here a minute.' A reluctant Charlie put his tray down and came over to the bar. 'You was on duty a couple of nights ago, you recognise this guy?' Charlie looked at the photo 'Yeah, he was wearing glasses though, table six, lousy tipper, so what?'

'You don't remember his name by any chance do you?' Gibson asked, then suddenly realised he'd blown his cover story.

The barman looked at Gibson and smiled 'Some friend huh?' Gibson started to think how he could recover the situation. Charlie looked confused. The barman said. 'It's okay Charlie, I'll take it from here, go back to your clearing up.' Charlie walked away muttering 'Jesus, Charlie come here, Charlie look at this, Charlie go away, fuck you Charlie…..'

The barman laughed and turned to Gibson, the smile now gone. 'Okay bud what's the score?'

Gibson reached into his back pocket, pulled out his wallet with his Private Detective Licence in it, took it out and showed it to the barman. 'Blew it there didn't I?' said Gibson.

'Sex or money?' said the barman. 'Sorry?' said Gibson.

'Well, it's either the wife or the business partner who hires a private dick, otherwise it would be the cops looking for him, am I right?'

'I suppose you are, and it's money, business partner.'

'Okay, so now we know what we're dealing with, but if you have his picture, why don't you know his name?'

'I know his real name but he's probably using a false name, that's why.'

'Okay, so what's it worth, for the name, the name he's using?'

'You definitely have the name?' said Gibson

'I guess I do, in that diary over there.' The barman pointed to a desk in the far corner of the bar 'Unless he was a walk in, but that's doubtful, we're booked up most nights.'

Gibson took two twenties and a ten out of his wallet and put the notes on the counter. The barman scooped them up, went over to the desk and flicked through a large diary to find the correct date, then ran his finger down until he found what he was looking for. 'Brian Jones, was the name the guy used. It's the only booking for one. And lookee here, he's made another booking for tonight, seven thirty, late diner your Mr Jones, like a European,' he said and laughed. 'You want I should book you in as well?'

'Ah, no thanks, I'll pass. I don't suppose there's a telephone for him is there?' The man looked at the booking again. 'Nope, nothing, not even a cell number'

'Okay, thanks, what's your name?' Gibson asked the barman. 'Jake, Jake Hardy.'

'Tell you what Jake, take another twenty for being so helpful,' Gibson handed Jake the twenty, oh and here's a five for the beer. I assume you'll keep this strictly between ourselves, you won't say anything to Mr Jones will you?'

'My lips are sealed as they say,' said the barman conspiratorially.

Gibson thanked him again and left, wondering and hoping the barman was as good as his word. He looked for a place to park later, somewhere where he would be able to see the entrance to the Oceana, then walked back in the general direction of Hemingway's Hideaway. He was hungry now and needed a proper meal to sustain him. He wouldn't be eating tonight he thought and started looking for somewhere to eat.

Fortunately he'd had the foresight to set the alarm on his cell phone before he lay down on his bed. The drive down and the big meal he'd just eaten sent him into a serious doze and he woke to the sound of his alarm, wondering where he was. He looked at his watch, *six thirty, time to go*. He drove to the Oceana and had to wait a while for a convenient parking space to become available, then settled down for the wait. At seven twenty, he saw in his mirror a man resembling the person he'd seen in pictures of Richard Boswell, walking towards the restaurant. The man looked around briefly before going through the entrance and up the stairs.

Phase one a success, Gibson said to himself, turned the car radio on and tried to find a talk radio station. He reckoned he'd be there for an hour at least probably longer. The question was, thought Gibson, had Richard Boswell walked to the restaurant from wherever he was staying, or had he driven?

Fortunately there were still plenty of people walking around the area when Richard Boswell finally emerged from the Oceana and hour and a half later. Gibson now had to make the decision whether to follow him on foot, or by car.

He decided to compromise and follow him by car until the next junction. He could hardly creep along in his car at a walking pace all the way back to where Boswell was staying, but equally if Boswell had parked a car some distance from the restaurant and Gibson had chosen to follow on foot, then he would lose him. He let Boswell walk a considerable distance before he started the car and drove down the street until he could see the next junction.

Boswell had walked past many places where he could have parked a car, including a small car park, so Gibson left his car in the next available parking space and got out to follow him on foot. Boswell was well in front by now and Gibson had to walk quickly to shorten the distance between him and his quarry. He slowed down when he was a comfortable distance behind him. Richard Boswell walked quickly and purposefully and never looked round. They were walking down a main thoroughfare called Flagler

Avenue and there were still plenty of people around. Gibson guessed the temperature was still in the high seventies even though it was approaching nine thirty, and people were variously driving around in cars, riding bikes or walking.

Boswell continued along Flagler, then turned left at Ashby Street. This was a much quieter road and Gibson had to drop back a little. They walked a further seven blocks, then Boswell turned right into Catherine Street. Gibson walked carefully round the corner on to Catherine Street, just in time to see Boswell go through a white picket gate and up the front steps of a small white two story hotel, a small distinctive sign outside the door with the name Purple Parrot in purple and green neon. Gibson stopped and considered his options.

He'd promised Bonnie he wouldn't go in alone and in any event, he had no idea what he'd do if he did go and confront Boswell. The man was almost certainly armed and he wasn't so that was reason enough to wait for the cavalry. *However,* he thought, *it wouldn't do any harm to try to find out which room Boswell was in.*

Gibson figured there was no risk in him doing this as Boswell had no idea he was following him, nor who Gibson was or what looked like. *I'll go in on the pretext of looking for a room* he thought, and strolled through the entrance door and into a pleasant and surprisingly roomy reception area. He'd assumed that there would be few if any staff around at that time of night and he was right. There was a room off to the left where the flicker of a television could be seen reflected off the walls, some sort of resident's lounge he guessed, but other than that the place was deserted.

He approached the reception desk and picked up a leaflet from the counter and pretended to read it. *No one around.* He leaned over the reception counter, lifted a ledger type book from off the desk top below and placed on the counter in front of him, then turned it round so he could read the entries. He knew the date that Boswell had driven into Key West, so he flipped the pages back to February ten and started to look down the entries, there he was, Brian Jones one single room for seven nights.

'People used to say I looked like him when I was young,' said a voice behind Gibson. 'So I thought he wouldn't mind me using his name, especially as he died in sixty nine.'

Gibson turned round to face Richard Boswell who was pointing a pistol at his middle section. 'Let's go up to my room and you can tell me who you are and why you're following me. You certainly don't look like the mafia type, but then what do I know?' Boswell's smile changed into a sneer 'Now move.'

Gibson walked in front of Boswell towards the stairway realising how badly he had underestimated him.

'Last door on your left, it's not locked.' Gibson went through the door. 'Sit on that chair.' Boswell closed the door behind him never taking his eyes or the gun off

Gibson. Boswell backed up to the wardrobe and pulled out a sports bag, then took some trainers out and threw one to Gibson who caught it. 'Unlace that,' said Boswell, and sat on the bed facing Gibson, the other trainer in his hand. They went through the same procedure for the next trainer. Boswell told Gibson to give him the laces.

'Okay,' said Boswell, 'turn the chair round and sit back down on it.' Gibson did as he was told. He now had his back to Boswell. 'Now, put your hands round your back and through the back of the chair.' Gibson again complied.

'I'm going to tie your wrists to the chair supports, and before you get any clever ideas, know that my gun is on the bed beside me. So if you try anything, I assure you, I can pick it up quickly enough to shoot you, and I won't hesitate should you be foolish enough you try anything funny. Got that?'

'Yes,' said Gibson

Gibson felt his wrists being tied to each of the chair back supports.

Satisfied with his work, Richard Boswell stood up and came round to face Gibson.

'Now my fine friend, did you really think I wouldn't spot you following me? You must think I was born yesterday. Okay now, who are you working for?'

Gibson was about to speak, when Richard Boswell held his hand up to stop him. 'Before you start, no bullshit okay,

I've killed two people in the last few weeks, so one more isn't going to make that much difference. Come clean and maybe, just maybe, you'll get out of this alive, understood?'

So he did kill Federal Agent Vogel thought Gibson, another great misjudgement of character. Gibson nodded.

'Okay, give,' said Boswell

'Okay, but first I have to tell you that you won't get away with this, and corny as it may sound, the police know I'm here looking for you, so they won't be far behind.'

'Yeah yeah, and there are fairies at the bottom of the garden. Now look friend, you're trying my patience.' Boswell turned round and grabbed a pillow from the bed, stood up and put the pillow roughly against the side of Gibson's head, placing the gun behind it, forcing Gibson over sideways, teetering on the legs of the chair. Boswell spoke again, this time with a hard edge to his voice. 'Now stop fucking about, you have ten seconds to start answering my questions, then the lights go out, understand?'

'Yes, okay,' said Gibson.'

'Sorry I couldn't quite hear you.'

'Yes,' shouted Gibson, 'okay I'll tell you.'

Boswell took the pillow away and threw it back on to the bed. Gibson straightened up and rotated his head to try to get rid of the ache and tension in his neck, then he spoke. 'It's a long story, but initially I was working for your business partner Jack Otterbein. After you'd staged that video execution and fooled everyone, Jack thought he saw you some weeks later and he hired me to try to find out if you were still alive.'

'Saw me where exactly?' said Boswell, his tone incredulous.

'On a CNN news report, you were seen helping to drag a woman out of a collapsed building in New Jersey.'

'Jesus Christ, I don't believe it.' Boswell sat for a while letting the implications of what Gibson had just told him sink in. 'So all my careful planning all blown apart by a chance event, that's just not....' Boswell ran out of words and was shaking his head.

'What, not fair?' said Gibson, 'you think it's fair to swindle your partner out of two million.......' Gibson's little speech was cut off by a back handed blow from Boswell.

'Shut your fucking mouth, you have no idea what you're talking about.' Gibson shook his head to try and clear it. He glared at Boswell.

'So how come he hires a British, what detective? I assume you are a detective of some sort?'

Gibson licked the corner of his mouth and tasted blood.

'Yes I am a detective, or was, I'm retired and I just happened to be on holiday, staying at Bay View and Jack persuaded me to help him find you, if you were still alive that was.'

'And were you in on the attack on me at the trailer park?'

'No, we were on our way to arrest you but someone got there before us, and as you well know, there was a shoot out and you killed a man.'

'You said we, so who else is involved?'

'The police, well the NYPD to be more precise.'

'NYPD, I don't get it, explain why the NYPD.'

Gibson told him about being on secondment to the NYPD some years previously and how he used his contact with Chief Romano to get a PI licence to look into his disappearance and how he was now working in conjunction with them to find him.

He nodded taking in the information, then asked, 'How come you knew I was staying at the trailer park?'

'Mary, from the boat yard, she gave me your cell number and we got your location using that,.'

'And the other guys, the ones who attacked me, nothing to do with you?'

'No, we had no idea who they were.'

'So how do you think they found me?'

'The same way I imagine,' said Gibson

'When you tracked me down, who did you tell, I mean before you came to arrest me, did you tell anyone? Who else knew I was at the trailer park?'

'No one, just me and the police,' said Gibson

'What about Jack, did you tell him?'

Gibson thought. 'Yes I think I did, yes I told Jack, but that was it, no one else.'

'And how did you find Mary, the marina, I mean how did you know I had a boat there? How did you know I had a boat in New Jersey at all, for that matter?'

'Gina, you told Gina.'

'Shit...,' Boswell was silent, thinking, then said, 'Okay I remember now, but I'm sure I didn't tell her exactly where in New Jersey, so how did you find which marina I had my boat moored in?'

'Elimination, the news clip gave me an approximate location so I targeted all the marinas within that area, simple really.'

'You really are a detective aren't you? I don't even know your name, what do I call you, Sherlock?'

'Very funny, no Gibson's my name, just Gibson.'

'Okay Gibson, how did you know I was in Key West?'

'Gina again, she told me you brought her here on a little trip one time.'

'So what? I could have gone anywhere, there has to be more to it than that.'

'Not much, call it a hunch, but you helped us confirm it.'

'I did? What the fuck are you talking about; I didn't tell anyone where I was going.'

'No, but you were caught on a security camera walking out of the car park where you dumped the FBI agent's car and where you also stole a licence tag. You were then caught on several traffic cameras driving a car into Key West on US1, February tenth, with the stolen tag on it.'

Richard Boswell's shoulders slumped and he looked down at the floor, then looked at Gibson, putting it all together in his mind. 'Anyone ever tell you you're just too fucking clever for your own good?'

'Yes, a few times, but only by people I usually end up putting behind bars, so I never took much notice.' Gibson replied.

'And the restaurant, the Oceana, Gina again?'

'Yes,' replied Gibson.

'Pretty girl isn't she?' Richard Boswell said, smiling weakly.

Gibson ignored the question and said 'Look, the police, the NYPD know I'm here, they know everything so if I don't contact them soon, they'll be down here looking for me, and more to the point, looking for you. You're a fugitive from justice Mr Boswell and you've killed two people, so think about your next move very carefully. With that kind of record they're likely to shoot first and ask questions afterwards.'

'I told you to shut up, now be a good detective and do as you're told.'

'Fuck you,' Gibson said in response. Boswell got up from the bed and wandered over to the window, deep in thought.

CHAPTER 24

Richard Boswell swivelled back from the window and looked at Gibson then looked back out of the window, stroking his chin.

Gibson spoke. 'What?' he said.

'You're here on your own right?'

Gibson said nothing, he couldn't see any advantage to confirming that he was on his own.

Boswell came over to Gibson and put the muzzle of the gun to his head. 'Look, there are two goons sat in a car out there and unless I'm very much mistaken they're hired hands, hit men, so make up your mind quick. If they're with you, I might as well shoot you now and take my chances, so what is it, are you on your own or not? And if I think you're lying, I'll shoot you anyway.'

Gibson realised Boswell was serious, the man was terrified. 'I'm on my own and I know nothing about the two men,' he said, 'but I'm telling the truth about NYPD knowing I'm here after you.'

'I don't give a shit about NYPD, now shut up while I think. You were followed' he said, almost to himself. 'They won't wait much longer, we'd better go.' He put the gun into his waistband.

'We?' said Gibson

'Yes we. I haven't finished questioning you yet, but we can't stay here. I'm going to untie you and we're going downstairs to find a way out at the back of this place, then we're going to get your car. I know where you left it, but have no doubt detective Gibson I will shoot you without hesitation if you try anything funny, okay?'

'Okay, I understand.' Said Gibson, 'you've made it clear enough.'

Richard Boswell went to the wardrobe and took out a sports bag, then began untying Gibson and let him stand up, then pushed him in front and said. 'We'll go downstairs and into the lounge and hope there's no one in there. There's some big windows we can get through, just hope they open.'

The lounge was empty and the windows opened easily enough. They were low so getting out wasn't a problem. They walked through a small garden and stepped over a picket fence on to the road at the back of the Purple Parrot. They weaved their way through a couple of small streets and were soon on Flagler Avenue.

It took them another ten minutes or so to get to Gibson's rental car. Richard Boswell told Gibson to get behind the wheel, never taking his gun off him, then opened the rear door, threw his bag on to the back seat and got in beside it, sitting behind the driver's seat.

'Now drive, the US1 north, how much gas do we have?'

'Just over half a tank,' replied Gibson.

'Good, that means we won't have to stop before we get out of the Keys. Step on it, we need to get as many miles between us and those two goons before they realised we've skipped.'

Once they were out of Key West and on the US1, Boswell checked periodically to make sure they weren't being followed. After a few miles he spoke.

'Okay, we don't seem to be being followed, but keep your eyes peeled. I might be the target, but they'll kill you as well so they don't leave any loose ends, understand?'

'I assume these are mafia people?'

'I think you assume right.'

'And they're trying to kill you because you went to the FBI about laundering their money for them?'

'Yeah, that and the fact that I ripped them off in the process'.

'Where are we going?' asked Gibson.

'To see your employer and my old business buddy, I need to ask him some questions, like why he's sicking the mob on to me.'

'You think Jack's behind the attempts on your life?'

'Who else? You said yourself that Jack was the only other person who knew my cell phone number, he must have told the mob and they must have used it to track me down to the trailer park, no other explanation is there?'

'Well other than someone at NYPD, so no I suppose it could point that way, but why would he do that?'

'That's what I intend to find out. But along the way I need to make a call, get these goons off my back.'

'You can do that, how?'

'A little thing called blackmail. I've lodged all the stuff I know about the money I moved around for the mob, with a lawyer, together with an affidavit, so if they kill me it all goes to the Feds. Trouble is, I haven't had the chance to tell them yet, so it's open season on me until I do.'

Gibson couldn't help but admire the tactic. 'Now, we have a good few hours' drive ahead of us, so tell me how you met Jack, the whole story, and leave nothing out.'

Gibson couldn't see what harm it could do, so he told Richard Boswell how Jack had discovered he was a retired British detective and then showed him the video of Richard's execution followed by the clip he'd recorded from the CNN news report on super storm Sandy and Richard's unwitting part in that clip.

'And what was Jacks motive for hiring you to find me,' he asked.

'It seemed pretty straightforward to me,' said Gibson, 'he was mystified as to how you could be dead, but then show up on that news clip weeks later, he seemed genuinely distressed and wanted to know if you were still alive.' Gibson went on to tell him the rest of the story, his trip to

New York, his visit to the offices of JARIC and to his apartment, then how he'd tracked him down to Bill and Mary's Marina.

Boswell stopped him now and then to ask about some detail, then when he'd finished Richard Boswell was quiet for a while.

'You said Jack was surprised when you told him about me being involved in moving mafia money offshore through the company?'

'Yes, he seemed to be, why?'

'Because he encouraged me, I didn't want to do it, but he said we should, or more to the point, that I should. You see, these people from Miami, businessmen or so I thought, started to use our financial services to transfer monies overseas, legitimate stuff as far as I could tell, then after a while they suggested I might do some more transactions for them and that they would pay a hefty premium for not being too fussy about where the money came from etc, etc.

Anyway, I said I'd consider it but I really didn't like the idea, so I naturally went to Jack as he was my business partner and asked his opinion, thinking he would say no, but he actively encouraged me, said it would be good for the company, and pointed out that I'd just gone through an expensive divorce and the extra money would help finance the way he knew I liked to live. So why would he pretend to you he didn't know?'

'I have no idea,' replied Gibson beginning to wonder if he'd been used as a patsy.

'I think Jack wanted to find me for reasons other than checking on my welfare, I think he may have wanted to find me for precisely the opposite reasons, and I'm going to find out the truth.'

Gibson thought to himself that he wouldn't mind knowing the truth himself. They drove on and Gibson decided to risk asking about the killing of agent Vogel.

'You said you've killed two people recently?'

'Yes I have, as you well know.'

'Well I know about the man at the trailer park, but I think it was fairly obvious that was in self-defence, but Vogel, why do you kill him?'

'The same reason. Vogel was trying to get his hands on my money' Richard Boswell laughed. 'Well maybe not my money strictly speaking, but you get what I mean? He threatened to let the mob know where I was unless I gave him some of the diamonds I'd got from Jack, but I knew it wouldn't stop at that, so I decided to run. I was planning to run anyway, so I just brought my plans forward.'

'Is there any way you can prove your story about Vogel trying to get his hands on the money?'

Boswell hesitated, no, it's just my word against a dead man so.... wait, yes there is, Vogel came into the bank with me, so I guess he would be on their security cameras, providing they keep copies for that long.'

'Being a bank, they might very well do that, but tell me more about the bank. Where was this bank and what happened next?'

'I'd kept the diamonds and a few other things in a safety deposit box in a bank in a place called Brick, so Vogel had to take me there so I could retrieve the diamonds to give him the share he was demanding, but instead of taking the diamonds out, I took out a gun I had stored in the box, and when we got back in his car, I pulled the gun on him and made him park up near the river, intending to dump him, steal his car and get far away. I managed to take his gun away from him, but he pulled an ankle gun on me, and fired twice before I was able to react, but when I did react, I shot him and killed him. I didn't make the play, he did, so…. At first I panicked, then I worked out a plan to make it look like the mob had killed him and kidnapped me. Did it work, did I fool anyone?'

'You did for a while, that is until you were seen on the security camera leaving the car park where you dumped Vogel's car.'

'Shit' said Richard.

Gibson took the opportunity of the break in the conversation to ask a question that had been bugging him for some time.

'The execution video.'

'What about it?' said Boswell.

'Well not that it's important now, but how did you manage to make it so convincing, I mean the impact of the shotgun blast propelling you back to the wall, I assume it was a shotgun?'

Richard Boswell sniggered, 'Yeah that was pretty cool wasn't it? I did a lot of hunting years ago and I mostly made up my own cartridge loads, that way I could be sure the load was to my preference for what I was shooting, you know heavy shot for bigger birds like Geese or Turkeys, smaller loads for partridge that sort of stuff. So I loaded the cartridge the guy used to shoot me with a combination of salt pellets and some normal lead pellets, that gave it just enough force to knock me backwards, make it look real, plus I wore a Kevlar vest underneath my sweatshirt, with a plastic bag full of pig's blood on top and the result was as you saw Like I say, pretty cool huh? Still hurt like hell though.'

'It was very convincing I give you that, but all for nothing in the end wasn't it?'

'Yeah, it wouldn't have been but for stopping to help drag that woman out of the house. Son of a bitch, you do a good deed and where does it get you?' he said to himself out loud, then he was silent for a while.

Gibson drove on then after a few more miles, Boswell said he needed a leak and told Gibson to pull into a wooded rest area coming up on the right. They both got out and relieved themselves. Back in the car Boswell told Gibson to wait before driving off and searched through his bag then brought out a cell phone, then rummaged through again and brought out a small notebook. He flipped through it and found what he was looking for and dialled. Gibson could hear the faint tinny automated voice asking the caller to leave a message. Richard spoke.

'Graziano, this is Richard, and yes I'm obviously still alive and that's the way I intend to keep it. Now listen carefully.' Richard proceeded to tell Graziano that he had lodged all the information he had with a lawyer together with an affidavit and how it would be released to the FBI should he meet an untimely death etc. He finished off by telling Graziano to call off his men immediately or else.

He finished the call and told Gibson to drive on. They drove in silence for a while then Gibson asked him when and why he'd decided to steal the mob's money. Richard told him that he feared the mafia would dispose of him at some point, so he decided to salt some of their money away in a separate account for himself, in preparation for his exit.

'I thought the execution video would be an end to it all, and I'd carefully planned my escape, the boat in New Jersey, new identity, new papers the lot, so what could go wrong? Nothing, until that damn storm fucked everything up,' he said bitterly.

'So you think Jack's working with the mafia somehow?' asked Gibson.

'Looks that way to me, but we'll know soon enough,' he said as they passed a road sign saying Naples fifty three miles.

It was nearly three in the morning when they pressed the bell on Jack's apartment door. Jack peered through the security peephole. Richard had stood to the side so Jack could only see Gibson. He opened the door and said in a loud whisper.

'Gibson, what the fuck are you doing ringing my bell at this....'

That was as far as he got before Richard Boswell pushed Gibson through the door and followed quickly pointing the gun at Jack and telling both he and Gibson to walk slowly to Jack's den. Jack had gone white at the site of Richard Boswell and he had started to speak but nothing came out of his mouth. He then did as Richard said.

'Sit down over there both of you,' Richard pointed at the sofa.

'Now Jack, what the fuck is going on?'

Jack took a deep breath and got some of his colour back.

'Me? What the fuck are you asking me for? You're the one who needs to explain, execution videos, demanding two million in diamonds, and you want *me* to explain?'

'That was only about money Jack, I didn't try to kill you. That's a whole different ball game - murder! It was you who got me into this mafia thing. At least it was you who told me to go ahead and launder their dirty money, I was against it but you persuaded me. "We'll make more money" you said, why? We didn't need to make more money, it was just greed on your part, then I realised once I'd started moving their money around, that they wouldn't let me live knowing all their secrets. I saw what they did to people when they thought they became a threat, when they thought you knew too much. I knew one day they'd decide it was too risky. Arranging that video, making it look as though I was dead was the only way I could think of, to get me off the hook. And as far as the ransom was concerned, I thought it only fair that I get some of the money I was owed, the company could afford it.'

'No it couldn't,' said Jack looking at the floor.

'What the fuck are you talking about Jack? We were rolling in it, profits every year since we started.'

'I cooked the books.'

'What did you say Jack?' said Richard Boswell

'I cooked the books Rick, been doing it for years. It never showed because we kept growing, in cash flow terms, but in profits, no. We lost money every year. I was able to cover it up by sort of misappropriating some of the cash flow, well quite a lot of it, and calling it profit. We had such a large amount of forward cash it was just too easy, but I knew that one day, maybe if we had a bad year, or the business shrank, then the hole in the money would become apparent but as long as the company grew, it was okay, well sort of okay.'

Richard Boswell looked incredulous. 'I don't believe this,' he said to no one in particular. 'So the mafia money?'

'Yeah,' said Jack, 'well, I had the cash at hand so I thought maybe I'd see if I could win some money gambling, I mean I read about all these guys who make fortunes playing blackjack, how the odds favoured the punter if you had enough cash to keep going.'

'You lost, I assume,' said Richard. 'How much?'

'Going on for a million.'

Richard let out a gasp, as did Gibson. Jack carried on talking.

'So that's how I got to know the mob. See I'd run out of ways to get the cash out of the company without someone noticing and I asked them for more time to pay and they refused. They knew all about our business and asked me about laundering money for them and that's how it all started. I couldn't do it and I told them that you were the financial whizz kid and that I was just a travel agent, that you handled all the overseas money transfers and stuff. I also knew you wouldn't wear it if I just suggested it, so we, that is they, suggested that they soften you up by starting with some legit stuff, then ask you to do some more risky stuff. I was fairly certain you would ask my opinion and you did, so that's why I persuaded you, why I pushed you into it. They said they would forget my debt to them if I could help them move some money around for a while, plus they'd pay well for our services and I thought it might fill the hole in the accounts, make everything right, then you pulled that video stunt and everything went to shit.'

'So why pay the money, the ransom?'

'They told me to, said they couldn't afford for some low life hoods to kill you for a couple of million, when you'd ripped them off for a lot more. They wanted you back so they could get you to tell them where you'd put the money you creamed off the top. They reckoned you'd stolen close to fifteen mill off them. But then you sent the execution video and you fooled everyone Rick. Me, the mafia, everyone. We all thought you were dead. Graziano was beside himself with rage. He told me I had three months to get someone to go through all your files and find out where you'd transferred their stolen money, every cent, and to get it back. I knew I hadn't got a hope, but I didn't dare tell them that, and then I saw you on that news clip, and well, you know the rest I guess.

'So your reason for trying to find me was to hand me over to the mob, knowing what they would do to me?'

Jack hung his head in silence for a moment and Gibson heard a small sob, then Jack raised his head and looked directly at Richard, tears slowly rolling down his face. 'They put pressure on me Rick, more than I could stand, they said they'd kill me if I didn't find you and they didn't get their money back.

Boswell looked at Gibson. 'And you didn't know any of this?'

'No.' said Gibson.

Richard Boswell held Gibson's gaze then turned back to Jack 'So all these years Jack, all these years you've been lying to me?'

Jack said nothing and looked at the floor. Then the door, which had been left partially open opened fully.

'You lied to me too Jack, you lousy shit,' said Mary Lou. 'And here I was, thinking you were a big shot businessman all this time, and now look at you.'

It was as though all the air had been sucked out of the room. Mary Lou stood there in a long flowing pink silken dressing gown, looking like a vision from paradise, Gibson thought, but he looked at her eyes, they were as dark and hard as flint. 'Are you going to tell him or shall I?' Mary Lou asked, looking at Richard Boswell.

'Tell me what?' said Jack looking confused.

'Well Jack, you're not the only one who's been lying, is he Rick?' she said, a brief sympathetic smile fading as she waited for Rick to respond.

Richard Boswell looked awkward and said nothing.

'Afraid of telling your friend, your business buddy? Well I'll do it then. You see Jack, Rick and I, we've had an arrangement so don't feel too bad about lying to us, we've been lying to you, probably about as long as you've been lying to us about the business. Ironic isn't it?'

Gibson turned to Jack who looked as if he'd aged ten years in ten seconds, his face was grey and he was having difficulty breathing. Jack looked up at Richard Boswell waiting for him to speak but he just stood there stock still.

'Come on Rick, tell him,' Mary Lou said, 'Rick and I, we're going away together, I'm leaving you Jack…'

'No!' shouted Richard Boswell, cutting off her little speech. No we're not,' he continued in a lower voice, and sat down on Jack's leather chair. He put his hand to his forehead rubbed it and looked at the floor, then turned and looked up at her. 'Sorry Mary Lou, but you and I, we're through, I know I said we'd run away, but it's too late, I've changed my mind. I can't do this to Jack. You and I.., we'd never be happy, it just wouldn't work.'

'What the fuck are you talking about' said Mary Lou, her face draining of colour, 'changed your mind? You son of a bitch,' her face contorted and ugly now, her voice increasing in volume, spitting out her words. 'Got someone younger lined up, Gina is it?' Then she screamed 'You double dealing bastard…' and suddenly she took a small silver pistol out of the folds of her nightgown. There was a loud bang and she shot Richard Boswell at nearly point blank range, then turned the gun on Jack and pulled the trigger twice more, shouting and screaming incoherently, out of her mind with rage. Gibson was slow to react to begin with, but was now on his feet. He threw himself across the room just as she began to turn the gun on him.

A shot careened past his ear and he collided with her knocking her to the ground. He was on top of her now, half in and half out of the doorway to Jack's den, he didn't hesitate and thumped her hard on the jaw twice. She was unconscious before the second blow hit.

Gibson stood up and went over to Richard Boswell. He was trying to stand, holding his hand to his lower left arm, there was a lot of blood. 'I'm okay' he said, 'I turned as she shot so she got me in the arm but my hand still works, 'Jack' he said, and they both went over to the prone form of Jack Otterbein who was slumped halfway off the sofa and the floor. His blood was everywhere. Gibson pulled him fully on to the floor and tried to arrange him into the recovery position then felt for a pulse. Richard was on the house phone asking for an ambulance and giving the address. He looked down at Gibson who shook his head.

'Give me your keys' he said to Gibson. Suddenly a gun was pointing at Gibson's face about two feet away. C'mon, we don't want any more shooting,' said Richard Boswell.

'You wouldn't shoot?' said Gibson.

'Richard smiled, maybe not, but it gives you an excuse to say why you had no choice but to hand over your keys doesn't it?' Gibson fished in his pocket and gave him the keys. 'Now, find something to make a tourniquet for this arm' They both looked around the room 'Get that curtain tie back, quickly,' said Richard. Gibson did as he was told and tied the golden platted cord around Richard Boswell's upper arm.

'See you around,' said Richard Boswell and went through the door, glancing down briefly as he stepped over the still unconscious Mary Lou. The night time silence suddenly shattered by the urgent siren noise of the emergency vehicles, getting louder as they screamed along the road towards Bay View.

CHAPTER 25

I t was six in the morning before the detectives let Gibson go back to his apartment and despite his exhaustion he knew he had one more thing to do before going to bed, so he brewed some coffee and took two big gulps before dialling the number.

Bonnie listened to Gibson's account in silence, then spoke.

'Boy am I in big trouble?' she said. 'I can't begin to think of the implications on my career when this gets out, if I have a career by then.'

'Yes I realise, I've been thinking about that Bonnie and I made some, shall we say adjustments to the story I told the detectives who've just interviewed me.'

'Oh, go on.'

'Well you remember that at the time I asked you to keep the information just between the two of us, the stuff about you seeing those pictures from the security cameras at the car park in Brooklyn and maybe recognising Boswell?'

'I do yes.'

'Well that's where it stays, I haven't said anything about that to the detectives here.'

'Right, okay, so what about the tracing of the car with the stolen tag, going into Key West?'

'What trace?' said Gibson

'Okay, let me think, I didn't tell the traffic cops in Florida what the trace related to so there's no reason to suppose they would connect it. Okay, so what did you tell the detectives, I mean how did you explain why you were able to trace Boswell to Key West? I assume you did tell them the whole story?'

'I did yes, more or less, including all the help I had from one Detective Bonnie Ledinski from NYPD, I just left out one or two insignificant details, that's all. As for how I traced Boswell to Key West, I convinced them I was a great detective who had a hunch. I made a big thing about the information I'd got from Gina, sort of exaggerated it a bit. They loved it, so I don't think we need worry about your career. There is one other person who knows though, Boswell himself, but I don't think he'll be telling anyone soon.'

'You are one smart son of a bitch Gibson.

'Well thank you, I'll take that as a compliment.'

'It was meant as one, so how about Boswell, how badly was he hurt?'

'Hard to tell. He was shot in the arm, but I think the guy's a survivor, so my guess is he'll somehow get his plan back on track.'

'And that plan is?'

'I don't know but I think it probably involves a boat, some money and probably a girl.'

'And what about the mob? They won't let him alone will they, even if we don't find him, the mafia will?'

'He's taken care of that. He told me he's lodged all the stuff he knows about the mob and their offshore money, with a lawyer, together with an affidavit, and if he dies in suspicious circumstances, he's told the mob that everything will be released to the FBI, clever stuff.'

'Hmm maybe, but he had already given the FBI some information, including details of the account where he salted away some of the mob's money for himself, so how does that work?'

'Yes, I asked him the same question, and he told me he was happy enough for the FBI to confiscate the money he'd siphoned off from the mob, gave them complete access details of his offshore account, so they'll get that at least. But he was just a bit too willing to give that bank account up, so I wonder if that was some sort of decoy account, and he has money stashed away somewhere else?'

'As for the information he gave the FBI on transfers he made for the various mob companies, I don't think the FBI will be able to recover any money from those accounts without further testimony from Boswell, and I doubt he's going to come back and offer to help them.'

'He thought this all through very well didn't he? He's almost as smart as you Gibson,' Bonnie laughed.

'I think maybe cleverer than me Bonnie, after all, he's got the money and probably the girl as well.'

'Do you think the girl is Gina?'

'Maybe, that would be a turn-up wouldn't it? Listen I'm going to bed now, probably for a week, so thanks again for your help Bonnie, I'll give you a proper update when I wake up and check what's going to happen to Jack's wife, talk about a woman scorned!'

'Okay Gibson, well just let that be a lesson to you, have a good sleep.'

*

He drove one handed across Alligator Alley heading for Miami. The blood from his wound had dried now but he knew he had to stop soon to release the tourniquet for a short while to let the blood circulate, and it would probably start to leak again. The pre-dawn sky was a curious combination of orange, grey and yellow as the sun began to peek over the horizon. There were only a few other vehicles on the road at this time of day so he decided to risk stopping at the next rest area.

Richard parked outside the rest rooms until he was sure no one else was in there and went in. He washed the blood off his arm and released the tourniquet. After a minute or so he felt the pins and needles as the blood flowed back into his lower arm. Only a small amount of blood leaked out of the wound, and he realised he'd been lucky. The bullet had missed the main artery. He pulled some sheets of brown paper from the paper towel dispenser and wrapped them round the wound then using his other hand and his teeth, he secured the tie-back cord over the towels to keep them in place.

He drove on in the general direction of Miami and stopped at a Wallgreens. He took his jacket out of the sports bag and draped it over his shoulders to cover the bloodied sleeve and the cord tie back. He bought some dressings, bandages, some wound cleaning gel, soap powder, bottled water, sandwiches and snacks then carried on to Carol City on the outskirts of Miami, a high crime area, and stopped at the first down at heel motel he came to, The Brightstar Hotel.

He paid cash for two nights and told the receptionist he wanted complete privacy, no cleaners and tipped him an extra fifty dollars. The money disappeared into the receptionist's pocket in a flash.

'No problem Mr...' the teller looked down at the register, 'Smith, have a real, nice day now.'

Once in the room, he took a long hot shower then inspected and cleaned the wound properly and bandaged it as best he could. He filled the sink with hot water, poured in some soap powder and left his shirt to soak, then got into the bed, ignoring the musty smell of the sheets and slept.

He woke up and checked his watch, three in the morning, then he went back to sleep and woke again at nine thirty.

Once again he marvelled at the recuperative power of sleep. His arm throbbed a little but when he inspected the wound it was clean and seemed free of any infection. He redressed it, ate the sandwich he'd bought the previous day and started to make plans in his mind for moving on. He now needed to find somewhere to stay for a week or so while the dust settled.

CHAPTER 26

Gibson had just under two weeks of his holiday left and he spent it variously fishing, sunbathing, and dinners and days out with Meg, plus some considerable time being interviewed by the police. Now that his investigation had come to a conclusion of sorts, he was able to tell Meg the full story. The publicity surrounding the shooting, and his part in it, made him something of a local celebrity, not the least with the residents of Bay View. And so, he was obliged to tell the story over and over again, and the more he told it, the more bizarre it seemed, even to him.

Jack's body was released a few days before Gibson was due to go home but he was spared the further distress of going to the funeral as Jack's relations had made plans for him to be transported to his home town where he was to be buried. Gibson felt a great sadness at Jack's death as he had really got to like him and he missed his jolly company round the pool. Mary Lou was held on various charges with bail set at five million dollars, which effectively meant she would stay in jail until her trial on charges of murder and wounding with intent.

The word was that Mary Lou would eventually be charged for the lesser crime of manslaughter, but it was likely she would receive a custodial sentence nevertheless. JARIC was put into administration and Bonnie told Gibson that the administrators were working with the FBI to try to unravel the various transfers of money, but that the task would be a tough and lengthy process.

When it came time for Gibson to leave and go back to the UK, Meg helped him with his packing, not that there was much to pack, then they loaded his one suitcase and hand luggage into his hire car ready for the long drive to Orlando and the flight back to Manchester.

Luggage packed away, they both stood awkwardly beside the car facing each other, the emotion of parting with Meg made it difficult for Gibson to speak. A single tear ran down Meg's face which made it even worse. They kissed, hugged and promised to email each other and Meg said maybe she'd come over to see him in the UK. Neither of them made any wild promises. Meg had hinted previously that she was too established in her own ways to consider any significant change at this stage of her life, but Gibson lived in hope.

He drove away and was soon on the Interstate for the long drive north. He suddenly realised he hadn't spoken to Jill for some time.

"That was some working man's holiday wasn't it?' He said to her.

'It certainly was,' she said, 'and she laughed, then he laughed, until tears ran down his face making it difficult for him to drive.

CHAPTER 27

He'd found a relatively cheap hotel on Miami Beach where he would be anonymous in amongst the throngs of visitors and tourist. He kept himself to himself and spent his days sunbathing and swimming, but after a couple of weeks he became restless and wanted to get the next part of his journey over with.

He spent a lot of time weighing up the risks of flying to Nassau in the name of Steve Forretti, against the different risks associated with hiring a boat to smuggle him into the Bahamas. In the end, he decided to risk flying. He reckoned it would be difficult for the authorities to cover all the possibilities of him travelling out of the USA. Also, the idea of being dumped on some remote shore on an equally remote part of the Bahamas didn't hold any appeal at all.

He decided to book his flight just a few hours before flying. If the flight was full, he would just try again the following day. He had no particular schedule he had to work to and considered that the shorter time he had a flight booking in the system the better. Once he was in the Bahamas, he would feel more secure. Despite its proximity to the United States, it was an independent country and a place where he could leave to travel to anywhere else in the world he fancied, without having to go via the states.

He chose to book on the last flight of the day, figuring that people were weary by that time and if by any chance there was any kind of alert out for him, the chances of anyone bothering to be on the lookout for him would be that much less. The first couple of days he tried to book a last minute flight he found they were full, but got a seat on the third day of trying. He booked a round trip ticket as he knew that he might face some awkward questions by immigration in Nassau if he only had a one way ticket.

He stood in line US immigration with his sports bag trying to look casual, feeling anything but and had to make a conscious effort not to look away when it came to his turn. He looked at how people were being treated, some were waved through with the most cursory glance at their documentation, others not. The official took his passport and looked up at him.

'Remove the glasses please Mr Forretti.' Steve took his glasses off and tried to smile, causally. 'May I see your travel documents please?' Steve showed the official his plane ticket. 'Purpose of visit?' the man said.

'Vacation,' he replied, feeling his stomach churning. The man looked up once more. *This is it* he thought *and began to wonder if there was any way he could escape.*

'Have a nice flight Mr Forretti. Next.'

Steve Forretti stood rooted to the spot for a micro second, then moved through the gate. He completed the Bahamas immigration card on the flight and tried to stay calm. The passage through Bahamas immigration was uneventful and soon he was outside the airport terminal hailing a taxi.

Once he was out of the airport he felt he was home and dry. He stayed for one night at the British Colonial Hilton, then the next day he wandered around Nassau. He passed two smart black policemen dressed in white fitted military style jackets, dark blue trousers and white pith helmets. They smiled and greeted him. He just couldn't imagine them apprehending criminals and getting their uniforms all messed up.

He wandered in and out of shops, and bought a couple of casual shirts at a Ralph Lauren outlet centre. Then he looked at a couple of house rental agencies until he found one with something that caught his eye, a small private villa on Paradise Island, just across the bridge from Nassau, remote enough for privacy but busy enough for him to blend in. He went in and signed a contract for a month and paid in advance in cash.

He moved in the following day and once he was settled in, he relaxed by the pool and began to think about where he might buy a house, and what sort of boat he would get. *But first things first* he thought. He still had some cash left, around fifty thousand dollars he reckoned, despite all his expenses to date. But he now needed to establish himself with the bank, where he'd diverted around five million dollars of his erstwhile client's money.

He phoned to make an appointment for the following morning with the business manager at the Commonwealth Bank on MacKay Street.

'Hello, how may I help you?'

'Hi, Mr Steve Forretti here, Chief Executive of Rank Export and Import. I'd like to meet with your business manager to discuss some financial aspects of the company's account at the bank. Tomorrow if possible?'

Okay, please hold and I'll put you through to the right department.'

'Hello Mr Forretti, I understand you wish to make an appointment with our business manager for tomorrow?'

'Yes please.'

'Okay Mr Forretti, well that would be with our Mr Glendenning. Just let me check his diary. Yes, I can offer you 11 a.m., if that's convenient for you?'

'Perfect, he replied.'

He arrived at the bank on time and was shown to Mr Glendenning's office.

Mr Glendenning was a smart tall balding black man, impeccably dressed in a cream suit. He welcomed Steve warmly and asked him to take a seat at his large leather bound desk, then sat down opposite. Richard Boswell had formed a company, Rank Export and Import Inc, and opened a bank account in the Commonwealth Bank to receive the funds. He'd made Steve Forretti the sole shareholder and Chief Executive Director. Steve could see the company name on the manila folder on Glendenning's desk, no doubt in anticipation of discussing his client's wishes.

'Now Mr Forretti, you will appreciate the necessity for me to check your credentials, especially as this is the first time I have had the pleasure of making your acquaintance.'

Steve put an envelope on the desk containing a letter of introduction on the company's letterhead, together with his passport. Mr Glendenning looked at the passport and the letterhead and then asked Steve for the account number. Steve rattled it off together with the amount and date of the last deposit of cash made into the account. Steve smiled and Mr Glendenning handed the documents back to Steve.

'You seem very relaxed, considering the circumstances,' said Glendenning, 'but I suppose it's just a matter of going through the motions, and all will be resolved satisfactorily in due course.'

'I'm sorry,' said Steve, 'going through the motions?'

'I do apologise, I thought you knew, I assumed that's why you were here.'

Steve was baffled and getting annoyed, but told himself to keep calm and said,

'Look Mr Glendenning, could you explain what you're talking about.'

'Yes of course, I do apologise. Well, the company you used to transfer your funds to your account,' He stopped talking briefly to look inside the folder, 'JARIC, well they've filed for bankruptcy, and apparently, are also the subject of an investigation by the FBI. I thought all their past clients had been informed, hence the reason I assumed you knew.'

'Yes, well I've been away on business, in the middle east, so I've been a bit out of touch,' said Steve. 'So how does that affect the funds I have in my account, I can't see what impact this JARIC company going bust would have on funds already transferred.'

'Strictly speaking it doesn't. And your funds are all intact, so there's no need to worry about that. No, it's just the inconvenience, and I'm sure it's very annoying, but the FBI has some sort of Court Order granting them the ability to freeze all funds transferred by this JARIC. Apparently the company may have been involved in laundering money. But all you have to do, is contact the FBI and establish the provenance of the funds transferred. Provide them with proof and the funds will be unfrozen. As I say, a relative minor inconvenience in the scheme of things, I'm sure you agree.'

Steve Forretti sat there in silence not responding. 'Mr Forretti, are you okay?'

'Sorry,' Steve said pulling himself together, 'I was just thinking of... Never mind, as you say a minor inconvenience, I'll get on to it right away. Steve got up out of the chair and Mr Glendenning came out from behind his desk and showed Steve to the door, where they shook hands and bid each other goodbye. He wandered round Nassau in a semi daze for half an hour then found a bar. Two hours later, the taxi driver helped him unlock the door of his villa. It was all he could do to remember the street where the villa was. He was just about capable of taking his clothes off before stumbling to the bedroom and slumping on to the bed.

He woke in the dark and made to get up, then moaned, *big mistake* he thought, and remembered. He got up slowly into a sitting position and stayed like that until he felt able to walk. He got up and walked to the shower, got in and turned the taps, it was cold. He shouted out, but stayed in until the water gradually heated up, then he slid down the wall of the shower and stayed there until the water ran cold again. He finally got to his feet again and turned the shower off, dried himself, and went back to bed.

The next day the early morning light woke him up. His head still ached but it was bearable. He made his way to the kitchen, brewed some coffee, spooned in some sugar and drank it hot, black and sweet. Sitting at the kitchen table, he started to recover. How long would it take the FBI to connect the dots and link the transfer to Rank Exports, and Imports Inc., and to Steve Forretti? *Maybe never,* he thought, *but even if they don't connect me with the five million, and Rank Exports, how can I get them to unfreeze the account?*

Maybe he could work something out for the future, maybe he could think of a way of validating the money? Take Steve Forretti out of the picture somehow? But for now, he found it just too complicated to think about. He needed money and consoled himself with the thought that he still had the diamonds, and they would provide him with a big enough pot to put him back on his feet.

He'd thought that the five million in cash, plus the two mill in diamonds would be enough for him to live a life of luxury for quite some time, before having to consider working. But now he realised he would need to cash in the diamonds and invest, to create an income. He'd been studying the diamond prices for a while and had a much better understanding of what he now thought of as a commodity to be traded, rather than just expensive jewellery. Prices had risen considerably in recent years he discovered, but were now bouncing around on a daily basis, so there was some judgement required on when to sell. But first he needed to establish if there were willing buyers of precious stones in Nassau.

There were certainly plenty of jewellers there, selling their goods to tourists, especially those spilling off the cruise ships on an almost daily basis. He decided to approach the largest retailer of diamond jewellery in Nassau, but first he needed to open a bank account with another bank to enable him to trade and make investments. There were plenty of other banks in Nassau. so he went on-line and chose Banco

Solunas who advertised 'ultimate discretion' as their byword.

He called and made an appointment with a Mr Norbert Grenville. The interview with Mr Grenville went well and Steve felt he could trust the man. Steve had taken his papers and he opened an account there and deposited a token ten thousand dollars in it. He returned to the villa pleased with his achievement, eager to take his first step in establishing a normal life, *albeit a normal luxury one,* he thought. He badly wanted to buy a big sailing boat, but before that he needed to establish an income to be able feel comfortable spending that sort of money.

He decided he would sell some of the diamonds the following day, possibly all of them if he could get a good price. He would deposit most of the money from the sale into his new bank account, ready to begin trading in stocks and commodities, then he'd buy a boat with the rest and join a yacht club, where he was sure he would be able to pick up useful information on what stocks to buy. He felt good and went to make himself another coffee.

CHAPTER 28

Driving across the Paradise Island Bridge into Nassau, he felt the strength of the morning sun through the open car window and breathed in the fresh sea air. He was gradually getting over the shock of being denied access to his five million dollars, and tried to put everything into perspective.

It was good to be alive he thought *and thanks to the diamonds, he'd soon be back in funds.* He was looking forward to resuming his commercial life. He'd always had a talent for predicting currency fluctuations to his advantage, and was confident he could apply the same skills to dealing in stocks and shares. All he needed was a decent sized pot of money to start him off. He found a parking space on Bay Street and walked the rest of the way to the main street, where most of the jewellery shops were located.

He was still prepared to be ripped off on the price he got for the some diamonds to begin with, but later he would find a respectable diamond buyer. Maybe he could send a sample to a big dealer in the states and get a price based on bigger quantities, *whatever,* he thought. He came to the first large jewellery store on Market Street and went in. The smiling lady assistant came over to him and asked if she could help.

'I'm selling not buying today' he said. 'Diamonds,' he added, smiling back, and asked if he could speak with someone who could provide a valuation.

'Just one moment please' she said, and went to talk to a diminutive, bald headed Asian looking man in a small glass walled office at the rear of the store. The man put the item he'd been inspecting down, removed his glasses. They were wire framed with a binocular like extension on one of the lenses. He looked down the shop at Steve, then turned back to the girl and gave his instructions. She came back and asked him to follow her.

'Come in, come in' said the man gesturing for Steve to sit down on the chair opposite his. 'Now what can I do for you this fine morning sir?'

Steve took the plastic bag out of his pocket and the man anticipating, rolled out a purple velvet cloth on the top of his desk. Steve poured the diamonds out on to the cloth. They sparkled brightly in the reflected light. The man looked at the diamonds, then at Steve's face and smiled.

'You want to sell these, or do you just want a valuation?' he said.

'Both, depends on what you're willing to pay.'

'I see,' said the man and put his glasses back on and picked up one of Steve's diamonds with some large tweezers.

'Do you mind me asking where you bought these?'

'Yes, I do really,' said Steve.

'I only ask because the young lady said you had some diamonds to value.'

'That's correct, yes.'

'Hmm,' said the man, 'you see, these aren't diamonds,' he said, taking his glasses off.

Steve looked at him in disbelief,

'What do you mean, not diamonds?'

'I'm afraid these are zircons my friend. Extremely good zircons, I'll say that. But they're zircons.'

The colour drained from Steve Forretti's face

'Are you all right sir?' asked the man. Then he waved the nearest girl over and asked her to get a glass of water. She came back and Steve sipped some.

'So, what are these worth?' he managed to ask, when he'd recovered, pointing at the sparkling stones.

'Difficult to say. First, you'd need to find someone interested in buying such stones. But, as a rough guide, I'd say between five hundred and a thousand American, at best.'

Steve looked at the man.

'You're joking…you can't be….?' then he started laughing 'Jack you fucking bastard, you lying cheating, double dealing...….' and then Steve Forretti was laughing so much, he couldn't speak.

He stood up and carried on laughing loudly, as he walked out of the shop. Customers and staff stopped what they were doing and watched.

The Asian man ran after, him trying to give him the zircons back. Steve finally turned and took the plastic bag off the man. Now, laughing hysterically, he walked out of the shop and threw the stones into the street. Then he fell to his knees on the sidewalk, bowed his head and started sobbing.

SHAKEDOWN

The expression Shakedown is said to have originated in the USA, to describe the actions of gangs of yesteryear. These gangs roamed the streets in search of victims, whom they would hold upside down, and shake the money out of their pockets, which they then stole. True or not, the expression Shakedown, is now used to describe obtaining money by extortion or blackmail – with or without violence. It's also sometimes used to describe the actions of cops who use intimidation or violence to extract information from unwilling individuals.